I0764612

Opulent

Opulent

OPALESCENT
Book One

Isabelle Gallo

Copyright © 2008 by Isabelle Gallo
All rights reserved. No part of this book may be reproduced or transmitted in any form or by any means, electronic or mechanical, including photocopying, recording, or by any information storage and retrieval system, without written permission from the publisher.

Summary: Struggling to remember her past, the life she had no choice but to abandon and forget, Chenille East must also discover who she is and who she was.

ISBN-13: 978-0-615-60069-7
ISBN-10: 0-615-60069-7

Printed in the United States of America

Contents

Prologue
Chapter 1 - Midnight
Chapter 2 - After the Storm
Chapter 3 – The Bat and the Bird
Chapter 4 – The Bridge of Secrecy
Chapter 5 – Ultimatum
Chapter 6 – Festivities
Chapter 7 – The Revelation
Chapter 8 - Sacrifice
Chapter 9 – A Total Blank
Chapter 10 – Lucian
Chapter 11 – Addiction
Chapter 12 – Unwelcome Company
Chapter 13 – Black Book
Chapter 14 - The Race
Chapter 15 – Journey
Chapter 16 – Taunting Nightmare
Chapter 17- Amour
Chapter 18 - Control
Chapter 19 - Supremacy
Chapter 20 - Royalty
Chapter 21 - Tetchra

Chapter 22 – Light the Way
Chapter 23 - Nalani
Chapter 24 – The Old Farm
Chapter 25 – Obsidian
Chapter 26 – Unmasked
Chapter 27 – Lock and Key
Chapter 28 - Misconstrue
Chapter 29 - Ally Conformation
Chapter 30 - Poison Kiss
Chapter 31 - Woken
Chapter 32 - The Lost Boy
Chapter 33 – Masterpiece
Chapter 34 - Over the Bridge
Chapter 35 - Torn
Chapter 36 - Out of Mind
Chapter 37 - For and Against
Chapter 38 - Tintinnabulation
Chapter 39 - Glass and Gold
Chapter 40 - Alias
Chapter 41 - Preparations
Chapter 42 - Prince of Light
Chapter 43 - Evaluation
Chapter 44 - Haunted
Chapter 45 - The Ball
Chapter 46 - After the Ball
Chapter 47- Arise Again
Afterword

Prologue

The universe now only consisted of two worlds: Earth, home to the mortals, and the immortal world, Catastrophe. Residing on Catastrophe were the vampires, werewolves, and strange creatures. Immortals could only get to Earth by a bridge known as the Bridge of Secrecy, a bridge suspended between the two worlds. One could only cross the Bridge when the moons of both worlds came together in an eclipse causing total darkness for one month. It would be only then when they could cross and feed on the lives of the mortals and return home. If an immortal made the mistake to stay longer than one month, they would remain on Earth until the next eclipse and most likely be *killed* by the mortals only to come back reincarnated in another life. This had been an agreement made between the two worlds.

The planet Catastrophe, nearly twice Earth's size, was not different from Earth but appeared darkened slightly more from Earth's small shadow. The creatures that resided on Catastrophe were not friendly toward the mortals who feared the immortal beings.

The vampires and werewolves, enemies since the day of their existence, were constantly at each other's throats. The wolves were submissive to vampires, the dominant species of Catastrophe. The vampires had proved themselves long ago as being smarter and faster. They were the merciless predators to the innocent people of Earth, after all. However, that did not mean that the wolves willingly bowed their heads to them. In fact, the wolves resented them. The wolves' vengeance and distaste was almost inevitable, reinforced by the fact that, as claimed by the mortals on Earth, vampires were liars and should not be trusted; being associated with one will only get you killed, but that is redundant.

So what happens when you become one of *them* and you have no choice but to coexist with the monsters that turned you into something you are not? Who do you turn to - or turn against?

Part 1

Platinum Moons

Chapter 1- Midnight

My eyes fluttered shut after a long while as cold air filled my lungs. Once opened, I looked out my bedroom window to see nothing but tremendous clouds drifting eerily across the darkening sky. The sky was bleak, the clouds like thick curtains hiding the setting sun. I sat at the edge of my seat, hoping the storm would pass by, even though I knew it would not.

"Chenille, come down here," my brother screamed from the kitchen.

"Coming," I mumbled as I trotted down the stairs hastily.

Immediately, my friend caught me in his arms. As soon as my vision evened out, I stared blankly at the person who had spun me nearly halfway across the room.

"Calvin!" I cried throwing my arms awkwardly around the vampire's neck. He had gone across the Bridge of Secrecy to Earth nearly three weeks ago and I had not seen him since. "You're finally back." I rested my chin on his shoulder, uttering a sigh.

"How have you been?"

I took a step back and cleared my throat. "I've been fine." My voice quivered nervously, causing my eyes to flash away with embarrassment.

"You haven't changed a bit, have you?" Calvin teased.

My face burned from his comment. Of course I had not changed. I was still getting used to my own awkwardness that had not yet diminished since becoming a vampire.

"Come on, the clan is waiting, let's not stand and chat all night."

My eyes flew impatiently to Zaire. *The clan can wait,* I thought.

Zaire has a tendency to get under my skin too

often, with his immatureness and interruptions of perfect moments. As an older brother, he has every right to protect me, but not kill me by being as insensitive as he is. I mean, about a year ago I came to him in panic, unable to remember anything. Aside from knowing my name and family relations, I lost my memory when I was turned into a vampire. Generously, he welcomed me warmly to this new world and allowed me to live with him in this dump of a place. That's right, no water, no electric, just a two-bedroom place with antique furniture and an old kitchen that we never use. Nevertheless, what more could one expect from a poor nineteen year old vampire or, rather, a subordinate older brother?

"I suppose… we should go." Calvin sighed as he made his way over to the door.

"Wait for me!" I called, trailing after him.

Once outside, I was pleased to see my fellow clan members gathered on our small patch of grass that we called our lawn in front of the house. They spoke amongst themselves, the hum of their voices occasionally breaking the silence. From where I stood, I could just make out the colors of the capes they wore in the growing darkness. Their capes were the only things that helped me distinguish one from another. I did not know their names. I only knew Amelia.

I could spot Amelia from over a mile away, with her long red hair and dark green cape, a smirk on her face. I could only imagine of what that manipulative mind of hers was plotting. Grabbing Calvin's hand in excitement, I quickly led him to where she was standing. As we approached her, she took no notice of our presence. It seemed as if an eternity had passed before she finally turned her head to acknowledge our existence.

"Hi, I didn't see you there," she remarked with a sly grin.

Impatiently I crossed my arms and glowered at her once her comment flew off her tongue.

"We've been here for the past five minutes," I said as

Calvin peered over my shoulder to glare at her.

Amelia and Calvin were bitter rivals from the minute I had introduced them and rarely put their differences aside to appease me.

Zaire's harsh voice broke the silence between us. "You are all aware that the eclipse of the two moons will be ending soon. All but stupid mortals will stay on their planet, meaning we may find a mortal or two on our land."

"What if none of the mortals show? What will we do then?" I yelled over the raging winds.

"If that comes to be the case…we will have to wait for the next eclipse."

"That could take months!" Amelia protested.

Calvin jabbed her sharply with his elbow. "It's too late to cross the Bridge now. We don't have much of a choice."

The vampires raged on protesting to cross the Bridge, while others, like me, stood quietly in the shadows, listening intently. I mumbled beneath my breath, shoving my hands deep in my pockets from the harsh coldness of the storm that was approaching. Calvin stood by my side and dropped his cape over my shoulders as I began to tremble from the cold drizzle.

"Are you cold?" he asked softly from behind me.

I wrapped the cape tightly around me and nodded in response. Hushed voices transpired to excitement that suddenly stirred around me. A group of people approached us.

"Probably a group of teenagers," someone nearby said quietly.

I could only wonder if they thought the same of us. The group headed toward us hastily and I braced myself hoping, *hoping* for there to be at least one mortal among them. A figure stepped from the darkness, into the illumination of the rising moon's faint glow and a series of gasps and frustrated sighs stirred the silence. The person leading the group took the hood of his cape off and looked straight at me, green eyes bright with intensity. All at once, my breath left me and I plunged down to meet the wet ground.

"They're vampires!" I yelled.

"I know," Zaire mumbled under his breath with a hint of annoyance and walked up to the person with the green eyes.

They talked in hushed whispers to each other and exchanged inquiring glances at me now and again. It was clear they were not oblivious to my small stumble. I stood up quickly to get a better view of them and looked over at Amelia who murmured a few words to herself, her eyes gleaming with exhilaration. She glanced at the other clan and quickly turned to me.

"Look at all of those vampires, and cute ones at that," she exclaimed.

"You are so predictable."

"Chenille," Zaire called, gesturing for me to come over.

As usual, I was very tentative, but approached with caution, my throat instantly tight with anxiety. My brother's gaze was hot, menacing almost, as I felt it burn into my skin. I wondered if I was in trouble.

"Hello, I'm Fitzray," the green-eyed leader said with a smile that nearly made me trip over myself again.

I took a deep breath before returning his greeting.

"I'm Chenille," I replied as I started to comb my fingers through my tangled brown hair, suddenly aware of my unkempt appearance.

"Why don't you come with us? We could use a bit of company on our little excursion through the woods," Fitzray said.

I looked at Zaire with a hint of skepticism. As usual I was looking for my big brother to offer some protection, but for the first time I saw him avoid my gaze carelessly.

"Go ahead, we're going home. I've been told that there will be no crossing the Bridge tonight."

I opened my mouth to contradict, but found that Zaire was already giving orders to go home. I looked over my shoulder to see Amelia rushing up to him. Without objection, Fitzray took my arm and led me to the edge of the woods.

Amelia was screaming her words over the raging wind, though I could barely hear them. "I'm going with them," she demanded.

"*No* you're not. You're going home like the rest of us," Zaire snapped.

She let out a growl through her teeth. "If *anything* happens to Chenille, I swear I'll-,"

"*Nothing* is going to happen to her."

"Where is that vampire taking her?" Calvin screamed, pushing Amelia aside.

"How should I know?"

As we went deeper and deeper into the woods, apprehension crawled up my spine making me feel colder than usual. It took me only a few minutes to realize that Fitzray's clan was gone. Only Fitzray remained. Feeling as uneasy as I was, I quickened my pace. Icy hands gripped my shoulders, making me come to an abrupt halt.

"Are you all right?"

"Where is the rest of the clan?" Trying to conceal my fear had failed thanks to my quivering voice.

"They went home. It's been a long couple of weeks crossing the Bridge and all."

A loud rustling in the bushes caused a chill to slice through me. There was a red haired woman standing in front of a clan. It was almost as if she had appeared out of nowhere. I almost mistook her for Amelia, but thought otherwise when I heard her voice: elegant, sharp, and threatening.

"You," she said, pointing a sharp fingernail at me, "come with us, you belong to our clan now."

I looked up at Fitzray and then to the woman confused. Fitzray was unmoved beside me, which only challenged the possibility that I was imagining her.

"What-," I began.

"Quiet, you belong to our clan now," the woman said again.

"Not if I have anything to say about it," Fitzray growled.

"Fitzray don't, please-,"

He looked at me, his harsh grip moving to my wrist. "I'll take care of this," he said quietly.

I wanted to stop him, but it was not my place to stand up to him and hold him back, especially since he was a vampire.

Once he left, two clan members grabbed hold of my shoulders and walked back, edging me toward the deeper, darker territories of the werewolves.

"Help, Fitzray!" I screamed as a black wolf stepped from the bushes and growled lowly, his teeth, gleaming white daggers, within striking distance of my hand.

Fitzray only looked back at me for a split second and turned to the woman. Something shiny in one of his hands caught the milky glow of the rising moon.

"No!" I screamed, but it was too late.

He dug his nails into her shoulder and pierced the knife he held deep into the woman's chest, killing her. The vampires that held me captive ran off in disbelief. The black wolf turned and rushed back into the woods.

Fitzray slowly walked up to me, his green marble eyes now inauspicious. He still gripped the knife in his right hand; blood stained it to the hilt. His other hand formed a fist and blood dripped off his knuckles onto the velvet soft moss below. The knife dropped to the ground, hitting a rock. Its sharp sound rang in my ears. I watched, paralyzed in fear as his hands slowly unraveled themselves from fists. They were trembling.

He stared at me blankly and took a step closer, his bloody hand gently touching mine. I felt the cold sticky liquid on my palm and the sickly launch my stomach gave me.

My eyes closed and I fell into a dead faint. I fell with a crash, gripping his hand. My head smashed hard against a large rock. A faint voice whispered in my ear, but a loud buzzing in my head drowned out parts of his words and words I was unaware of saying.

"You are going to be fine. I am here. No, I am not going anywhere. I won't leave you," was all I heard.

Chapter 2 - After the Storm

A warm ray of sunlight flooded into my room for a brief moment, just long enough for the light to warm my face, waking me. I tried to recall the night before, wondering if it really happened. I shifted slightly and something gently touched my arm. My head pounded painfully against my skull. Fitzray sat on the edge of my bed. His marvelous green eyes settled on me.

"What happened?"

"You passed out," he said quietly, "and you hurt your head pretty bad, so I took you here, to your house. When I turned to tell your brother Zaire about what happened, you begged me to stay and I did."

Without warning, the door flew open and Amelia stood in the doorway, her eyes narrowed to glare daggers at Fitzray.

"*You*. What did you do to her?"

Before he could reply, Calvin rushed through the door at Amelia's heels. He let out a sharp hiss when he caught sight of Fitzray. Fitzray loosened his grip around my arm and growled in response.

Zaire appeared from behind Amelia and Calvin and grabbed their shoulders, dragging them both down the hall before either of them had a chance to speak to us.

"I suppose I won't be going over the Bridge."

"I'm afraid not. Maybe another month."

At the sight of my disappointment, he let out a sigh and smiled, running his icy fingertips down my arm.

"So how long have you been a vampire," he inquired softly.

"Not all that long, barely a year."

"I suppose you don't know much about the vampire ways

here."

"No, this world is confusing to my everyday life. Zaire hasn't been of much help either."

He chuckled softly and held out a rose in one of his porcelain hands. His hand was bleeding from the sharp thorns that protected the beautiful flower. He studied my expression for a moment in silence.

"For starters, vampires aren't supposed to faint at the sight of blood."

"I didn't faint at the blood. You *petrified* me. You...you murdered an innocent woman. It had nothing to do with the blood," I said, casting a glance toward the bloodied rose in his hand.

"I wouldn't call her *innocent.* Her intentions were worse than you think. "

"How would *you* know?" I spat, insulted.

"Listen, I've been around long enough to know when Hell's about to break loose. I stopped that from happening. I did you *a favor.*"

"You still murdered a woman."

"She brought that upon herself. Besides, she'll come back in another life," he said with contempt.

My hands flew to my head that pulsed with discomfort, causing a groan to escape my lips.

"I have something at my house that can help with the pain." Fitzray offered suddenly as he rose to his feet.

"Can I come with you?" The words slipped off my tongue so slickly, but if I could harness them and take them back, I would have. I was in no condition to travel.

"If you must, I won't stop you."

He helped me to my feet and I tightly gripped his hand for balance. I should have sat back down, but instead I fought to stay on my feet. Something in my head told me to appear strong before this potentially dangerous vampire. Here, on Catastrophe, it was survival of the fittest and I was not taking any chances. I could not have the appearance of prey. I could not appear weak.

While he guided me outdoors, I tried desperately to masquerade my lingering mortal-like qualities. It was cold and I could not help but shiver. The fact that I was clutching Fitzray's hand like a child did not make it any better. Fortunately for me, he did not appear to be paying much attention.

He snaked me through the woods as a cold drizzle began to fall. It became foggy and I strained my eyes to find him. We had not walked very long, but I was tired and I wanted to go home already. Fitzray shouted something and I turned around.

With the fog rolling in thicker still, the path before me was barely visible. The dense fog prevented me from seeing a large tree root in my way, which, when I stumbled over it, forced me into cold water.

Cold water, ice-cold water, encased my being. All of my senses were completely gone, and despite my attempts, I just could not break the water's surface. My head was spinning while water went up my nose. I swam upward, stretching my arms at full length, hoping to grab onto anything at all, but there was nothing. I thought I was going to break the surface when a force pushed me back down. My body was numb as I fell into the dark depths of my subconscious.

The cold water submerged my thoughts for a long while until something warm touched my face, forcing my eyes open. Fitzray was bent over me. His raven, shoulder-length hair hung down, his head inclined toward me. My hands clutched a soft carpet. Fitzray's back was to an ignited fireplace that illuminated the room and cast warmth around us.

"Are you okay?" He asked, placing his other hand on my face, his wet hair tickling me.

In an instant, he was gone and a few seconds later, he sat on a large red velvet chair in front of me. My tongue felt heavy in my mouth. He silently handed me a large mug. The liquid that filled the mug was bitter and I quickly handed it back to him.

"It's for your headache. It will help relieve the pain, trust me."

My head still hurt, but the pain no longer clouded my thoughts as it once did. I took another sip of the drink and made a face of disapproval, swallowing quickly though it left a bitter taste in my mouth.

"Why are you going through so much trouble for me? You must have better things to do then to tend to my needs," I said at last.

He shrugged. "You need some looking after."

"I don't need your help."

"Now, now, let's not be resentful. After all, I *did* just save you from drowning."

"I didn't *need* your help. I could've saved myself if you hadn't plunged into the water to save me."

He straightened up and leaned against the chair slickly. For a moment his gaze rested on the bottle he held in his hands.

"If that's what you think."

"I mean…I don't even know you."

"Oh you don't?" He laughed quietly to himself.

I looked at him with a new sense of perplexity.

"I'm just messing with your head." He said after a few suspenseful moments of silence.

"I…should be going home." I handed him the mug, my head jerking in the direction of the door.

His hand gripped my shoulder and I turned back to face him. He did look familiar in some way.

"You should rest," he insisted.

"No, honestly, I'm fine."

"Should I come with you?"

"No, stay here. I will be fine."

He shrugged on his cape and set the bottle down on the velvet chair.

"What are you doing?"

"I'm coming with you."

"So you're going to walk me home?"

"Well, *can* you walk?"

"I think so." With Fitzray's hand offering leverage, I was able to stand without much difficulty at least.

Outside it was misty and cold. The first signs of daybreak erupted through the clouds of the passing storm, making me realize that I had spent the whole night unconscious in a stranger's house. This only pushed me faster and I did not stop until I saw my brother's old shack. I never thought I would be so relieved to see it in my life.

"Thank you," I said quietly.

"You don't need to thank me. I'm just keeping an eye out for you," he chimed in a near-mocking tone.

"Still, thanks."

Once I turned to open the door, Fitzray called my name. I was not out of the woods yet.

"Come back to my house later. I'll tell you all about the insanity of this obscure planet."

I smiled and walked inside, not giving his words much thought. "I'll see you later then," I called back in attempt to appease him.

Zaire was not there when I entered the house so I went up to my bedroom. Amelia and Calvin sat on my bed half-asleep but became alert when they saw me.

"What happened?" Amelia shouted loudly, practically jumping up.

"Well, I was nearly killed by a couple of clan members and a werewolf...and nearly drowned in a lake, but that's not any new news on my account."

"I knew that guy was trouble!" She cried.

"He's not all bad," I struggled to justify. "He saved me today."

"Well, just as long as you're ok." Calvin mumbled, barely listening to me anymore.

"Well, now that you're here safe and sound, I'm going home. It's like four in the morning and I am exhausted. But this conversation is *not* over!"

Once she left, I looked at Calvin, his sleepy eyes coming to life before me. Tiny orange sparks glittered in his black eyes, like dying embers that caught fire again. When his eyes took their radiant orange glow, he stood up and stretched, letting out a yawn.

"I'm going home too." He said, quickly kissing my cheek.

"Good night."

"Yeah, good night, sweet dreams…see you tomorrow I guess," he cooed and sluggishly left the room.

Silence enveloped the room as soon as my friends were gone and in the moment of peace, I rested my aching head against my pillow and fell asleep.

Chapter 3 - The Bat and the Bird

Sunlight beamed off the tips of my eyelashes and warmed my face, slowly waking me from deep slumber. I sat up and stretched out my arms, inhaling a deep breath of dust. Light bounced off the decaying walls and illuminated the corners that showed off their cobwebs. I could almost see all of the dust particles swarming around me.

Recalling my encounter with Fitzray the previous day, I changed into jeans and a warm sweater. I walked outside and noted that the moons were separating; the sun's rays were breaking through. Since no one was home again and I had nothing else better to do, I figured I would take Fitzray up on his offer.

Desperately, I tried to recall the way to Fitzray's house and shortly found myself lost in the woods. It only took a deep growl to send me running as fast as I could, causing me to stumble over branches and brush. I nearly fell into the creek again. Then I saw it - two large metal gates opened to a large driveway.

This must be it, I told myself as I looked up at the huge house.

I arrived at the door, hoping it was the right house and knocked as loudly as I could.

"Come in!" I heard Fitzray shout from a distant room in the house.

With relief that I was at the right place, I walked in, dazzled by what I saw. The windows looking out to the front porch were open, the light from the morning sun flooded through them and the white scarves hanging on the curtain rod above them swayed in the breeze. It was much larger inside than it appeared outside with its high ceiling and grayish white marble tile floor. In the distance there were two red velvet chairs and a plush white rug was stretched out before the majestic stone fireplace. The polished wood staircase followed, leading up to the second story of the house. I looked to my right where a black leather couch remained in front of a plain coffee table. Not far from that, an archway led to the kitchen. Thunderous music played, echoing through every room.

"Fitzray?" I could only hope he heard my voice over the music.

"In here," he hollered from the kitchen.

I had to admit, for a vampire, he had an enormous kitchen. The kitchen was probably twice the size of the first floor of Zaire's house, with its mahogany cabinets and granite tops, an island located in the middle of the room. A small silver birdcage was located on a stand in a far corner.

He turned to me and smiled, apparently happy to see me. He was wearing a white button down shirt, the sleeves rolled up to his elbows and a pair of black pants. It seemed he was dressed a bit formal, but I decided it was best that I did not comment.

"Hey, did you get lost?"

"How can you tell?"

"Lucky guess," he said, eyeing me. I ran a hand through my hair; leaves and twigs were tangled and twisted in a big mess on my head.

"Oh…well." I started to claw the leaves from my hair and felt reddened to my face, green eyes still staring.

"Do you need some help?" He reached out to pull a tangled twig from my hair.

"No! I'm fine. Trust me, this happens a lot." I stumbled back quickly, throwing up a hand to prevent him from coming any closer.

"I suppose it's just something to get used to."

My eyes flicked to the nearest object, the birdcage, wanting to change the subject. "Do you have a bird?"

"No, I don't have a bird."
"What is it then?"
"Charlene," he called.

At that moment, a beautiful white bat flew into the room and landed on his shoulder. A heavy white coat of fur covered her body. Her eyes were sinister.

"What a miraculous creature," I said with a smile.

All of a sudden, she flew from Fitzray's shoulder. Her exposed fangs gleamed while she flew at her full speed toward my face. Before her fangs took off my nose, Fitzray launched forward. He held her tightly in his hands as she struggled, her wings firmly pressed to her body. She screeched sharply and bit her master's hand with full force, still struggling to break free and glowered at me, the intruder.

Fitzray rushed up to the cage and threw her inside, slamming the door shut. His cool blood dripped from the deep puncture wounds on his right hand as he proceeded toward the kitchen sink. He placed his hand beneath the cold water that spilled from the faucet.

"I'm sorry…she…she's usually good with strangers. I don't know what happened."

"I thought…she was a fruit bat."

"She looks like a fruit bat, doesn't she, but she's not, she's a vampire bat. She was the daughter of my mother's bat."

"*Was* the daughter of your mother's bat?"

"My mother was killed on a trip over the Bridge a long while ago, as well as her bat who had tried to protect her."

"I'm so sorry."

"It's all right."

I glanced at his hand that was still gushing blood.

"I'll be fine," he said, following my gaze.

He turned off the water and placed his hand gently on the counter. With his pointer finger and thumb, he pinched the broken skin together and once he removed his fingers, the wound was gone.

"How did you do that?"

"It takes a great amount of power for a vampire to heal wounds. It's a great advantage to be able to heal your victim's skin so there isn't a trace of stolen blood. Only a few vampires have this ability."

"Is that so?" I inquired, half-interested, working the twigs out of my hair.

"You know, you had a long scratch running up your arm when I pulled you from the creek, and I healed that."

"Thank you…again."

"Anytime," he purred, taking a step toward me, "now come, let me…explain some things-,"

A loud rumble shook the house. We ran to the window to find that the two moons, Earth's moon and our moon Clesta were moving back together in their eclipse. The sun disappeared behind the clouds once again.

"What does this mean?"

"I'm not sure. The eclipse isn't over…but it has begun again. This only happens once every hundred years or so, an eclipse lasting longer than one month."

"So what do we do now that the eclipse is longer than usual?"

"I am going to cross the Bridge again."

"I want to come with you."

"Have you crossed the Bridge before?"

"No but-,"

"Then I cannot let you come with me. You are still too young of a vampire to cross the Bridge anyway. In time when you learn to defend yourself in this world, nevertheless in the mortal world, I will bring you across the Bridge myself."

"But that's not fair! I must go over the Bridge of Secrecy. Please Fitzray, let me come with you. I'll be safe beneath your wing."

"No, you will have to wait for your time to come when you become a bit more experienced."

I crossed my arms and stared at him with frustration. "That's not fair."

"*Life's* not fair. I am leaving tomorrow and you are staying *here*."

"I just have to go over the Bridge! Don't deny my only wish-,"

"No. As much as I would like to take you over the Bridge I *can't*."

I would not be going; I would have to wait at least a year more. I sat on the soft couch and sulked.

"Now, don't be like that," he said, his hand brushing the side of my face. "I have much to tell you and show you of this crazy world."

"Humor me."

"Ok then, if you insist."

He clasped a cold hand to the side of my neck, which sent me into a dream-like state. I saw a man, perhaps in his early twenties holding a baby with brown eyes, wrapped in a black blanket. Around them were tombstones. On the stone before the man was the name Luna Silver.

A flurry of clouds filled my head as a new vision rose. Fitzray was walking down the halls of a busy hospital. He entered a room with the name Doctor Silver in boldface letters on the door. He then sat at his desk and rubbed his eyes from exhaustion. Once again a new vision formed. This time Fitzray knelt beside the man shown in the first vision whom was dying. Fitzray's eyes were greener than I had ever seen them before and then my eyes flew open with a gasp.

I know this vampire. I know him from somewhere, somehow. He seems so familiar, I thought.

"What was that?"

"That was the bond of two vampires coming together. The visions you saw were past experiences of my life."

"Luna Silver, was that your mother's name?"

"Yes."

"And you're a doctor?"

"Yes, well, I'm a healer."

"I'm not surprised, with you and those healing powers, it's no wonder you've taken up medicine."

"I belong to a special group of vampires. We heal the wounds of newly-turned vampires that cross the Bridge."

"In the third vision there was a man with you…and your eyes were so bright."

"That man was probably my father, probably when I was turned into a vampire."

I turned to look at him over my shoulder. "What do you know about me?"

He walked around the couch and sat next to me.

"You were once rich when you lived in the mortal world, on Earth, but then you left your family and crossed the Bridge when you became a vampire. You are and will always be eighteen. And you…you like me more than you know."

That doesn't make sense. I've only known him a couple of days, I thought.

He looked at me and smiled as if reading my mind.

"You know me from somewhere. I'm familiar to you." His tone was low, hard to decipher.

"Yes, I know you. I've met you before, haven't I?"

"You tell me."

I tried to recall, but found no answer. I knew him, but I still did not know how.

"Maybe some fresh air will jog your memory." He took my hand and led me outside.

The brisk air stung my face, refreshing me. Fitzray held my hand tighter and kissed me lightly on the cheek without warning.

"What? What are you doing?" I yelped, breaking from his grip.

Something gave a startled cry at my feet. Quickly disregarding what he had just done, my eyes searched for the source of the cry. Through the growing darkness, I could just make out a small shape that was a baby bird. I gathered it in my hands and stood up. It was a blue jay, with striking navy blue feathers and distinct black and white pattern over its wings.

"I haven't seen blue jays ever since I left the mortal world. Where do you think it came from?"

"I'm not sure. Perhaps he was brought here from another vampire or werewolf."

"Let's get him inside, it's cold out here."

Once safely inside, I sat before the comfortably warm fireplace, the little bird nestled in my hands. Fitzray picked up the little creature and set it in a blanket. The little bird's black eyes studied him and he opened his mouth, letting out a cry for food.

"What can we feed him?"

"There's some bread and milk in the kitchen, but I think it's best if it rests. First thing in the morning he should be fed."

"Can you tell if it's a boy or girl?"

He studied the bird's wing and ran his fingers down the small feathers.

"It's a boy. You can see by the way his feathers are arranged," he said, pointing to the feathers to show me.

"He's so young. He's probably only a couple of weeks old."

"What will you name him?"

"I don't know. I had a parrot when I was younger. His name was Valiant."

"That's a nice name." Fitzray purred close to me.

"Such a cute little hatchling you are," I cooed quietly to the little bird.

"Hatchling," Fitzray exclaimed, "I almost forgot."

He grabbed my arm, pulling me to my feet. "What," I cried back, struggling to break free from his grip. "Let go of me!"

"Leave the bird here and come with me!"

He hastily led me up the polished staircase to his room. On the nightstand next to the king sized bed there was an egg, roughly the size of a melon. It was settled on a pile of hot coals and rocked from side to side every so often. Standing out from its light blue surface was a sharp point where cracks branched out over the top of the egg.

"What *is* that?"

"It's a dragon egg," he remarked, annoyed, as though I had asked a stupid question.

I snickered and shook my head. "A dragon egg? A *dragon* egg? Seriously, you're kidding right? Dragons don't exist."

"You think I'm *joking*?"

"Well, I don't think you're *serious*."

"Dragon scales have become as popular as jewelry on Earth."

"What has that have to do with-,"

"Dragons hide in their lairs in fear, but the mortals still find them and slaughter them. During their stay on Catastrophe, during an eclipse, they carve off, cut and polish the slaughtered dragon's scales, leaving the dragon's body to rot." He shook his head in contempt. "We have enough to deal with," he grumbled.

"What do you mean?"

"Well, the mortals claim that we are taking too many loved ones over the Bridge during the short eclipses and we should be reaping consequences because of it. There is also the constant tension between the wolves and us. And the dragons. Nothing seems to get resolved around here."

"How did you get that egg?"

"Vampires steal the eggs before they can be found and brought up by some mortals who only want their scales. We don't need precious scales. Dragons are great protectors and serve loyally to their masters who raise them. This egg was gifted to me by my father's dragon before he died."

Silence fell over us for a moment, just long enough for a small crackle to break the silence. The white crack on the egg grew, splitting further down the opal-looking egg.

It rocked, nearly sliding off the nightstand and then there was an explosion. Eggshells flew across the room. I turned my head and shielded myself from the sharp, hard shell.

The baby dragon lay on the hot coal exposed to the world. A sticky layer of membrane covered its body and its eyes were closed and helpless. It held its head high and flicked its light pink tongue through the air, its claws kneading at the coal as it uttered a soft squeak.

"What does it want?" I inquired quietly.

The baby dragon squeaked in response and clawed at the coal upon hearing my voice.

"He's heard your voice. Go to him." He gave me a gentle shove toward the creature.

The little dragon screamed louder and louder with every hesitant step I took toward him. My hands wrapped around the soft white body that was no larger than a newborn dog. It stopped crying and snuggled its frail little body in my hands. It lifted its head up toward my face with some difficulty, its tongue flicking out again and let out a soft squeak. Its eyes opened and it looked at me.

"He's yours now."

I wheeled around in disbelief. "No, he's yours. You take him!" I placed the dragon in Fitzray's hands and it immediately cried and moved its head as I backed away.

"I've taken care of him when he was an egg, but now that he's heard your voice, knows what you look like-,"

"No! *You've* cared for him. He's yours, *you* take him!"

"I can't take him! He will keep crying if you don't take him. Dragons are like birds, the first one it sees is its parent. And he saw *you*. I can't take him now. He wouldn't trust me. He's *yours*."

Hesitantly I gripped it in my hands again. The dragon let out soft peeps, nuzzled at my stomach and clutched my shirt with its talons.

"Don't let him out of your sight. He can barely walk and will remain as weak as he is for at least a few weeks."

"It's a boy?"

"Yes." Again, he gave me a look that marked my question as a stupid one.
"I have to name him something."
"I was going to call him Minx. Here, on Catastrophe, Minx means *the cherished one*."
"Minx," I repeated quietly to myself. "Can dragons talk?"
"Yes, they can be taught to mimic when they reach two years old."

The small clock on the wall read midnight. "It's getting late. I have to head back home."
"You don't have to go, not back to that old house. You can stay here. It's too dark for you to travel by foot. Besides, you'd probably end up in the creek again."
"I don't know." My eyelids became heavy as Minx let out a few soft cries. I could feel his soft breathing beneath my hands.
"I'm leaving tomorrow."
"No, I want to cross the Bridge."
"I'm sorry, but it's better this way." His voice faded into the quiet of the room and before I knew it, I was asleep.

Minx's loud peeps woke me the next morning. I could not find Fitzray anywhere.
"There you are," I said with a sigh of relief, spotting him in the kitchen.
"You're up early. I hope I didn't wake you," Fitzray said.
"I thought you left already."

He had on a long cape, a bag slung over his right shoulder. A white dragon the size of an adult cat rested on his left shoulder.
"I wouldn't leave without saying goodbye."
"Who's that?" I nodded toward the dragon.
"*That* is Moonscale."
"I didn't know you owned a dragon."
"Yes. He's coming with me and so is Charlene, so you don't have to worry about her. Give some milk to Minx."
"How long will you be gone?"

"Not long, a couple of weeks at most. And you are welcome to stay for as long as you want while I'm gone."

"Thank you."

"See you later." He called over his shoulder on the way out.

"Yeah, see you soon."

Chapter 4 -The Bridge of Secrecy

I stood looking at the Bridge of Secrecy, made from the finest stone of both worlds. There was still time to cross the Bridge and Fitzray would never know. He would be returning soon so I would have to act fast. Two weeks was long enough.

Valiant perched on my shoulder while Minx rested in my hands. Fitzray approached the Bridge so I ducked behind the nearby bushes and waited for a while. Once he was out of sight, I leaped from the brush and stepped gingerly onto the Bridge. I knew Fitzray would bite my head off if he found out I was crossing the Bridge. That thought alone made me quicken my pace. Fortunately, I was the only one here.

There was a sudden shout. My name rang in my ears, making my hair stand on end.

He saw me.

Without a second thought, I sprinted ahead. Glittering stars glowed in the space above me, lighting the way. The running steps behind me sounded closer, louder, and faster than my own.

A weight lifted from my shoulder and a loud cry hit my ears.

"Valiant! No!" I screamed. Charlene took him away.

Valiant will be fine. It's only a distraction to make me stop. I have to keep going. I have to make it over the Bridge. Fitzray cannot stop me, not now.

"Chenille stop," Fitzray yelled.

I tightened my grip around Minx and kept up my pace. Without warning, he collided into me, the force throwing my body into the stone.

"Are you insane? There are wolves crossing this Bridge. Do you want to get yourself killed?" He held me in place so it was difficult to avoid his infuriated glare.

"No, I just want to cross the Bridge. I want to go to the mortal world! I want to see my family again!"

The vampire breathed hard over me. "You will have to wait."

"No! I don't want to *wait*. Take me over the Bridge," I demanded.

"*No*. I won't let you go."

"Please," I begged, warm tears blurring my vision.

Fitzray shook his head, easing his weight off me without another word. He held my hands and led me off the Bridge back to the immortal world. Once we were in the confinement of his home, he released me.

"Why won't you let me go over to Earth? *Please,*" I begged.

He let out a sigh and rubbed his head. "Fine, I will go with you across the Bridge." He said it quickly. He was just trying to appease me with his words.

"What's the catch?"

"The catch?"

"I'm sure you want something in exchange."

"Exchange," his tongue formed the word slowly as if he was conjuring up a plan with it. "Fine, I will take you over the Bridge for a small *exchange*."

"And what would that be?"

"Just a taste of your blood is all."

"*My* blood, but I am a vampire. Why would you want *my* blood?"

"There is no rule stating a vampire can't have the blood of another."

"But why, I mean, who wants immortal blood?"

He shrugged. "Some like it hot some like it cold. Blood is blood."

"I thought the whole point of crossing the Bridge was to feed on the mortals."

"It is, but right now on Earth the mortals are snowed in.

No one is outside. Living in total darkness for nearly two whole months with the sun hidden behind the moons makes it cold there on Earth. And since we are bound by an agreement to respect Earth, property of the mortals', we can't break their doors down." A faint smile crossed his lips. "You still want to go?"

The fireplace beckoned me over, inviting me to sit before it on one of the velvet chairs. "When will we leave?"

"Tomorrow, if that's not too late for you."

"No, it's not."

"Do you remember what it's like to be bit by a vampire?"

One of his hands gently touched my shoulder and his fingers dug into my shirt.

"No, I don't." My voice trembled with unease.

"It hurts. You feel an indescribable pain when fangs break through the skin on your neck. And then when you feel your blood draining, *draining*...and there's nothing you can do," his voice trailed off. "I'm surprised you don't remember."

He walked around the chair and stood before me, the flames casting an eerie shadow over his face.

He's just trying to scare me so I give up and we don't have to go over the Bridge. I'm not scared of him. Besides, he would never bite me.

He edged toward my neck and Minx cried out, sensing something was wrong.

"Whenever you want to reconsider, just let me know."

His fangs pressed against my neck with a purr. The hairs on my body stood on end with a chill of fright. They dug deep beneath my skin and I became immobilized by shock. If his instinct kicked in, I knew he would suck my body dry.

His hands held me in place. He was too strong and my very strength was draining from me. He could kill me if I let him, but if I stopped him, I would not be able to cross the Bridge. He could not stop himself now. He allowed his fangs to sink deeper and uttered a wicked chuckle. I felt the warm blood spill down my neck, half stunned, but realized the pain was subsiding. With the air I had left in my lungs, I screamed.

Immediately he pulled himself away gasping and looked at me, fighting his instinct to go back for more.

"Why didn't you…stop me?"

There was no way for me to respond. I could not speak. He backed away and put a hand to my neck in silence.

"I'm sorry I thought… I thought...hey? Are you feeling ok?"

"No…no."

"Take it easy now. You are going to be all right. I didn't do *too much* damage."

He slid me off the chair and set me on the carpet. His hands caressed the side of my neck so gently, so passionately enticing and foreign to heal the wound he inhumanely created.

"You could've killed me, killed me! I could have been reincarnated in some different form, maybe even a wolf!" I cried out, finding my voice.

"Don't be so overdramatic. I wouldn't have killed you."

"Oh really? If I didn't stop you-,"

"I would've stopped myself. I just broke the skin, that's all."

He pulled me close to him, fixing me in a strong embrace. I pressed hard against his chest to get away, but my effort was futile so I surrendered.

"You know, you're not supposed to trust vampires. There's a good reason for that," he said softly and drew my face close to his, offering a hesitant kiss.

All at once, some of my memories returned. Memories, good and bad returned as if they had never left. Tentatively I looked up at Fitzray. He was my friend. I knew him before I turned into a vampire. I had been in love with him.

"I remember now," I said quietly, "you visited me during

every eclipse. And then, I was turned into a vampire and I never saw you again."

"We were supposed to get married actually."

"Why didn't you tell me?"

He snorted. "You have enough to deal with. You would not believe me if I told you. I knew you would figure it out on your own anyway."

"Then was it you who had bit me and turned me into a vampire?"

"No. I wanted to, but I was too late."

"Do you know who did it then?"

"Yes. I'm not telling you though. If you don't remember who he is then it's best you don't."

"Will you at least tell me his name?"

"His name is like poison Chenille. I'm glad you don't remember him. I'm glad you don't remember what he did to you. Anyway, he is irrelevant. We're crossing the Bridge tomorrow, first thing in the morning."

Chapter 5 - Ultimatum

Finally, I stood before the wondrous Bridge of Secrecy with Minx in hand and Fitzray at my side. Fitzray stood closer than what I would have liked. One hand was gripping my right arm while the other fingered the hilt of the knife at his belt.

"How long did it take to make this Bridge?"

"It took about two hundred years to make but that's only because the mortals had to finish it."

"Were we ever at peace with the mortals?"

"At one time, yes, the mortals didn't mind us, but over the years we have become very greedy creatures. We've been taking so many mortals over the past few past years that they declared that we could only cross the Bridge at the time of an eclipse. If we disobey their wishes, they will slay any immortal creature on Earth after the eclipse."

"What about the dragons? Do you think we can save them?"

"I'm not sure. Gems are a big part of the jewelry business on Earth. The mortals would not be happy with us if we cut off their supply."

"What would they do to us if we did so?"

"They would probably proclaim war or blow up the Bridge."

"What good would that do? I mean, if they blew up the Bridge they wouldn't get any dragon scales."

"But *that* would cause *us* to suffer. With vampires and werewolves, the protectors of the dragons, now gone because the Bridge was destroyed and none could get across to feed on the mortals, the other creatures wouldn't know what to do. The mortals would probably wait a few hundred years or so until the vampire and wolf race were gone and then build another bridge so they could kill all of the dragons they would need. They would probably take over this world *too*."

"So what does that mean then? No matter how you cut it, the dragon race will diminish? What about the other creatures on Catastrophe? Couldn't they help?"

"Well the dragons will someday be protected. I'm not sure *when* or *how* or *who* will come up with such a plan to protect them, but I'm sure that day will come."

"And the other creatures, what about them, could they help?" I repeated.

"I'm sure they could, but they refuse to. They have said repeatedly that the vampires and wolves are the ones who *cross* the Bridge and *need* the Bridge and that we are the reason why there *is* a Bridge to begin with, making the mortals have access to our world. They want no part of it."

I hugged Minx close to me. "That's selfish of them."

"It is, but they have a point."

"What if-,"

"Stay close and keep your voice quiet," Fitzray warned, cutting me off as a distant howl echoed across the Bridge. An immortal man, an assumed werewolf, and a big gray wolf approached us.

"Look here, a couple of vampires. How lucky for us," the man said.

"Yeah and look there, the girl's got a little dragon! It *is* our lucky day," the wolf said.

I looked down at Minx and nudged Fitzray. "What do they want with Minx?"

"I don't know," he replied in a hushed voice.

"Why don't we take a look at that dragon? It looks so helpless."

"Back off," Fitzray growled.

The wolf let out a growl in response. "Oh now leader of the fangs has something to say about *us*? Let's see if your bark is worse than your bite!" The gray wolf launched and backed him up against one of the Bridge walls.

There was a loud scream and Fitzray and the wolf were out of sight. Only the immortal and I remained on the Bridge. I swallowed hard. Tears gathered in my eyes.

Fitzray was right, right all along. This werewolf will kill me right here. By the time Fitzray gets back, I will be a pool of blood at his feet.

He strode toward me, his dog-like teeth exposed as he started to transform into a wolf. I turned and ran as fast as I could, the monster close behind. I stopped once I saw Fitzray.

His back was against the high side of the stone bridge. The gray wolf's claws extended deep into his neck. Blood dripped from the deep gashes.

Paralyzed, I helplessly watched as the wolf's teeth came close to his face and snapped his jaws viciously.

"No!" I screamed. Minx slipped from my hands onto the Bridge.

The gray wolf turned his head and leapt toward me, leaving Fitzray.

"Go! Go Chenille, run!" Fitzray said hoarsely. His hands clutched his bleeding neck as he fell to his knees.

I hesitated and bent down to pick up Minx, but the wolf snapped at my hand and I quickly withdrew it, stumbling back. I fell against the cold stone unable to move. The gray wolf walked close to Minx and carefully carried him away in his mouth, joining the other wolf.

"No, no Minx, they have Minx!" I whispered in desperation, my throat dry and sore.

Without my consent, my eyes closed, shielding me from the horror that now walked away with my precious dragon.

A high fever woke me hours later, my eyes stung, my lips burning. My eyes opened slowly. Tears flooded over my lids. I was on a small bed with clean, crisp white sheets. The smell of over-sanitation filled my nose at once, but I disregarded it. Fitzray sat on the corner of the bed with his head in his hands. A pale scar on his neck was the only evidence that I did not dream the incident on the Bridge.

"How are you doing?"

"I...I don't know. I feel really hot." I felt around the bed, suddenly panicked. "Where is Minx? Where's Minx!"

"Minx was taken away by the wolves. I tried to stop them, but I couldn't."

"No, no! This is my fault! Oh, my poor Minx is out there in the cold world with those wolves!"

"It's *my* fault. I shouldn't have taken you over the Bridge. I knew something would go wrong."

"We have to go find him," I said, sitting up.

"You will have to wait," Fitzray said, pressing lightly on my shoulders. "The doctors are still trying to figure out why you passed out and why you spiked such a high fever."

We waited for what seemed like hours in silence until finally, a striking vampire, dressed in a long white lab coat entered the room.

"Ah, Chenille East, I ran a few tests and I think we've got our answer." He nodded toward Fitzray. "Have you kissed her within the past few days?"

His face deepened to a glow and he cleared his throat with a nod.

"That explains it then. A vampire possesses a poison, I'm sure you are well aware, and you must have had an allergic reaction to it. It's fairly common with young vampires."

"And my fever and symptoms, will they go away?"

"They will subside soon."

"Does that mean I will always be allergic to his poison?"

"No, you will soon be immune to his poison and no longer get that allergy, but that doesn't mean you are immune to *all* of the vampire poisons. Each vampire has a different poison and causes a different allergy, that in which may range from burning of the lips to slurred speech to paralysis and in the rarest of cases, death."

"Death?" I got a chill at the very thought of such a strong poison.

"It is mainly caused from a very, *very* strong vampire feeding off a mortal."

I sank back into the warm sheets and noted the doctor's bright blue eyes and caramel brown hair.

"Ah, I didn't recognize you in this light, Caspian." Fitzray laughed. He turned to me with a smile. "This is Caspian, a fellow clan member and partner in crime."

"Right, sorry, I didn't introduce myself."

"Nice to meet you."

"Caspian is the City's finest doctor."

"Is that so?"

"I suppose it is," the doctor replied humbly.

"Could you tell me where to go for help to find my lost dragon?"

Caspian stuck one hand in his coat pocket and shifted his weight over to his left foot. "Well, since you're already here, at the City of Lights, you could go to the reservoir and look for Taj'. He should be able to direct you from there."

"Taj'?"

"Yes, I know Taj'. He'll help us," Fitzray assured me.

There was a sudden cry from a distant room in the hospital and Caspian flew toward the door.

"I'd love to chat, but as you can see I am needed elsewhere. Good luck, you are free to go, and feel better." He smiled quickly and left.

"Come on, let's go!" I sat up quickly and peeled the white sheets off my burning body.

"Take it easy, we'll find Minx, don't you worry. Just try to rest a bit."

"I don't care! I have to find Minx!"

He sighed and helped me to my feet. Reluctantly he offered me a hand, which quickly transpired to a full arm around my waist due to my inability to stand up straight.

"Let's go, this is the last day of the eclipse," I urged, more to push myself forward.

The crisp warm sheets lingered behind me, called out to my tired bones. If I returned to rest it would only be another minute - another minute I could not afford to lose.

Outside, it was cold and a harsh wind chilled my skin to my bones. If not for my urgency to move on I would have stopped to admire the glorious city. Unfortunately, I did not have the time.

"The City of Lights," Fitzray said with a gesture to the skyscrapers that crowded around us.

Large old lampposts lined the streets, making the buildings around us visible as though it were day, despite the heavy overcast and shadows cast from the two moons.

I had been in this city only once or twice since the walking distance from the house was too far and Zaire never offered protection to me from the strong werewolves and vampires that lurked.

"I know where we must go."

After a while of walking, my pace slowed almost to a stop and we sat on an old wood bench to rest. Each time I struggled to go on, but the vision of Minx and his loud cries were still fresh in my mind and Fitzray's words helped sustain me.

"We are almost there, you are doing great." He would continue to say. More than once he had offered to carry me or to stop, but I knew it would only slow us down.

"The reservoir, there it is," Fitzray said at last and led me to its edge.

A mermaid sat on a large stone in the middle of it and turned to us skeptically.

"Hello. What brings you here?" She inquired, her peremptory gaze falling on Fitzray.

"I've come for Taj'."

"Humph," she tossed her head, her blond hair cascading down her shoulders like a soft gold wave. "You've come to see *that* old lizard? Oh, *please*."

"I must speak to him."

She sighed in frustration and crossed her arms before she dove into the water impatiently.

Huge waves rolled over onto the land before us and splashed at our feet. A massive column of water shot up to the sky, revealing a licorice black snake with silver spikes down its back.

"Fitzray my good friend," the snake exclaimed, bending his head down to our eye level.

"Hello Taj'," Fitzray greeted with a large, flawless smile.

Taj's huge eye moved slightly to look at me.

"You're a beauty." His thunderous voice made the ground quiver.

"This is Chenille."

"What an elegant creature you are."

"Oh, thank you."

"What brings the two of you here?"

"My...my dragon was kidnapped by a couple of werewolves and I need help to find him."

The snake lifted his head, as big as an elephant, and flicked out his tongue. "Savages!" The snake said, spraying out a streak of water. "Not to fear, for I know someone who can help."

"Who, a fortuneteller or a sorcerer?"

"No, no dear, they don't exist!" The snake shook his head. "Princess Pearl."

"*Princess*, how can a princess help?"

"Do not underestimate her. She has a way with her powers."

He looked at Fitzray with his large bronze eyes.

"Do not look into her eyes. She can hypnotize any man. She can control his actions," he warned.

"Where can I find her?"

"Go onward through the City to the border of the woods and you will find a path that will take you to a river. Follow it until you see the Frozen Waterfalls and you shall find her there."

"Thank you very much Taj'."

"Good luck to you both. And if she gives you trouble, tell her that Taj' sent you."

Taj' took a joyous leap back into the water, disappearing under its glassy surface.

"Come on Fitz, let's get going." I pulled on his hand and walked with him through the busy streets.

"You know," he said slowing down, "they say if you go to the very top of this building, you can see the moons so clearly that you can even count the craters on their surface." He stopped to look up at the tall building.

"But we don't have *time*. We need to find Princess Pearl."

"We will find her, I promise." He looked at the building again. "Come, why don't we go and see?"

"But Minx, my *poor* Minx," I said pulling him away from the building.

He tightened his grip on my arm. "You're right. We should go and get him."

If you made it out of the woods in one piece, a worn dirt path cut through the dense greenery heading north. The path, tediously long, exhausting, and occasionally covered in overgrowth, presented us to a pond. It was here where the Frozen Waterfalls existed as a natural monument. The water that seemed frozen in time hid a rock wall. The raging torrents and white, misty froth that licked the edge of the pond ceased to move, captured in space and time as though it was a simple scenic picture.

Fitzray's eyes studied the ground while he stood beside me. We stood before the Princess who sat in the center of the pond. She was surrounded by three vampires all who sat by her on her rock, their eyes glassy and irresponsive. Pearls covered her neck and wrists and even a tiara with silver pearls rested on her head. Her delicate pixie-like nose turned up while she rested an icy stare on us. She was dangerously beautiful.

She was not a vampire, as I expected, but a mermaid. Her blonde hair hung down into the water, her turquoise eyes refusing to move from us.

"What do you want? Can't you see I'm busy," she snapped.

Mermaids were selfish, haughty creatures who thought that those who walked on land should pity them. Mermaids, classified by their degree of conceit, made stumbling upon a good-natured mermaid unlikely. In fact, the majority of the species frowned upon it.

"So *you* are the famous Princess Pearl? It's a pleasure," I said quietly.

Her lips remained neutral, though she eyed me suddenly, causing me to shrink back behind Fitzray.

"Who sent you here?"

"Taj', he sent us."

"Is she telling the truth?" She chimed, near mocking, in Fitzray's direction.

His head jerked to the side to avoid her glance. "Yes, Taj' sent us because he said you could *help*, not criticize. Tell us where our dragon is."

"My, my, isn't *someone* a little *demanding*?" Her pale pink lips turned up slightly. "But, since you seem so insisting, what's in it for *me*?"

"What do you want?"

"Nothing you can get me," she said in defeat, "my powers are not as strong as they used to be. And that means Taj' will never fall under my spell."

"Taj' is a good friend of mine," Fitzray said. "I'll put in a few good words about you to him so that way you won't even need a *spell*." His mouth twitched as though he suppressed a laugh.

"You would really do that for me?"

She touched the many pearls that hung from her neck and then her eyes became tearful. "You're probably lying," she accused with a scowl.

"Oh no, once I tell Taj' all about you and how truly *wonderful* you are, he will reconsider."

This time Fitzray could not suppress a chuckle from escaping his throat. The Princess eyed him suspiciously, probably suspecting that he was mad.

"You're making mockery of me!"

Still amused, Fitzray turned to me. "Come on, she's not going to help us."

"But what about my dragon?"

"If she doesn't trust my word now, then I don't think she'll trust us at all."

"No wait, don't leave. I will help you." Desperation filled every word she forcefully uttered.

"Yeah, you help us first. Help us find our dragon."

She frowned, looking into the water. "It doesn't look well for your dragon."

"How do we know if you're telling the truth?"

"Your dragon's name is Minx, right?"

"Yes, that is his name."

"And how do I know Taj' really sent you? How can I be sure that you even *know* Taj'?"

"Taj' is my old friend. I've known him for years," Fitzray said.

"Oh really?" She inquired, leaning forward on her rock. "Then you probably know how old he is."

"He's been around since the Bridge was built. I can't give you an approximate number."

"Then tell me how you met."

Fitzray's gaze rolled down to meet the water's icy surface. For a moment, he stared blankly, perhaps stalling time to conjure up his thoughts. He was wasting precious time.

"I was a sailor once. I sailed the seas of Catastrophe for many years with my friend Caspian." His mouth turned up with recollection. "That was in another life. Anyway, one night a vicious storm crossed our path. Caspian and I, along with our crew, stopped at nothing to fight the wind, though we were hardly successful, as you could imagine. Our crew rebelled against us. One thing led to another and they threw me overboard. Caspian jumped in after me. Even though we were both good swimmers, we did not last very long in the raging waves. I accepted the fact that I would probably meet my death, but somehow Taj' found us. He saved Caspian and I, brought us to shore, and we've been friends ever since."

"Your story seems truthful but…it seems you don't have an Eternal Mate. And if that's so, then how did you have a *past life*?"

"Well, you're right about me not having an Eternal Mate, but reincarnation was possible thanks to Caspian. Caspian was a healer then and still is. He always has some herbs with him, herbs that induce reincarnation and herbs that prevent it. He uses them sparingly since he only has a limited amount. He gave me a rare herb after Taj' pulled us to shore. It somehow enabled me to have another chance at life."

"I've never heard of such a thing in my life. Aren't vampires immortal anyway?"

"Yes, when they have an Eternal Mate."

The mermaid shook her head in defeat. "Whatever. All I know is that your dragon is being kept in the tallest building in the City."

"Thank you," I groaned with relief.

She shrugged and turned back to the vampires surrounding her. One of them in particular looked familiar to me.

"*Calvin*?"

Pearl turned to the vampire I was staring at. "Oh, is he *yours*? You can have him. He is of no service to *me*." She said, shoving him toward me.

He looked dazed as a cloud drifted over his orange eyes. "That mermaid promised me that she would help me…and now here you are," he droned, still in a trance.

Calvin studied me and wrapped me in a warm hug. "And you're ok. I thought something happened, I thought you were lost. I thought that green-eyed murderer took you from me."

"No Calvin, I'm ok."

"Minx is being kept in the highest building in the City of Lights, where the moons can be seen perfectly. Too bad the eclipse is ending," Fitzray cut in, snapping my attention back to more important matters.

"There will be other eclipses."

With little interest in the eclipse, I focused on the matter at hand. We had lost more than enough time.

"I am getting hungry, how about you guys?"

As hungry as I was, I could not stop now, so without a word I proceeded on toward the City.

"You go on Calvin. We'll meet up with you later."

He shrugged and made his way toward the City, heading in the direction of the nearest restaurant. Instead, Fitzray and I made our way closer to the tallest building in the City where Minx was.

"So tell me, how does marriage between vampires work? And what was that Eternal Mate stuff you were talking about?"

"*Eternal Mate stuff,*" he exhaled, probably stalling to gather his thoughts. "The vampire that turned you is referred to you as your Eternal Mate. If you had a relationship with someone else there would be a fight and the winner would be your mate for all eternity."

"So the guy that turned me into a vampire is out there?"

My spine quivered as an uncontrollable shudder wracked my bones.

"Yep, he's probably looking for you right now as we speak."

I shivered again and bit my lip. "And what if he wins?"

"You mean, if your Eternal Mate wins? He would be your mate for all eternity. He would basically control you and unfortunately you wouldn't have a say."

He shook his head and I figured he was brushing away his thoughts as I was. "We're here." He made a motion toward the building.

The building was deserted and quiet, odd for such a popular tourist attraction.

"How will we find Minx?"

"We are not leaving until we find him, so don't worry."

We searched the quiet, abandoned building with no signs of the werewolves that were responsible for my dragon's kidnapping.

"Pearl said he would be at the top," I recalled, pointing to the stairs.

We walked up the stairs since the elevator was not working, to our inconvenience, and found him before we arrived at the very top of the countless stairs.

The small huddled creature was just within reach. Minx lifted his head with a cry. He tried to hide in the crook of my arm, afraid and cold when I picked him up.

"He's not hurt and the wolves aren't even here. It's too good to be true. It shouldn't be this easy." The vampire's gaze scanned the abandoned floor skeptically.

I shrugged in response as the little dragon clung to my shirt.

"No, something's not right here," he continued.

There was a loud crack and, an earthquake, it seemed, caused us to fall over. The building shook. Smoke came through the walls and surrounded us. It filled my lungs and made me weak.

"We have to get out of here!" Fitzray grabbed me, nearly dislocating my shoulder in the process.

"What's going on?"

"The wolves are doing this," he said as he led me up to the roof. "It's a trap."

He tightened his grip around my waist, leading me to the edge of the rooftop. Creatures that roamed the streets and those who traveled on the backs of dragons stopped for a brief moment to look up at us. There was no chance for me to refuse to jump. Fitzray pulled me down with him.

As we fell, the black smoke that smelled of volcanic ash broke through the windows and drifted out into the city. I did not hear my screams, or those of the frightened immortals below. Minx had struggled in my hands, his cries drowned out by the bomb-like explosion from behind. The mushroom cloud blew off the top of the building, sending debris and large shards of metal to scrape the wind and flew at the innocent below. The building then fell, causing even more destruction than the explosion itself. I braced myself, awaiting the crushing impact on cobblestone.

A throbbing in my head jerked my eyes open. I was alive. Something firm moved from under me and I rolled my eyes to see what it was.

"Fitz?" My voice was hoarse.

"Are you all right?" His voice was slurred and barely audible.

He gasped for air and I turned my face to look at him. I was crushing him. My head throbbed painlessly and my arms bled, but I did not feel anything, nothing at all.

Somehow we were not molded into the cobblestone and suffering the consequence of shattered bones. Lucky for us, a passing dragon broke our fall.

The dragon's head swiveled around and it shook us off. Helpless, we slid off and braced ourselves for the road. However, we did not crash into a road. Water surrounded us, breaking our second impact. I inhaled it and it choked me. The water filled my mouth and blurred my vision instantly. I couldn't move, and I was sure Fitzray couldn't either.

My eyes opened after a long couple of moments and a familiar voice boomed, "Do not fear my friends! I've got you!"

* * * * *

The landscape around me was opaque and dreadful. My ears picked up a voice in the distance. Fitzray called out to me. He smiled once he caught my glance and beckoned me to come. Once I went to reach out to him, my hand smashed into something. A glass wall separated us.

He cocked his head in surprise that I could not get to the other side. Suddenly a tall figure appeared from behind him. A sword swung high above his head.

"Behind you!" I yelled.

Fitzray looked at me, confused. He could not hear me. I stumbled back and shouted again; this time he read my lips and turned to face the figure. Blood stained the glass wall as the sword mercilessly stabbed his chest. My bloodcurdling scream played back to me. Fitzray's lifeless body fell and he failed to make another motion.

The figure responsible for Fitzray's demise only smiled slickly. His cloak hood covered his face. He walked up to the glass and pressed his fingertips to its surface.

Shards of glass rained on me. The wall shattered and disappeared at his slightest touch. I expected him to pounce on me and kill me too, but instead only approached me and pulled me to my feet.

"What have you done? Who *are* you?" I stammered.

Ignoring my questions, he leaned close to my ear. His words came slow and clear.

"I killed Fitzray."

His voice fell upon my ears as smooth and warm as silk. Every syllable was so clear it caused my skin to ripple as if he had touched me with his murderous hand instead.

"Who are you?" I managed to say again, forcing the words off my tongue.

A devious smile revealed two pearly, nearly translucent fangs. "I am your Eternal Mate." He remarked softly, almost greedily while his hands drew me close to him.

"You're lying," I hissed through my teeth.

A chuckle formed in his throat and left his mouth so effortlessly that I tensed with envy. "I wouldn't lie about that," he whispered, his lips brushing the side of my face. "You are mine. And I love you more than anything," his voice trailed off.

I could almost taste his words, laced with artificial sweetener, on the tip of my own tongue. He was a good liar but he would have to try harder than that.

Chapter 6 - Festivities

A final dose of morphine was our farewell gesture from the hospital. After a couple of long weeks under close speculation it was finally decided that we could leave.

For two weeks, the doctors needlessly quarantined us. We both suffered a few broken bones, although vampires were always notorious quick healers that could make fast recoveries, faster than any mortal could.

Despite two weeks of separation, Fitzray and I had nothing to say to one another. We arrived at his house in silence. We helped each other climb the stairs to the master suite and, in exhaustion, stumbled into the room. Calvin and Minx waited for us on the edge of the bed.

"You guys are so lucky," he said, one of a hundred times since our incident. "You landed right in the reservoir and Taj' was right there and-,"

"Relax Calvin," I moaned, placing my fingers against his mouth. With difficulty, I took a seat beside him on the bed while Fitzray rested on his back beside me.

"We have some unfinished business to take care of," Fitzray grumbled.

"And what is that?"

"The mermaid and our...*proposition* remember?"

"Right, I almost forgot. Do you think it will work?"

"Probably not."

"When will we go?"

"Tomorrow, when this blizzard clears, we will go and meet Taj'."

"Chenille, Amelia wanted me to give you this." Calvin handed me a small, formal invitation.

"Amelia is having a dinner party tomorrow night."
"I'm up for a dinner party."
"Will you listen to yourself? We just got out of the hospital."
"Exactly, we've been confined in dull, sanitized rooms for weeks." He did not even have to insist. I knew we would be going.

Calvin rushed his goodbyes, noting the inclement weather, and left us alone. With Calvin gone there was not much else to say and Fitzray turned his head away from me and fell asleep. Unfortunately for me, the previous nightmare kept me up.

It was early, so early that the sun was not up yet when we got up, but luckily, the blizzard cleared, revealing a bright blue winter sky. Snow covered our path, hindering our walk to the City.
"Why do you think those wolves came after us?"
"I'm not sure."
"Those wolves wanted *my* dragon. Who could be after me, I mean, I haven't done anything."
"I don't know, but we'll soon find out."

When we reached the reservoir, Taj' rose from the water and peered down at us, expecting our arrival. "Hello my friends, you look well."
"Hello Taj'!" I had to yell for the large snake to hear me. His head stooped low to meet our level.
"Where is your dragon the orange-eyed one saved?"
"He's home. It's too cold out here for him to travel."
"We have a favor to ask you."
"Anything my friend, anything at all for you," Taj' said.
"Will you come with us to the Frozen Waterfalls?"
"Having trouble with Princess Pest?"
"On the contrary, she has invited us to her lands."
"Sounds too good to be true. She has never been sympathetic to anyone but herself and those who fall in love with her. I pity them the most, I do."
"Maybe she's changed." I offered.

"*Changed*? You humor me."

"But it's *true*."

He looked over at me and flicked out his red tongue. "I must see this for myself then."

He slithered out of the water. His long black body coiled behind him.

"If you would like a ride," I turned to Taj', "come right ahead."

"You're too kind."

"Just be careful of the spikes and you will be fine."

His body came up to my hip. His head came down and nudged me on with a boost.

"Onward to the Waterfalls," Taj' said.

As slick as oil on water he glided over the land while Fitzray covered ground by foot instead.

When we caught a glimpse of Princess Pearl, we found her sulking on her large rock in the middle of the frozen pond. Her vampires were out fetching the best pearls they could find and she was alone. Her eyes lightened as soon as Fitzray approached her.

"You came back," she said with a hint of relief.

"I came with a friend," Fitzray added, nodding back toward Taj'.

Her small hands clasped together and rested beneath her chin. "I knew I could count on you."

Once I dismounted off Taj's back, he approached the Princess slowly and cast a wary glance at her. I reported to Fitzray's side, quietly watching as the snake slithered up to the edge of the pond.

"Taj' there is something I have to tell you."

"What? You have troubled someone and you want me to help? *No*."

"No, no not that! It's just, well, you see…I know we have worked together to help the immortals in their time of need but-,"

"*We?* Since when was it the two of us? You could care less for the immortals and you know it," the snake spat impatiently.

"But it's not about the immortals Taj', it's about us. I haven't told you how I truly feel."

The snake peered closer at her. "How do you feel Pearl?"

There was a long silence as she nervously combed her fingers through her hair.

"My powers are fading Taj' and I am growing old. I may not look so, but they are failing, you can see that. I was once able to lure *mortals* from over the Bridge, although recently I have had only enough power to capture a few hearts, not one of them yours. I do not want them. I will release them, for you."

"You *arrogant creature*!" He rose up and flicked out his tongue in disgust. "I would *never* love a thing of your individuality."

"Please, Taj', give me a chance."

He shook his head and turned to us. "Is this a joke? A tradeoff?" His eyes narrowed in fury. "I trusted you!"

"She promised to help us, if we helped make you fall for her."

Taj' eyed her sharply. "Is that true?"

She looked away at the water's frozen surface, her mouth open though unable to speak.

"You have exasperated me in the past, but this is your worst."

The Princess's vampires returned and shoved beautiful strings of pearls in her face. They crowded her, all showing her what they'd found. They attempted to adorn her with beautiful things that were worth more than the skin they rested upon.

"Taj', wait!"

"Do not send one of your captives for me, I will not respond. Your tail must ache from that rock you have been sitting on. If you must talk to me, you will come to me personally."

"You don't understand Taj', I love you and no other! I

don't love them," she cried, pointing to the immortals surrounding her.

"Is that because your powers are gone, like you've said, and you know one day you will have no one? I am outraged and I am sorry for you. I do *not* love you."

"Please…Taj'-,"

"Have fun with your vampires Princess. Good day."

Angrily, she shoved the immortals away from her. They fell back into the icy water and scrambled to their feet as she screamed at them to leave. They retreated, slowly coming out of the trance she had cast on them. Then they were gone.

"You speak of the truth, for me," the snake inquired half-heartedly.

"Yes, for you," she said.

"One day I will reconsider, but not today, not today, for I speak the truth as well." His steady bronze gaze rested over her. "You know where to find me."

Quickly he slithered off, back to his home, the reservoir. She turned to us, her face flushed pink. "If you may ever need my assistance you know where to find *me*."

"Come on, we're going to be late for the dinner party."

For the first time in weeks, I returned to my brother's house. My brother of course was not home, though that did not concern me. I returned to the dump of a place for one thing and one thing only - a decent dress to wear.

It was among my small collection of Earth-made clothes, worn clothes, that I found a dress. It was my only dress and it was the best I owned, though I felt I might be better off buying something Catastrophe-made. That meant spending money, money I did not have. I would have to settle for what I had.

The tight-fitting ball gown dress had acquired many compliments on Earth. It still fit me perfectly, clinging to every curve that made up the shape of my upper body. Despite the slight stench of mothballs, it was perfect.

The dinner party would be at Caspian's home. Fortunately, it was not hard to find. Predictably, Fitzray was the first one to greet me. He did not have the slightest hint of discomfort regarding his broken ribs.

"Oh look at the two of *you*, dressed up like you were going to some prom together," were the first words that spilled from my best friend's mouth once she caught sight of us.

An unavoidable nervous laugh left my mouth. "Amelia, please don't embarrass me tonight," I whispered.

"It is good to see you're doing well Chenille," Caspian said quietly, wrapping an arm around Amelia.

His eyes swept over me as if he could see right through my dress to my healing bones. I wrapped my arms around myself, suppressing a shudder, suddenly feeling naked in the presence of the City's finest doctor.

"Are you all right?" Fitzray's concern snapped me back into my body, taking me back into the mansion. Caspian's eyes settled elsewhere, so I felt my breath return to me.

"I'm fine."

"Come on then, let's sit. You shouldn't keep your guests waiting," Amelia chimed, gazing up at Caspian.

Succulent fruit, meat, cheeses, and greens from both worlds decked the banquet table. The tile floor served as a dance floor for the hundreds of guests. Formality among the guests was expected. It was a privilege to stand in Caspian's home.

Considering the lives he saved and the countless surgeries he performed, he was a highly respected individual. Although he remained trapped in a body that resembled slightly over twenty, his eyes never failed to present the strange depths of knowledge he had behind them. He walked with his head held up out of self-respect.

The immortal women flocked him but as soon as Amelia took her spot beside him, they gazed down at her as if she was unworthy to be so close to him. She was *ordinary*. She was an outsider, completely unassociated with the medical field as her companion was. Once the rumor of Caspian being Amelia's Eternal Mate proclaimed true, the women retreated in envy.

"Amelia and I will be performing the Ceremony tonight," Caspian announced later that evening.

The majority of Caspian's guests congratulated him while others barely showed interest. The women only gazed down at my friend as an unworthy specimen.

"What exactly is a Ceremony?" I asked under my breath, fearing for scrutinizing eyes to turn in my direction.

"It's a bonding ritual," Fitzray replied simply. "In order to be reincarnated a Ceremony must be performed. One should only perform it with their Eternal Mate, but some of us break the rules. Still, Eternal Mates are destined to bond with each other. That is why a vampire seeks out the mortal he turned into his vampress. It's courtship."

"That's not how it's done on Earth."

"Oh really? What do you call marriage then? It's a similar concept."

"But a Ceremony is so complicated, isn't it?"

"It's as complicated as you want it to be."

"Doesn't it entitle drinking each other's blood?"

"Yes."

"Doesn't that seem *strange*?"

"Not to me. I am not surprised that bothers you, in fact, it should bother you. You are still young. I've been a vampire for years."

"But you haven't performed a Ceremony."

"No I have not, nor have I taken a mortal to be my own."

"Would you?"

He hesitated. "I think it's a little late for that."

"What do you mean?"

"You wouldn't understand." He gave me a smile that mocked my inexperience.

"Mock me now, while you can."

"Chenille, you and I both recognize your innocence. You

and I both know there are some things you don't need to know. Let's face it, you are not ready for a Ceremony. If I asked you right now, you wouldn't know what to do with yourself."

"Is that a challenge?"

Without another word, he took me to the nearest empty room. This was a challenge more than I bargained for. Caspian and Amelia were not the only ones that would have a completed Ceremony by the end of the night.

"We shouldn't be doing this. Not here, not now."

"You brought it up."

"But this should be Caspian and Amelia's day. If they found us here-,"

"Who cares?" Fitzray grumbled, loosening the collar of his shirt.

"What if someone finds us?"

"No one will find us. No one will even suspect that we're missing."

"Are you sure about this?"

"You don't trust me?"

"I barely *know* you."

"You know me. You just refuse to acknowledge the fact that you've known me for years before you were turned."

"I guess you're right. I'm just…a little nervous."

"That's perfectly normal. May you be mine forever," he said, pressing his lips to my throat.

There was no time to speak, no time to think. By the time a drop of blood hit my lips, there came a pounding at the door.

"Open up! I know you're in there Chenille."

"It's Zaire," I whispered frantically. "How did he find me? What do we do?"

"Stay quiet."

How typical for big brother to show up now at my inconvenience. If Fitzray hadn't been holding me so tight, I would have opened the door and throttled him.

"Chenille if you don't open this door-," he yelled,

pounding on the door so violently that I held my breath.

When he finally managed to open it, Zaire only stared at us, his face glowing crimson.

"You are coming home with me right *now,*" he growled.

The silence hung over us for a moment, for I was too afraid to speak. My only thought revolved around the possibility that Caspian lingered nearby.

"Get up Chenille or I'll drag you home by your hair," my brother spat, his growing anger adding an edge to his voice.

Fitzray moved away from me unwillingly, creating enough space for me to sit upright. Zaire caught his breath, probably noticing the blood on my neck.

"Zaire, it's not what you think-," I started instinctually, trying to cover up his suspicion.

"Is this *him,* the one responsible for turning you into a vampire?"

Every one of my brother's muscles tensed so quickly that I thought he would launch at Fitzray at that moment and rip him to shreds.

"No," Fitzray answered for me.

"Y*ou* stay away from her," he growled, probably suspecting that Fitzray was lying.

"Leave him alone Zaire."

His eyes settled back on me. "I've heard enough from you."

That was the last straw. I scrambled off the bed and pushed my brother aside to escape.

Without another word, I left the festivities behind me and traveled out into the woods. Alone for now, I knew Fitzray and Zaire were not far behind. Regardless, I ventured on, away from them both to seek some answers in solitude.

Chapter 7 - The Revelation

The Bridge of Secrecy, isolated, suspended between the two worlds, served as a refuge where I could be alone. The stars glittered endlessly, poking holes into the black blanket of the universe overhead. The air remained stiff and cold as it usually was here. I had no intentions to cross the Bridge, at least not tonight. For a while, I could mull over my thoughts while Fitzray and Zaire continued on their path to find me.

With a start, I caught a glimpse of a figure in my peripheral vision. The figure's dark cape gave me the impression that they had materialized out of the darkness.

"I didn't see you there."

His words hung in the air for a while. I could have said the same to him. He approached me slowly, cautiously, giving me a few quiet seconds to study his bold, captivating face.

His black hair swept over to one side, framing his intensive eyes, innocent among his darker features. He resembled the stranger in my nightmare.

"Who did this to you?" It took me a moment to register how close he was and that his hand nonchalantly rested on the side of my neck. "Who bit you?"

"I…I don't know," I stuttered, "I mean, my friend…my friend did it."

"So much of a friend he is," the figure replied with a coy smile, revealing two pearly fangs. "Was this done on purpose?"

"Yes."

"I see." He dropped his hand slowly.

"Why do you care?"

"Why shouldn't I care Chenille?" My name slipped off his tongue so beautifully that it did not concern me how he knew it in the first place.

"You know my name."

"Yes, I do. Why wouldn't I know your name?"

"I don't know *you*."

"My name is Pete." His words flowed together seamlessly, sending me in a daze for a brief moment as he spoke. He blinked slowly, tilting his head with interest. "I'm surprised you don't remember me."

"I've met you before?"

Pete laughed humorlessly. I felt myself shrink back, suspecting he was already thinking less of me.

"Well, you should know who I am," he said impatiently.

In silence, he removed a knife from under his cape and sliced his hand. Black blood spilled out of the wound and black blood, I knew, belonged to powerful immortals. Pete was the leader as King of the vampires - King of Catastrophe.

"I'm sorry I...I didn't know," I stammered, about to curtsey when he grabbed my shoulder with his bloody hand.

"That is no excuse. You should know your Eternal Mate."

I froze. "Excuse me?"

"Chenille!"

I stumbled back, away from the King, my Eternal Mate, my eyes locking on Fitzray. Moonscale ran alongside him. Without thinking, I ran to him, nearly colliding into him once I reached him.

"It's him," I cried, on the verge of tears, "it's the King. He claims that he's...he's my," my voice trailed off. I clutched his shirt in desperation, hoping he would wake me up from another nightmare.

"The two of us need to finish what we started," Fitzray said softly, gazing in Pete's direction.

"No, you don't have to finish anything. Just forget him and take me away from here," I begged frantically.

"I don't have much of a choice."
"You can't go. He's too strong. His blood runs black in his veins Fitzray!" I cried, holding him tighter, willing him not to leave.
"I won't die Chenille," he said calmly, giving me a nervous smile. He took my hands in his, prying them from his shirt. "I'll be fine." I knew he was lying.

Chapter 8 - The Sacrifice

Pete slowly made his way toward Fitzray.

"I haven't seen you in the longest time, brother."

"The two of you are-,"

"That's right. You see, we were all good friends once. I was born a vampire and Fitzray was not. He was just a mortal, like you, until our father turned him into a vampire. When he met you, he claimed you as his own, while I killed the previous leader of the vampires - our father. And *you*, I wanted you just the same. So I bit you and made you mine before Fitzray could. I knew you would run from your home and Fitzray would have to go and find you. But you are mine now, *my* Eternal Mate, and I have complete permission to rid him from these planets once and for all." Pete glared at his brother; his hands were fists at his sides.

"You can't do this!"

"I can do anything I want."

"What is all this quarreling about?" Taj' called, slithering up to us.

"Taj' what are you doing here?"

"Pearl said she foresaw a fight here, on the Bridge. Let's not be starting anything now. I don't want to see anyone get hurt," Taj' said softly.

"We're not starting anything," Pete said.

I clutched onto Fitzray's cape. "Don't do this. He's too strong."

"Let's end this now Pete."

Fitzray grabbed the knife from his belt and threw it as hard as he could before I could stop him. Pete moved, but not quick enough and the cruel blade sliced his shoulder.

Just as Fitzray walked up to him to do further damage, a man made his way toward us. It was Zaire.

It was my brother in the flesh, with a face like my own. It brought tears to my eyes at the very sight of him, though my heart sank as he looked me over with hardly any interest. My big brother was finally here to rescue me, I thought - I hoped.

"I'm ashamed of you Chenille. When you came to me nearly a year ago, I thought you had the potential to change. When Dad realized there was nothing that could change you, he wanted you killed. Your dragon's kidnapping was a plot to your demise. But I *let you* get away…I couldn't kill you - my only sister."

"What…what in the world are you talking about?"

"You were turned into one of *them*. *They* are the cause of this. They will *pay* for what they've done."

"Pay?"

"Chenille, look at me. I am your brother, your blood, and a part of the pack whether you'd like to believe it or not. So please understand…what I do is out of love - for your own good." His gaze turned to rest on Fitzray. "This is your fault."

"No Zaire, he's not my-,"

My brother's body transformed to resemble that of a large charcoal black wolf. He was a wolf. According to him, my family members were all wolves. They were a pack. And I was not a part of it.

He launched, nails extended, teeth exposed. Just as the wolf sunk his claws into Fitzray's chest, Taj' wrapped his tail around the wolf's body and flung him over the side of the Bridge in one swift movement. My brother's howl rang out as he plunged down into the oblivion of the universe.

There was no time to mourn my brother. Fitzray was nearly dead at my feet, blood pooled around him, his eyes half-closed. I fell to my knees, ran my hands over his ripped shirt where the wounds spilled blood at an alarming rate. I was sure the wounds were deep enough to pierce his heart, but I couldn't be sure.

"Fitzray say something…please."

"I'm sorry…Chenille."

Tears spilled over onto my face. "Are you…you're not going to die are you?" He didn't answer. "Oh please, please don't leave me."

"I will be reincarnated in another life."

"Are you sure?" Pete asked, his voice sounding almost as heartbroken as my own. He bent down to gaze over his brother and shook his head. His eyes flicked up and he slowly lifted his brother up into his arms. "I'm sorry to disappoint you then."

"PETE, NO!"

Moonscale lifted off as Pete threw his Master over the side of the Bridge. Pete grabbed his knife and slashed it through the dragon's wing. The dragon uttered a cry and he fell, spiraling down with his Master.

"You will pay, malevolent creature! The mortals will murder you once I drag you over the Bridge in my mouth! You will not be able to hide! For your own kind shall rebel against you! You will pay! We will show no mercy!" Taj' screamed.

Pete reached down and pulled me upright, forcing me to stand. I tried to keep my distance from him, but I was too distraught to fight him and wept against him since he was the closest thing to weep on.

"Chenille belongs to me now. You kill me and she will go down with me, I promise you."

And like the daisy, the flower of death, shall all cower and plea for mercy in its presence, as I had in Pete's arms during the night of the last eclipse.

* * * * *

Part 2

Through the Moonlight

Chapter 9 - A Total Blank

"Where am I?" Sitting up, I found myself surrounded by darkness, all except for the pulsing glow of black poison on my hands.

"I'm glad you are awake." A voice said from the darkness.

"Who are you? Who am I? Where am I?"

"I am Pete, your Eternal Mate. And you are Chenille East," the voice replied.

"Where am I?"

"What does that matter?"

"I don't remember anything."

"You don't have to remember."

I shook my head. Something was wrong.

"How long has this happened?"

"What?"

"How long have I been so forgetful? Have I always been so forgetful?"

"Yes, but don't worry, I'm here to guide you."

"What is an Eternal Mate?"

"An Eternal Mate is the one who turned you into a vampire."

"Vampire? I am a vampire!"

"Must we go through this every day?"

"I am a vampire?"

"Yes, and you will always be mine."

And the vampire kissed me, my head becoming fuzzy and I forgot my name - again.

I recalled days like those when I could remember nothing, but my memory slowly surfaced. I still knew nothing of my life. Pete never told me anything. Whenever a familiar face or name popped in my head and I told him, he only laughed and said I shouldn't be concerned.

I trotted beside Pete, stumbled over the volcanic-like rocks, and breathed in the cold clean air.

"I saw a man with green eyes in my dream last night."
"Doesn't ring a bell to me," Pete mumbled.
"Well, I remember the dream. It felt so real."
"You shouldn't overreact, it was just a dream."
"But it *meant* something, I'm sure of it."
"It was nothing, trust me."
"But Pete-,"
"*Trust* me."
"I do."
"Good, now let's go inside, it is getting late."

*****

Chapter 10 - Lucian

"Well won't you look at that? There is a new moon in the sky," Lucian mumbled quietly to himself.

"Not a moon Sire, but a planet," his dragon said, joining him on the Bridge.

The planet was black, like a piece of coal in the sky with red smoke radiating around it.

"What does this mean Sire?"

"It means…there is but another planet for Chenille to be kept and we must go there. Come Jasper, we have much to do."

"You have spent a lot of time looking for her."

"I know, but I must find her. I don't have much of a choice."

"How do you expect to find her?"

"I know someone who can help us."

*****

"I would like to help you, but I am afraid I too do not know where Chenille is. Pete took her away and she has not been seen since." The old snake peered down at Lucian with dismay. "Though we might have some luck if we ask Pearl."

"Very well," Lucian said.

The black snake led him through the thick fog to the Frozen Waterfalls where Amelia, Caspian, and Calvin waited. Princess Pearl, a powerful mermaid whose heart was as cold as ice, sat on her rock, refusing to assist them.

"Pearl, can you help me? I am searching for Chenille."

Pearl turned away and tossed her dull blonde locks of hair over her shoulder. "What good will it do if you look? What makes you think we will find her now? Who are you anyway?"

"I am Lucian, cousin of Pete and Fitzray."

"We are all still searching for her," Taj' said quietly, "we mustn't give up hope."

"What do you know of the new planet in the sky?"

She turned to Lucian and frowned. "I know nothing of the new planet, I'm afraid."

"Can we go there?"

"If we know nothing of the planet, how can we go there? We don't know what lives there."

"Or *who* lives there."

Everyone turned to Lucian skeptically.

"What if Chenille is there," he continued.

"There is a chance, although I can't promise you will find her there, especially since it is an unknown planet."

"An unknown planet to *us*," Amelia said.

"She could be trapped there," Caspian added thoughtfully.

"And if that is the case, how do we get there?"

"Why should we *go* there?"

"We won't know what...or who is there if we don't look," Calvin snapped.

"He is right. We have to look and see for ourselves."

"But how will we *get* there?" Pearl whined as she pressed the issue so they would not have to go.

"I don't know, but we will find out."

"We should have others come with us, some powerful creatures to back us up incase anything happens."

"And put *others* in danger?"

"If Pete is on that planet with Chenille, we won't have a chance against him. We need all the help we can get," Lucian said. "Amelia, Caspian, Calvin and I will get the strongest of vampires we can find."

"And you Pearl?"

"I will get some mermaids and see you tomorrow," she mumbled and crossed her arms.

"Let's go."

"Wait, how will we get there?"

"The dragons of course," Lucian said quietly.

"Lucian, why do you care about Chenille? Do you know her?" Amelia inquired.

"No, I don't know her but...Fitzray did and he was my cousin so...it's in my nature to protect her, I suppose. I know she meant a lot to him."

"Do you think we will find her?"

Lucian shifted his gaze to the redhead surprised at her concerned, almost harsh tone. He looked at her, sensing there was aggression hidden in her question. The demand for the save return of her friend was apparent in the way she tightened her jaw.

He knew she did not really trust him but he suspected that she would leave the concern of her friend in his hands at least until they reached her, if they did. He could tell she would break apart buildings to find her and that it wouldn't make a difference to her if a half-blood of a vampire would lead her or not.

"I don't know." He replied honestly, but simply. "We will find out once we get to Pete's planet."

Chapter 11 - Addiction

The vampire took off his leather jacket and dropped it over my shoulders. The poison that seeped onto my lips, once so bitter was now so sweet. It was like vanilla, but with the caffeine-like substance that made me crave it more. The more he kissed me, the more I forgot and the more he had control over me.

I shook my head and broke away from his grip.

"How about that Ceremony you promised me," Pete whispered.

"Ceremony? What Ceremony?"

"The Blood Ceremony, the ceremony that will make me immortal. Not even a sword shoved through my chest will kill and reincarnate me. But as for you-,"

"Pete…I…Blood Ceremony? No. I don't want a *Blood Ceremony.*"

"It is not your place to have a choice."

"That's not fair!" I shook my head and pushed him away.

"Trust me. I won't hurt you. Close your eyes and *trust me.*"

I obeyed. My head became light, my body numb, as though I did not even exist. Just as my eyes closed, I knew my memories would diminish. He quickly gathered me in his arms and lulled my jerky head.

"Here," he said placing his wrist before me.

I stared blankly at the deep scratch that ran down his arm, oozing black blood. He pressed his arm to my lips, but I turned sharply at the taste of the toxic, sour tasting blood. I coughed loudly and looked up at him.

"That is disgusting."

"Continue," he ordered and pressed his arm back to my lips again.

It was horrible, and I choked, but found my head was beginning to clear. Fragments of memory came to me and one thing became obvious – I did not love this vampire and I needed to go back to Catastrophe, my home.

With this in mind, I refused to continue with the Ceremony. I just knew it was not supposed to be like this. The Blood Ceremony confirmed a bond. What *bond* did I have with Pete?

"Continue," he demanded once I refused yet again.

"Fitzray," I whispered.

"What? What did you say?"

"Fitzray," I whispered, "I know that name."

Pete uttered a deep growl and tossed me off his lap, onto the floor.

"Don't you dare say that name ever again," he raged. "If you know what's best for you."

He stood up and looked down at me with an icy glare. He grabbed my wrist, pulling me to my feet and held me tightly in place.

"What will you do to me?"

"I will make you forget," he laughed and tried to kiss me when I turned away.

"I don't love you," I spat.

"You don't have to, but it can only help since there is no way you can escape me. Why do you think I created this planet?"

"So I will never go to Catastrophe again?"

"What for? You have a planet all for yourself."

"But I have no past…no *life*."

"Yes you do, but you have no need for it. You have started a new life."

"You mean *you* have started a new life?"

He shook his head and frowned. "I have used far too much power for it to be considered that *I* would be starting a new life. I have used my power for both of us."

"Well, I want my old life back."

"It's too late for that."

* * * * *

"Ready the dragons! Take your positions! We're going to fly over the Bridge!"

"I've heard that space is cold," Pearl whined and held her beautiful fur coat tightly.
"That it is," Taj' said.

Lucian clutched his cape in one of his hands to prevent it from smacking against Jasper while the hard winds continued to blow. In his other hand, he held onto one of Jasper's blue spikes that ran down his neck.
"Are you coming Taj'? We could use you."
"I am afraid your dragons will not be able to carry me. You must go on and leave me here."
"Nonsense, you won't be a problem for our dragons."
"If you are sure I won't be any trouble-,"
"Not at all."

The snake turned away as Lucian continued to shout his orders to the battalions.
"How will we find her on that planet? Do you know how long it might take," someone began to protest.
"We will split up and look for her. The planet is smaller than Earth so it shouldn't be *that* hard to find her." Lucian said and quickly mounted his dragon, as the rest had done. "Now take your formations, let's go!"

The vampires, now all on the backs of their assigned dragons all waited for his command.
"Fly over the Bridge!"

In the first row Lucian, Amelia, Caspian, Calvin, Pearl and the werewolf girl, Prusaious, braced themselves for takeoff. Next were the strongest of the vampires atop stalwart dragons. The dragons had very little space to get over the Bridge wall and many barely made it over. The dragons' stomachs skimmed over the apex of the wall, resulting in great thrusts from their back talons to prevent themselves from crashing.
"Get behind me," he yelled. The dragons flew behind him in formation.

Prusaious moved up near Lucian and smiled sweetly, keeping a firm grip on her dragon's spikes. He glanced over at her and sighed.
"What do you want Pru?"

"Lucian, do you think this is such a good idea, the whole trip to this new planet? I mean, what if you get yourself killed?"

"Why are you worried about me?"

"I have known you for nearly five years now, as an ally of the vampires, and you are like a little brother to me. I had to look after you all those years. Why wouldn't I be worried about you Lucian?"

Lucian shook his head and shifted uneasily on the rough surface of his dragon's back.

"You have the highest risk of us all to be killed." Prusaious continued. "I mean, you are more of a mortal than any vampire I have ever seen. Why, you are a mortal with fangs. You have absolutely *no* taste for blood nor do you know the vampire ways. Although you *do* have the compassion no mortal possesses, that will not make up for what you need to stand up against Pete. I just don't think you are strong enough."

"I am not *going* to stand up to him."

"Oh?"

"I just have to take Chenille back to Catastrophe and avoid him."

"What! You want to try to bring her to Catastrophe where Pete will find her, take her back again, and then hunt you down? You don't stand a chance. He'll kill you before you leave the planet!"

"He won't kill me."

"You are a mortal!"

"I'm not a mortal!"

"Oh sorry, a mortal with *fangs,*" she snapped, aggravated.

"I will save her."

"Do you plan to take on Pete too? Because you shouldn't expect your plan will work. He *will* find you and by all means he *will* have you dead."

"I have the strongest vampires of Catastrophe and their dragons behind me. How can my plan fail?"

"That doesn't matter! It doesn't matter that you have an army of immortal creatures! You don't get it! He is so strong he can kill every single one of them without hesitation. He is not only the leader of the vampires, but that of the planet he has created and who knows what lurks there."

"How does he have so much power?"

"He has killed his father and his brother who both possessed royal blood. If Chenille were to complete the Blood Ceremony with Fitzray, he would be back by now, reincarnated. And so I hope she has not completed *any* Ceremony with Pete."

"But I thought Fitzray and Chenille already performed the Ceremony together."

"They began to, but I heard that it wasn't completed. Had they completed it, Fitzray would be back by now. He would be able to stand up to Pete. And that would leave Fitzray and Chenille as the leaders of Catastrophe."

"I hope she hasn't performed the Ceremony with Pete yet."

"We will find out soon. The planet is coming into view."

"Go back and tell the others to prepare for landing. I'm going to go ahead to check out this place."

*****

Chapter 12 - Unwelcome Company

I looked up into the sky, foggy with dark ash clouds. A white dot appeared on the horizon. One of Pete's black dragons lifted off and flew towards the white object in the sky. Pete was asleep. It was late and feeling restless, I came to gaze at Earth and Catastrophe from afar.

The dragon roared and came plunging down, as did the white object. It drew closer until it was clear in the sky and I ran from it, realizing it was about to crash. It was a dragon. A figure sat on its back, commanding its every move.

Pete's dragon suffered a bite from this huge white one and sliced its wing, causing them both to plunge down. The black dragon, paralyzed, simply fell and collided into the hard ground as the white one struggled to fly, barely glided down, and crashed as well. The figure flew off the dragon and collided into the ashy ground, sending up a cloud of smoke.

Is this an intruder? I thought, slowly making my way toward the figure.

"Are you all right?" I asked.

"No." The figure said and sat up with some difficulty, one hand clutching his injured, bloody arm. The color of his blood was dark, a clear sign that he was of some royalty.

"Let me help you." I tried to take his hand, but he quickly turned. "Let me help you," I repeated.

"Who are…are you…Chenille East?"

"Yes, I am, now if you could just let me-,"

"Chenille? Chenille where are you? Get over here!" It was Pete.

The boy froze, sat as still as a statue. Even his breathing stilled. "Who are you? What is your name?" I whispered.

"I am...Lucian, Fitzray's cousin."

There is that name again.

"Chenille!"

"I can't leave you here, you're hurt."

"Don't worry about me, just go. Meet me here when Pete is asleep."

"But your arm-," I began.

"Go!"

Slowly I made my way over to Pete, resisting the urge to look over my shoulder at Lucian as I did so.

"Where were you? I heard a loud noise and-,"

"That was thunder, nothing to worry about." I pushed him back through the doors of the palace.

"It didn't sound like thunder, it sounded louder."

"It was thunder." I struggled to make my voice sound convincing.

He laughed quietly. "You look so shaken."

"*You* look so disheartening."

He smiled and pressed his lips to my neck. "Must I make you begin the Ceremony?"

I laughed. "You can't make me drink your blood. It won't happen."

"How about Fitzray? How was *his* blood?"

"Who *is* Fitzray?"

"No one important," he grumbled.

"Well, whoever he was, I'm sure his blood was *delicious* compared to *yours*."

"Why you-,"

"I have no trust in you and I don't *want* to drink your thick, acidic blood. That's why I don't *like* it. I don't *like you*."

"Of course you do. I am all you have."

"That's not true! And I would prove it to you if you took me to Catastrophe-,"

"I will *never* take you to Catastrophe. Everything you would ever need and want, I can give to you," he spat.

"Well, I *want* to go to Catastrophe."

"Except *that*."

I crossed my arms impatiently. "I want to be left alone for the rest of the night."

Just as I turned, his hand grabbed my arm.

"Why must you be so difficult," he scorned. "I only do what I do out of love," he chimed, practically mocking. I realized, *remembered*, that those were the last words my brother said before he was killed. "I do love you."

I looked away in disgust from the vampire. A part of me wanted to echo his words, but another part of me would have pierced my heart if I had. His poison had control over me, which made me echo these words repeatedly without me realizing it. Each time I had said them, he kissed me and gave me the poison I craved, but in doing so, he lost more of his poison to control me. At the same time, he became more and more powerful from the sense of the fake love he was receiving from my words.

I broke away from his grip, this time refusing to echo his words. This was a first, the sense of my independence from him, and he growled loudly at my rebellion. My gaze focused elsewhere, to the stairs, and I made my way toward them.

"Come back."

Tossing my head, I swaggered up the stairs. As I proceeded away from him, he angrily ran after me.

"You cannot disobey my wishes, Pete."

"And you cannot disobey *mine*."

Once I made it to the top of the stairs, I settled my feverish glare over him.

"I am Queen of the vampires. Not even *you* can overpower *me*."

"Oh yes I can. Since I am King and you are mine, I can easily overpower you in every way."

He prowled up the stairs like a tiger, like a beast, stalking prey. I dug the heel of my shoe into the hardwood floor and the stairs disintegrated, splitting beneath Pete's feet. He plummeted down, now that the stairs were gone, and landed flat on his back.

"As I said, leave me be for the rest of the night," I called down to him.

He yelled, but I knew he was not hurt. He probably had no more than a bruise. I walked quietly down the hall with a smirk and entered the master suite. Alone at last, I took a seat on the edge of the bed and marveled at the sight of the huge moon Clesta with its deep yellow-orange glow beside Catastrophe.

Is Lucian a threat to me? Should I trust him? How does he know my name?

An icy hand wrapped around my throat as the bed sagged from the weight of my Eternal Mate.

"I am sorry for the way I acted," I said quietly, frightfully, hoping the grip around my throat would loosen.

"Don't let it happen again."

"Pete."

"Hmm?" His hands moved to my shoulders, slowly wrapping around me.

"Are you tired?"

"No."

I rubbed my eyes. "I am."

"You should be. You destroyed the stairs."

"Are you hurt?"

"No. I am not harmed from your childish mistakes."

"Forgive me?"

"As always," he said with a kiss.

I felt my head ease, my memory erase, but kept the thought of Lucian. I knew the loss of his poison would weaken him and soon cause him to fall asleep as if under anesthesia. To my relief, he fell asleep within a few short minutes. I made the slightest movements as I rose from the bed and walked out of the room. Even if he woke up, he would be too weak to chase after me.

I grabbed my cape on the way out and shrugged it on while the chilled air struck my face. I didn't have to travel far when I saw Lucian and the white dragon. They were not alone.

A vampire with long red hair ran up to me and hugged me tightly. "Chenille, you're ok."

"Who *are* you?"

"I'm Amelia...remember? *Amelia*?" She spoke to me as if I was a child, but I could see she knew me well.

"No, no I don't."

"What about Caspian?"

A vampire with striking blue eyes walked up to me. "I am Caspian. Do you remember me?"

I shook my head. I was also introduced to Calvin, Prusaious, Pearl, and Taj'.

"These are your friends," Lucian said. He paused, an anxious glance shooting toward the palace. "Is Pete asleep?"

"Yes, he's asleep."

Friends. I bounced the word around in my head for a moment.

"Why are you here?"

"We have come to take you back to Catastrophe."

"Really? You would really take me there?"

"We are going back tomorrow since everyone is tired from the long trip here." Lucian replied, answering my question.

The large group of vampires separated into small groups where they formed circles around constructed fires. I sat next to Lucian and the snake, Taj'.

"Can you tell me...who Fitzray is?"

Lucian took a deep breath before he began. "Fitzray was my cousin. He loved you very much, believe it or not. He was killed by Pete."

"You don't remember him?" Taj' asked, surprised.

"I don't. I wish I could but my memory has faded."

"How?"

"Poison, I have been poisoned."

"Poisoned by Pete?"

"Yes, the poison in his fangs is so wonderful. It's so addicting that I can't help myself, but I lose some of my memory as soon as it hits my lips."

"We have to keep you away from him."

"How did you get here? How did you find me?" I sat on Lucian's lap and looked up at him as a child eager to hear a nursery rhyme. He did not seem bothered by it, so I remained where I was.

"We flew on the backs of dragons and I found you. I saw one of the black dragons and suspected there would be something there for it to protect. I was right. The beast nearly killed me."

"Is that your dragon? The big white one?"

"Yes, that's Jasper."

"You know, we do have someone that has been waiting to see you," Taj' said, diverting my attention away from Lucian.

"Who?"

Taj' slithered away and came back a few moments later. A dragon with icy blue scales stood next to him. A blue jay was perched on one of the dragon's light brown horns. A smaller orange colored dragon was at his side.

"Who are you?"

"This is Minx," Lucian said gesturing toward the blue dragon.

"Who is the bird?"

"Valiant," the bird chimed and flew to my shoulder.

"We have found that Valiant is not a blue jay," Amelia said. She paused for a moment to see if I was confused or if I had remembered what a blue jay was.

"What is he then?"

"He is a phoenix."

"He doesn't look like a phoenix."

"You should see him in the morning, that's when he changes. He is a blue jay a lot probably since he can't mimic when he is a phoenix."

"And this is an old friend of Fitzray's." Lucian added as he showed me the beautiful white bat that flew to him. "This is Charlene."

The bat swelled up nearly twice her size and side-stepped from Lucian's hand over to my shoulder to perch beside Valiant.

The smaller dragon clung to my cape and nuzzled me beneath my chin. I looked at its brilliant orange scales with its pink wings the color of a grapefruit. Its veins resembled the inside of an orange, thin and filled with sweetness.

"Who is this?"
"That is Citrus," Minx said.

I looked up at the blue dragon, unaware it was him who had talked, and moved my fingers down the tiny yellow spikes that ran down Citrus's neck.
"Citrus was found as an egg. She also would have belonged to Fitzray," Minx said, flicking out his tongue to speak.

I looked up at Lucian; the flames from the fire's luminous glow danced in his golden eyes. It was surprising how much he looked like Pete with his black hair and shining smile, but all at once, he appeared as his total opposite. I rested my head on his shoulder, allowing a sigh to escape.
"So is this how my old life was? Surrounded by friends?"
"I'm sure it was."

A haughty girl came over and sat across from me, smiling boldly.
"So you are Chenille, Queen of the vampires?" She asked in a sweet, elegant tone.
"Yes, I am."

She gathered her black hair in her hands and began to tie it up with a piece of dilapidated leather. "I'm Prusaious." She chimed, resting her weight on her elbow to examine me, probably disregarding the fact that she had introduced herself to me already.

A loud pulsing noise echoed in my ears, not my own pulse, for mine was so faint it was barely audible to me. This pulse belonged to someone else.
"Do you *smell* that?"
"Smell what?"
"It's so sweet," I snuggled closer to Lucian. "What are you wearing? Did you bathe in honey? You smell almost...sort of like a...like a *mortal.*" My head swelled with dizziness from the scent.

He shifted slightly and looked at me cautiously, already leaning away from me.
"*Exactly* like a mortal." I rested my palm on his throat just to feel the beating of a pulse. He scrambled to his feet,

practically throwing me off his lap. He obviously was not taking any chances. "How is that possible? A mortal vampire?"

"Yes, it's rare but possible. And since I am one, I am a reject to both the vampires and the mortals."

"I never thought that was possible."

He sat back down and sighed. "Me either."

The vampires around me began to nod off beside their dragons, as did my friends. I settled down before the fire and rested my head against Minx's warm body. Lucian sat up and watched for any sign of Pete, his eyes heavy with fatigue.

"Lucian, Pete won't wake up. Try to get some rest," Prusaious mumbled in a lethargic voice.

He had mumbled something back to her, but I was so tired I did not even register what transpired between them.

Lucian looked back to me. "I know what you must be feeling. I know all about vampire poison, even though I don't possess that much myself. It's because of poison that I am a half-mortal."

"How so?"

His hand came to his forehead, his face darkened by the shadows, but I could see his uncertainty of where to start. "I was bit by someone I knew very well," he paused to smile, "and someone you knew very well."

I glanced up at him puzzled and when my eyes blinked in astonishment, he nodded and laughed quietly. "Fitzray. It was an accident of course. When he told me of his father's death I swore I wouldn't tell anyone about it, but then Pete caught us by surprise and entered the room. He'd heard everything."

"So what did you do?"

"It was Fitzray who made the first move. He accused Pete of their father's death, which was confirmed as soon as Pete strolled into the room with a devious smile. He was laughing. Infuriated, Fitzray launched at him and since Pete was faster, he collided into me instead. He bit my hand, nearly bit off one of my fingers in the process." He uttered an amused, tired chuckle. "It was all unintentional though, once he finally realized it was me. By then he had nearly beat me half to death."

I smiled. The image of Fitzray from my dream preoccupied my thoughts for a brief moment. "He was a good fighter, wasn't he?"

"One of the best I've ever seen."

"How did you become a half-mortal then?"

"Fitzray wasn't done in his transformation becoming a vampire so his poison wasn't fully developed. When he bit me, it wasn't strong enough to kill me but it was enough to give me the appearance of a vampire. I have the blood of a vampire, and a little poison, but nothing more."

I sunk back against Minx, satisfied with his story.

"Do you miss him?"

"I don't remember him much because of the poison," I remarked softly.

"You will remember again, I will make sure of it."

Chapter 13 - Black Book

Something warm rubbed beneath my chin, waking me. It was Valiant in the form of a brilliant phoenix. He had dark ruby feathers on his head and body. His tail feathers looked like the train of a peacock, but instead they were light pink with yellow eyespots. Lucian grabbed my hand and pulled me to my feet.

"We are leaving."

"There is something in the palace I need to get," I mumbled lethargically.

"Why didn't you get it before?"

"I will be quick, I promise."

Before he could stop me, I was already at the palace door. I took the back steps up to the second floor. Then I slipped into the library. There was a knife on the small table, where it remained untouched since Pete last used it on the Bridge. I picked it up and hid it beneath my cape, my elbow knocking a book off the bookshelf. I picked up the black book, held it in my hands and fingered the bold silver lettering on its cover entitling *Vampires.* Curiously, I turned to the first page. It read-

All have heard stories, myths, and legends, but with careful research and examination, evidence shows that vampires are real creatures.

I turned to the next page; the writing was by hand with ink splotches here and there, although the pages were in perfect shape. I closed the book and hid it beneath my cape as well, while quickly making my escape from the palace.

Why would Pete even have this book?

Once outside, Minx came up to me and helped me onto his back hastily. We did not have much time.

"Let's go to Catastrophe!"

Minx moved to stand beside Lucian who already looked down at me from atop Jasper's back.

"Did you get what you needed?"
"Yes, I have everything."
"Did you wake Pete?"
"I don't think so."
"Good. Follow me."

Valiant and Charlene flew over to me and took their spots atop Minx's horns.

"Ready the dragons," Lucian called.

I stayed beside Lucian and watched as Pearl shrugged on her fur coat. She caught my glance and smiled. "What are you gawking at?"

"Pearl, stop your discourteous behavior!" Taj' roared.

Pearl looked down quickly. "I was just joking with her," she sniffed.

"Leave her alone Pearl."

"Yes Taj'."

Lucian studied me for a moment. "Are you ready to fly?"

"Yes. Take me home."

"Ok let's go! Start flying," he ordered.

Uneasily, I held onto Minx's neck. He ran, lagging behind Jasper, being not nearly as fast. He extended his wings, braced them for flight and before I knew it, we were airborne. For a moment, I thought the thin skin that made up his fragile looking wings would fail to carry the tremendous weight of a dragon. The dragons all took off, each row at a time, and flew steadily behind us. After a few minutes of smooth flying, I knew we would be all right after all.

"I told you my plan would work!" Lucian chimed.

"You have to get home first," Prusaious shouted back.

I took out the black book and flipped to the next page with one arm tightly wrapped around Minx's neck.

Chapter 1 - Identifying a Vampire

A vampire's eye color can be red, gold, purple, black orange, green, etc. Their fangs, razor sharp canine teeth, can rip through flesh and bone and are a vampire's greatest asset. Vampires mainly tend to feed on mortals. The most common site of a bite is at the base of the throat near the collarbones, near the middle of the throat, or on the left or right side of the neck. This ranges from below the ear to the shoulder. The marks left are roughly an inch or so apart. A vampire's fangs will sink to desirable depth, which can cause paralysis.

Chapter 2 - Vampire Poison

Vampire poison is created in the vampire's fangs and will drip onto their lips to numb a wound. A male vampire has strong poison that may cause reactions to different vampires and humans. Only he has the ability to turn one into a vampire. A female vampire, or vampress, has weak poison that has little or no affect on victims and vampires.

"What are you reading?" Lucian inquired, snapping my attention away from the book.

"Oh, just a book I found."

"What is it about?"

"Vampires."

"Oh." He quickly turned away, suddenly more interested in the vast space spread out before him.

I turned back to the book and flipped through the pages, stopping at one chapter in particular that caught my eye.

Chapter 15 - Transformation

Transforming into a vampire requires the poison of a male vampire. (See chapter 2). It is common that a vampire can bite a young boy by simply getting angry with them and suffer the consequence of a bite in the process. It would only take ten minutes or so for the poison to set in and react with human blood cells. With the poison mixed in, it gives the boy a craving for blood since poison destroys healthy cells. This is in all cases for vampires. This does not require a Blood Ceremony, for the poison would simply set and the boy would fall asleep for a few hours.

Turning a girl into a vampress is a slightly more complicated process. A vampire may feed for hours at a time, but six hours of consistent feeding is ample time for the poison to set in to ensure transformation. A vampire would be well overfed after only a couple of hours and therefore must sustain himself another several hours to turn his victim into a vampress, thus must have a very good reason for it. A vampire can only turn one victim into a vampress. During the experience, she is likely to be awake during the process, but will forget it all the next day. It is even common for a new vampress to forget ever meeting the vampire that turned her. In some cases, a newly turned vampress can suffer memory loss, which, over time, will recover.

The vampire would leave until she is fully conscious and then return to find her again. He would then complete the transformation with a Blood Ceremony. (See chapter 18). After the Ceremony, the vampire has total control over the relationship. With newly acquired power, a vampire is stronger and can kill any vampire or mortal that gets in the way of their relationship. The two vampires are Eternal Mates.

I closed the book and leaned against Minx.

"You should get some rest, it will be a while before we get to Catastrophe," Lucian said.

"What will we do once we get to Catastrophe?"

"Yeah Lucian, what *will* we do once we get to Catastrophe?" Prusaious chimed.

"I want to take you to some places you may find familiar."

"Why?"

"No not you! Chenille."

Prusaious crossed her arms and led her dragon banking to the right, away from us.

"Where will you take me?"

"Just a few places you should recognize."

Once we landed, I stood on the Bridge as the vampires and dragons parted in their separate directions, relieved to be standing on solid stone. My friends went about their business, trusting that I would be safe in Lucian's hands for the short time he promised to look over me.

He took me to a house where there was a marble tile floor with a huge fireplace and velvet covered chairs. He led me through the house and showed me every room, waiting for me to remember something, but I did not. He put a fire in the fireplace and closed his eyes.

"Lay down on the rug."

I obeyed, as usual, but not without hesitation.

"I want to try something." He moved to sit beside me.

"You fell into a river once and nearly drowned, but Fitzray had saved you. Then you met Charlene and found Valiant and cared for Minx." He opened his eyes and smiled.

"How do you know that?"

"I knew Fitzray and I am part of his family so I have access to his memory, or, at least, the memory he had. I can tell you anything you need to know about him."

I closed my eyes. "We go way back."

"You do. Now I want to try something...maybe I can share some of his memory with you."

"How?"

"I am not sure if this will work...just stay still."

He slid his lips to mine in one swift movement and my head drifted off before I could think to move away. Lucian kept a warm hand to my forehead and shushed me quietly. I jerked up cautiously, afraid. Pete was the last to kiss me and inflicted too much damage in doing so. I was on my feet, breathing heavy with sudden panic, unable to tell if his expression was a threat to me or not. He stood up to take hold of my hand.

"You can trust me. I saved you from Pete. I took you home. That must count for something."

It was true, but suffering emotional and physical distress from another vampire made my stomach churn uncomfortably even staring at *his* promising face.

"All I want to do is help you." He sighed. "Fitzray *is* a part of me in a way."

I sat back down keeping one hand on his wrist to keep a check on his pulse. The rhythmic throbbing was elevated slightly.

"Be still," he ordered.

I saw a man with black hair and green eyes, a wolf, and the two of us jumping off a building roof. I saw myself with a vampire I knew very well performing the Blood Ceremony with me...well, at least trying to attempt it. I saw Fitzray's experiences, the ones he loved and hated. I saw Pete and their conflicts, their mother gasping her last breath, and their father dying beside Fitzray.

I broke away from Lucian, my breath in gasps, unable to endure it anymore. The visions came over me so fast I was sure only a few short moments had passed.

"What…did you see?"

"Everything."

"No, you didn't see everything. I will show you *everything*."

He kissed me again and this time I was on the Bridge. I saw Pete and Fitzray. A knife slid through a dragon's wing and the sound of my own scream rang out. The fear I felt, even now, watching it replay, was so real, like a loud beat in the heart of death. Fitzray's body fell over the wall, the long howl of the black wolf rang out, and then Pete kissed me and I forgot everything.

"No!" I screamed and turned my head. "It can't be true, Fitzray is dead! Pete killed him! I didn't think it was true…I didn't believe you when you told me. I didn't know. I didn't remember him." I wanted to cry at the very thought.

"You remember?"

I shook my head from the memories I wanted so desperately to forget.

"It's all right," Lucian whispered.

He rested on his side beside me and watched me quietly.

"Perform the Ceremony with me," I whispered.

"Maybe I shouldn't have done that," he replied doubtfully. "Besides, I couldn't do that even if you wanted me to."

"Yes! Yes you can!"

"No, I *can't*."

"Why?"

"Our love for each other does not run solemnly in our bones and therefore couldn't be carried out. And I am more of a mortal." He sounded panicked.

"It doesn't matter-,"

"Yes it does. You see, I don't have a taste for blood, and if you bit me…I could die."

"I wouldn't let you die. I wouldn't kill you."

"I'm sure you wouldn't do it intentionally," he laughed nervously. "Why do you want a Ceremony anyway?"

"You can keep me safe. With a Ceremony, Pete wouldn't be able to perform one and I would be safe from him for good. If Pete finds me, he will make me perform the Ceremony with him. I would rather perform the Ceremony with you."

"Listen, all I can do now is keep you safe. I can't guarantee anything. Besides, I'd rather not take the risk of performing a Ceremony if it means I can keep you safe for another day."

The heat of the fireplace took its toll and I rested beside Lucian. I was safe for now.

Before I could settle into a deep sleep, Lucian stood up, swiftly grabbed my hands and pulled me to my feet. Dazed as I was, he guided me outdoors where the moon still sat in the sky. He took me through the woods and spoke nothing as I rubbed my eyes, trying to wake myself.

"Lu…where are you taking me? It's late."

"It is a surprise," he said.

I thought he was about to start the Ceremony itself but quickly thought otherwise, considering the conversation we had earlier. My feet soon crunched over pure white sand and I could hear the crash of waves that sent salty sprays of water to the stars.

"If you told me we were going to the beach I would have brought a bathing suit or something."

"You don't need anything to come to the beach at night." He made his way toward the blue water.

"What are you doing?"

"Going for a swim," he replied and began to wade out into the ocean.

"You are going to get your clothes all wet."

"So?"

He looked at me with a smile and then yelped, disappearing beneath the water. I ran to the water's edge and looked for him, but there was not even a ripple over the lazy ocean. I could only strain my eyes in the dim glow of moonlight, but saw no trace. Yet, he was part mortal, and he could not hold his breath forever. There was a sharp pinch to my ankle and once caught off balance from fright, Lucian leaped in front of me, pushing me down into the shallow water. I struggled for a moment, feeling the water rush over me, when I saw a beam of white moonlight that illuminated the water as though the sun was there. I sat on the sand, still under water and looked around a moment longer until I finally went upward to get a breath of chilled air. Lucian was not far from me when he too popped up for air and I, being just within reach of him, grabbed his sleeve so he turned to face me.

"What did you do that for?"

He laughed. "See? You don't need anything."

"Yeah but now we are sopping wet!"

"And?"

"*Sopping wet* on a cold, sandy beach in the middle of the night," I droned.

I mumbled quietly and gathered the hem of my dress in my hands to trudge my way to the sand. Once on land I fell to my knees and crawled over to drier sand. I brushed the wet sand that clung to my skirt and already felt the harsh stick of the ocean water. Lucian made his way over to me and sat close, his body blocking the light wind that gave me chills from the bitter feel of the salty ocean. I hugged myself tightly and saw him move beside me, clutch his cape in one hand, and wrapped it around me. There was a low whimper from behind and just as I turned my head, so did Lucian.

"Get down," he said in a hushed whisper.

I crouched low onto the sand and looked in the direction where I had heard the noise, following his gaze to a sandy spot illuminated by dim moonlight. There was a gold creature with a pointed snout and large pointed ears, almost fox-like. It sniffed the air for a brief moment and then rested in the cool sand.

"What's that?" I whispered, unsure if the creature was vicious or not.

"That is a nellina."

"Will it attack?"

"No, it's harmless."
"What is it doing here?"
"It lives here. Actually, it lives in deep burrows in the sand. They are very rare."
"What do they do?"
"Well you probably can't see from here but it has wings that blend in with its fur. It can only glide short distances at a time, and it's because of that they rarely ever fly, unless threatened."

I studied the frail fox-like creature and then looked at Lucian who had turned away from me.
"What do they eat?"
"They eat whatever they can find," was all he said.

I moved slightly closer and at once, he stood. "We should be going."

At his hasty movement, the nellina rose to its feet, shaken, and dashed off with its red-gold wings spread out at its sides. It lifted onto a cool breeze and disappeared from sight within seconds.
"What did you do that for? You scared it away!"
"We are leaving." His voice sounded stern, almost angry.
"But...but we just got here."
"Look at yourself. You're shaking so hard I can hear your teeth chatter."
"Well-,"
"Come on." He put out a hand. I looked back into the vague sky for the nellina and once convinced it was not going to return, I took his hand.
"Why did you even take me here?"
"I thought you might remember more, but you haven't, so we are leaving."

Confused, I allowed him to take me home where he lit a fire in the fireplace while I showered and changed into a pair of warm pajamas. While the fireplace warmed downstairs, I sat on the bed in the master suite fingering the cotton sheets just as they had been since I had last seen them.

A heavy weight in my chest formed and soon I was choking back heavy tears from the memories Lucian had showed me. I shook my head and fingered the blanket. Unlike before, I now realized how it was so soft beneath my fingertips. It was strange how I noticed these things now, when I had been exposed to them so many times before.

"I wish he came back…I wish nothing ever happened. Oh that stupid, arrogant fool," I sobbed.

There was a quiet knock at the door and I looked to see a tall figure in the doorway. With my imagination and memory taking over, I shook my head in astonishment.

No, no it can't be.

I raced over to the figure dressed in Fitzray's clothes. It was as if he was standing before me. I ran over and wrapped my arms around Lucian who noticed what was going on and hesitantly stepped back. Still, I grabbed onto his shoulder, pulling him toward me. I could smell Fitzray for the first time in months. I remembered what he smelled like, what he sounded like, what he felt like. It all came back to me as I breathed it all in slowly.

"Fitzray, you came back. I knew you would, I knew nothing could happen to you. You didn't die. I knew you didn't die, I knew he couldn't kill you."

I grabbed the candle from the nightstand and anxiously wove it before his face, still holding his shoulder. Instead of the marble green eyes I expected and yearned to meet, I saw gold. My smile faded. I moved the candle away.

"You thought I was Fitzray, didn't you?"

"You…his clothes…I am sorry I-," I cut myself short, quickly releasing my hold.

"No, I didn't know you would react that way. But, that is no excuse. I should have known better."

"It's just…they fit you so well." I looked away, afraid to meet his gaze again, afraid to see gold rather than green. Afraid to see him and not Fitzray.

"Let's go where it's warm downstairs."

Once I was in the presence of the flames, Minx came over and rested his chin on my lap. Charlene, who was out of her cage, had flown down to Lucian's shoulder.

He held his arm before his chest and with one simple command, the bat flew onto his arm and then he placed her before the fire beside me.

"Never have I seen Charlene so obedient…she would never do such a thing if I had asked." I talked quietly as if I was talking to myself. I really did not want to engage in conversation with him.

"I have known her quite a while," he admitted, "you shouldn't be surprised." He sat on one of the red velvet chairs, his hands balled to fists on the arms of the chair.

I watched the flames waver and allowed them to captivate me by their movement for a long time, until he spoke again.

"How is the fire suiting you?"

"Well."

Minx lifted his head. "If you would like to sit with us you may." He called out.

Jasper came in from the kitchen and rested beside me as close as he could manage with still leaving enough room for Lucian to sit near me if he wanted. The dragon's scales were cold as ice and he trembled ever so slightly beneath my hand, yet he refused to lay his head on my lap, almost in respect for Lucian.

"Come and sit Sire."

Lucian hesitated but slipped from the chair and sat next to me. Once he wrapped his arm around me and I rested my head on his shoulder, Jasper had then placed his chin on my lap.

"Where is Citrus?" Minx asked, suddenly alarmed.

Jasper lifted his head and the dragons rose to their feet in search of the little dragon. After several minutes, Valiant flew to one of the velvet chairs and exclaimed, "Citrus!"

Sure enough, there she lay, curled on the chair like a little cat. The bat flew up to perch beside Valiant and the dragons moved around the room. Tension grew to stiffness in my muscles and the constant pulse against my shoulder did not help. I turned my head to see if Lucian was looking at me and sighed, unsurprised that I was right.

"I'm not going anywhere. I won't leave you." Lucian said with a kiss. This time, it did not bear memory like before.

Chapter 14 - The Race

The shifting movement from Lucian woke me up. The sun was not even up yet.

"Lu? Where are you going?"

"I have to go to the City."

He stood and straightened out his cape. "Do you want to come with me?"

"Sure, I'll come."

Onward we sluggishly made our way to the City. The stores, still closed, remained locked and the streets were peacefully empty, but all the same, strangely vacant. Loud voices echoed from up ahead and I decided to check to see what was going on, my curiosity getting the better of me. Just as I turned the corner, Lucian grabbed hold of me.

"Where are you going?"

"I want to know what's up ahead."

"I can't leave you out of my sight." He grumbled to himself.

"Come with me then."

Beyond the corner, there were two vampires. Each one held a horse. They were odd looking with small horns protruding from their foreheads and stubs for wings sprouting from between their shoulders.

"What are those?" I called.

One vampire turned his head. "These are Catastrophe-bred horses. They are born to run."

"Where do you get one of these?"

"They are not commonly found in these parts-,"

"Do you want to go for a ride," the other interrupted.

"Well…I don't know-,"

"We would give them to you half price."

One of the horses walked up to me, bent his head down and playfully nipped at my shirt.

"No!" Lucian growled and pulled me away from the animal, shielding me with his body.

"Hey, if you could even ride one, we'd give them to you for free!"

I shrugged from Lucian's grip and walked up to the vampires.

"You've got yourself a deal."

Lucian sprinted toward me while I managed to get up on one of the horses.

"Relax Lu. I rode dozens of horses when I lived on Earth."

"But you are not dealing with an average horse from Earth," he protested.

I snickered and grabbed hold of the horse's mane.

"All that horse wants to do is run!"

The horse did not hesitate. At the very word, he darted off. Lucian quickly mounted the other horse and the chase was on.

I could steer him only enough to clear sharp turns, but other than that, he had a mind of his own. The street below me whirled by, but I clung to the only comforting thought that the horse's hooves still clopped against cobblestone. I knew I was still in the City. Lucian was catching up and the horse ran even faster with the thought of racing the other horse. I cleared another sharp turn into an alley with a dead end. The horse turned on his haunches, barely pausing, spinning on a dime, and ran from the small street. Lucian was catching up, nearly behind me, and my horse was getting tired. Lucian at last got in front of me and banked off to another street with my horse closely following.

At the end of the street, the vampires stood waiting. Lucian's horse came to an abrupt stop before them and my horse slowed, but not fast enough. As he reached the other horse, he reared up onto his back legs. I clutched desperately onto his mane, holding on as best I could, but I slid helplessly onto the stone. The other vampires then controlled the horses as Lucian rushed over to my side.

"Chenille, are you hurt?"

"My wrist!" I cried and got up slowly to examine the damage done.

Lucian walked over to the other vampires and yelled; his profanities echoed in the streets. From where I crouched, a huddled mess, I could see they only smirked at him. Without another word, he walked briskly over to me and looked at my wrist. It was bloody, painful, and already beginning to swell.

"I'll take you to the hospital. It's not far from here."

"No, just take me home."

That was what he did, for some reason respecting my wishes. Once we went back to Fitzray's house, I sat on the bed in silence. Antiseptic and a few different splints surrounded me.

"I don't have the skills of a healer, but Fitzray taught me a lot."

He took a needle and a spool of thread, setting it all in front of me. Carefully, he took the needle and held it above the candle's flame.

"What are you doing?"

"You need a couple of stitches."

"But…but the wound isn't that deep Lucian."

"It's deeper than you think."

I squirmed in place while he put the thread through the needle and proceeded. He removed the ice from my wrist and I turned, feeling the bite from the needle.

"Why did you do that?"

"Do what?" I peered at his working hands and turned again.

"Why did you want to ride that horse?"

"I thought…I thought the horse was tame enough that I could ride it like a horse from Earth."

He said nothing, but I could see his jaw tighten and he kept his eyes to my wrist. He took a breath and finally spoke.

"If you had gotten any more hurt…what if that animal landed on you and crushed your skull? What would I have done? You are lucky you didn't break anything. You are lucky your wrist isn't broken," he snapped, suddenly infuriated.

Once I looked at him, he placed the thread on the nightstand. He was glowing crimson in the heat of the candlelight. Harshly, he wrapped a splint around my wrist tightly.

"I'm sorry."

He did not look up from his work. He sat in silence until he was finished and then sat thoughtfully beside me. He rolled his eyes over to me to study my expression while I pressed my lips together to prevent myself from smiling. His serious face softened for a brief millisecond. He could not see that I was biting my tongue, suppressing a laugh, but I was sure he saw it was obvious because he turned away immediately. His jaw tightened again as though he remembered he was still angry with me, or figured that he was supposed to be.

"They didn't give us the horses. They said if we rode them they would give them to us." I said hesitantly, breaking the silence.

"They used us, well *you*."

"What do you mean? There wasn't any money involved or anything."

"We were simply a form of entertainment."

He said something under his breath, something I did not hear. He then laughed at his own remark and turned to see if I had heard what he said. When he saw my blank look, he turned away, his smile fading. He looked straight through me, not even at my face.

"What are you thinking about?"

It took him a moment to come out of his daze and comprehend what I had asked and then turned his face from me instantly, embarrassed.

"Nothing, nothing at all," he said and glanced up to see if I was convinced.

I knew what he must have been thinking. He probably thought I was crazy, not just in general, but considering how sick I had been feeling earlier that morning. That was the whole reason he wanted to go into the City so early in the first place.

"You are mad aren't you? You wanted me to stay home and you didn't want to wake me. You just needed to get the medicine and come home before I suspected you left at all. And now you wish you didn't take me with you."

He nodded his head and smiled hopefully. "At least you look better. Do you feel any better?"

"No, I feel the same."

"Do you want me to go?" He was on his feet, knowing what my answer would be. I did not even have to nod my head or make the slightest motion for him to leave.

I never felt so sick since I had the flu years ago. I was a mortal then. The nauseating pain was hard to overcome. It was hard to sleep at night. It was impossible to eat even when my stomach signaled a want for food just for a moment because I knew I would regret to have eaten. I could only take the pain if I rested on my side and closed my eyes, even when I knew I would not fall asleep. I knew I was sick when I could not sleep and was up staring at the ceiling in discomfort. I opened my eyes to look into the light of the candle, wishing to feel hypnotized by its movement so I could just sleep and not feel the harsh symptoms. Waiting patiently for Lucian to come back was a daunting task since I counted each dreaded minute that passed. When he finally returned, I forced myself to sit up.

He handed me a glass of water, as I expected, and poured some green colored powder into the glass. The water looked repulsive, so much that I did not see how it could make *anyone* feel better.

"It should help with your symptoms, but that's all I can do for you."

I drank it down slowly waiting for my stomach to reject it, but it settled instead. "I can't believe I felt so good before, but now I just feel so sick."

"It's getting worse, isn't it?"

"I can't be sure. All I know is it's not getting any better."

He stared at me with astonishment but I did not know why. He was deep in thought. Perhaps he knew something I did not know or maybe he was suspecting something. It might have been that he was recalling some virus and thought it contagious. He held one of his hands in the form of a fist and started to shake his head.

What could he possibly be thinking? Did I see fear in his eyes or was it just the light of the candle? I could not tell.

"If you still feel bad tomorrow I will take you to the healers." He seemed to be insisting and I did not want to argue with that.

"Whatever you want Lucian."

He seemed vexed at the tone of my voice. "Is there something you're not telling me?"

"What are you talking about?"

"You know what's wrong."

"No, I don't. I am not a doctor."

"The healers will know what is wrong." His voice settled again.

I turned away from him, waiting for him to say something else or for him to leave.

"I will be downstairs if you need me."

I was startled at how close he had been to me to whisper into my ear. I was startled even more when I heard him chuckle as he left. It was a nervous chuckle, I could tell. Something was scaring him. I did not blame him.

For some reason I just knew I would not be feeling any better by morning. I would be going to the healers. Lucian suspected something was wrong and I was not telling him something. Little did he know, I had something that could not be cured by medicine or diagnosed by the healers. And if they failed to tell him, I would have to tell him myself. I would have to tell him or he would find out on his own.

"Lucian!"

His figure filled the doorway in an instant. His speed was impeccable for a half-mortal. He came over to sit beside me, almost with hesitation. I caught a glimpse of his tired face and held my breath, unable to say another word.

"What's the matter Chenille?" After nearly a minute of silence, I could tell he was losing patience.

Opening my mouth to speak, I failed to utter out a few simple words and took in a breath instead. He had to repeat his question again before I could find my voice. I swallowed hard, taking in another breath of discontent.

My eyes filled with tears and I struggled to hold them back, trying desperately to refrain from adding fuel to the fire. At the sight of my fear, his eyes became wide and suddenly frightened too. His hands flew to mine and he froze. He held his breath, and though he remained painfully still, I saw him nearly shaking out of his skin. Whatever nightmarish, unimaginable thoughts he conjured up before he probably assumed true now.

"It's just...my family," I blurted. "I never had a chance to go over the Bridge and see my family. I miss them."

Lucian's body relaxed instantly, although he eyed me with uncertainty, as if certain I was not telling him everything.

"You're just homesick," he said softly. "All right then, I will have it arranged so you can see your family," he replied stiffly, his eyes locking onto my own deceit-filled eyes.

*****

Chapter 15 - Journey

Lucian arranged that I would meet with my parents as soon as the following day. We received the news that they were eager to see me. After all, they had not seen me in over two years. I wondered if they had heard of Zaire's death.

After much debate, I managed to convince Lucian to allow me to meet with my parents alone. Of course, if he wanted to accompany me on the trip to Earth, I would not object.

With growing uncertainty adding to the weight on my shoulders, Lucian and I hastily made our way over the Bridge to Earth. It was almost painful to be on Earth's soil again. Even the cool winter air was different here - crisper, not as sweet, almost oxygen deprived in comparison to Catastrophe's clean atmosphere. A part of me, probably the remnants of my mortality, found comfort in stepping foot here. If only still a mortal, it would take more than some sweet air to sway me to leave here.

The simple abode my parents invited me to was below my usual standards. Their humble mansion was the house I grew up in, although even *that* seemed plain in comparison to the new luxury that surrounded me back on Catastrophe. When I walked into the dining room the first thing I saw was the long dining table, every seat occupied by a werewolf family member. The chatter among them stopped and they all looked at me. My father rose and welcomed me in a hug, though it was probably more to appease my mother who instantly embraced me after my father moved away. *She* was not displeased by my presence or by the fact that I was not one of *them*.

My father was always very robust-looking to me. His simple Earth clothes did him injustice, though his eyes carefully scrutinized my own foreign clothes, expressing his distaste without having to say a word.

"Chenille is here," he exclaimed as if the family had failed to acknowledge my presence. "You can go and have a seat near Timothy."

Timothy had always been my favorite cousin. Surprisingly, this was a memory that surfaced easily. His blue eyes flicked up to greet me before he uttered a word and I tousled his blond hair without thinking.

"I haven't seen you in the longest time!"

"I know! How old are you now, eighteen?"

He shook his head. "Nineteen."

"We have a lot to catch up on."

Something sharp jabbed into my back, making me turn. It was my Aunt, the crazy one. Her boney finger poked me to catch my attention. She had her black hair situated to look like a mountain was on her head, gold earrings dangled from her ears and a silver necklace with rubies practically choked her. She kissed the side of my face, leaving a sticky red imprint behind.

"Oh darling I haven't seen you in ages," she chimed and, to my relief, turned away from me, having already wasted enough time acknowledging me.

"I can hardly imagine of what she looks like when she is a wolf." I whispered to Tim.

"Oh, I'm sure you can. Don't even get me started."

"I'm sure glad I'm not a wolf."

"Oh that's right, you're a vampire." He lowered his voice to a whisper. "Your dad isn't happy about that. He wants you to be a part of this family. He wants you to be a werewolf."

"What can he do? It's not like *he* can turn me into a wolf."

"Have you performed the Blood Ceremony with another vampire yet?"

"No, why?"

"Damn."

"What? What's wrong?"

"Have you ever heard of arranged marriages?"

"Yeah."

"Well your dad is going to sort of…going to make you perform a Ceremony. It's called a Moon Ceremony and it is performed on the night of a full moon. Think of it like an arranged marriage. You will be bonded to whatever wolf your father chooses."

"And tonight is a full moon. I don't believe him. That's so typical," I said through my teeth.

"I'm going to help you, don't worry."

"How will you help me?"

"Leave that to me."

"Family, we have gathered to discuss some issues on Chenille's behalf."

"Wait, before you start with that, can someone please tell me how it's possible that you're here, being wolves and all?"

"And by *here* you mean on *Earth*?"

"Yes."

"You see, since you were born a mortal we made an agreement with the other mortals. Your mother was a mortal when she had you. We promised the mortals to have you raised as a mortal, without Catastrophe's influence, unlike Zaire, who was born a wolf. We suspected you would one day join our pack, which was fine with the mortals. Many vampires kill to kill, but we take mortals strictly to bond, not to feed. And so the mortals made an exception and appointed me as head wolf of Catastrophe and allowed me to remain stationed here."

"Zaire had to be sent to Catastrophe because we weren't ready to show our identity to you. We were going to have you bonded by your eighteenth birthday, but we could not protect you from everything. Somehow, someway, a vampire slipped under our radar." My mother said quietly.

"So you sent Zaire to do your dirty work for you?"

"Zaire was our last option…our last chance to save you."

"*Save* me? Zaire is dead now because of you!"

"I've heard enough!"

My father stood, immediately causing me to back away from my seat. He pointed to my cousin.

"End this now Timothy!"

To my horror, my cousin fell to his hands and knees in obedience. He transformed into a wolf before my eyes, without thinking. His silver-white coat mesmerized me for a brief moment.

"Go on Timothy, what are you waiting for?"

My cousin's gaze fell on me, filled with regret. I knew exactly what was happening.

"You...you can't do this. Family members can't bond!" I cried.

"Denver, please do something-," my mother began, only to be silenced by a simple warning glance.

"I don't want to be a wolf. I don't want to be one of you. And you can't make Tim change me," I stuttered, frightened.

"Timothy!"

My cousin stood on his hind legs, his massive paws pressing me up against the back wall. Struggling, screaming, I tried to move my cousin away, although, to my relief, he did not make any further motions. He exposed his teeth, his eyes almost pleading to continue my cries of horror. He had other intentions and for my own sake, I played along.

Lucian's figure flashed into my peripheral vision. At the sight of my sudden urgency to leave, my cousin released me, retreating away as if I had just injured him. The distraction gave me just enough time to make it out of the house with Lucian – in one piece.

Chapter 18 - Blood Ceremony

A Blood Ceremony is analogous to that of mortal marriage, but more complex. The bond of two vampires creates a Blood Ceremony. Each drink the blood of the one they love. The two vampires, Eternal Mates or not, can perform this ceremony anywhere at any time just as long as they both have pure trust in each other and both agree on performing the Ceremony. If one of the vampires dies after a successful Ceremony, they will reincarnate into another form. If not in their original form, but that of another such as a dragon, the new reincarnated vampire will find their Eternal Mate.

However, the Ceremony must be renewed every time reincarnation takes place to ensure that another successful reincarnation will occur if an Eternal Mate is killed again. Failure to renew a Ceremony will result in total death for the killed Eternal Mate without hope for reincarnation.

Chapter 16 - Taunting Nightmare

"Bow before your new leaders, the King and Queen of Catastrophe!" Jasper cried as he flew over the heads of the thousands of vampires that gathered in the front yard of the palace. I walked with Lucian onto a balcony that overlooked the bowing creatures.

"It is an honor to stand before the many faces my family has grown to know. Pete no longer rules over you. His planet no longer exists."

"What happened to him," a voice cried up to us.

"He perished along with his planet."

"How? By who?"

"We're not sure, but do not be afraid. He will not be coming back."

"As your new leaders, we have great pride in...great pride in-,"

"Chenille? Chenille, are you feeling...Healers! Get the healers over here!"

Prusaious ran out onto the balcony with several vampires behind her.

"Chenille will be fine. Finish your speech," she insisted, barely flicking her eyes in my direction.

"Is she going to be all right?"

"She will be fine, finish the speech!"

Prusaious led me away, as if I was more of an obligation to her. Once in the palace, Prusaious made me sit down. A wave of exhaustion fell over me. A few healers and unfamiliar faces surrounded me. I could hear Lucian's voice, barely, but I could hear it.

"What do you mean you won't let me come in? I am King, you must let me through!"

"I am sorry sir, I cannot let you pass-,"

"No, let me in! Chenille is in there! I need to know what's going on!"

"Lucian," I cried, "where are you?"

"Calm down Chenille," Prusaious said calmly. She grabbed my hand, not so much to comfort me, but more to prevent me from scrambling to my feet.

"Where is Lucian?"

"Let me pass!" I heard him cry from behind the door.

"Lucian, where are you?"

"Stay still Chenille!" Prusaious scolded.

"Where is he?"

"Clear the way."

The healers moved aside as a vampire took his place at the foot of the bed in which I lay. He had his cape hood shielded over his face, the handle of Fitzray's blade held firmly in one hand.

"That's not Lucian! Where is Lucian?"

"Let me in! What's going on in there?"

"The child won't take my throne," the vampire spat darkly.

"No!" I screamed.

The blade came up, pointed down in my direction and slid through the air towards the target the vampire aimed for - me.

In a flash, I was on the Bridge of Secrecy. Confused, I rubbed my arms, surprised I was all in one piece. Pete was there, standing as the antagonist in my intrusive nightmare. He strode up to me before I could even move, his wicked smile leaving me immobilized.

"You look…different."

"I…well I-,"

"You bear a child."

"Yes."

"Whose child is it?"

"Mine."

"And?"

"Yours?" I said with a shrug.

He shook his head. "It has a blood beat."

"So?"

"No child of mine would have a blood beat." He fingered the knife in his hands, the same blade that I had just seen.

"You wouldn't dare."

"You wouldn't be harmed-,"

"You are malevolent."

"If that child is born, I will be kicked from my throne. And if he performs a Ceremony, so will you."

"You have no throne. Lucian is King now."

"Is he?" His lips curved up, exposing his fangs deviously as he jutted out his chin.

Hesitantly, my eyes turned in the direction to where he motioned. A stream of black blood flowed on the beautiful white stone at my feet.

It isn't possible. It can't be.

There was a faint gasping sound in the distance and following it, I saw the dark stream, once a shallow puddle, now an *ocean* around me. I fell to my knees, my legs unable to support my weight from the shock. A frail body was huddled before me on the stone.

"No," I whispered, "Lucian, no."

"Leave me...here on the Bridge to die. Go back. Save yourself, save the baby. With the power I have left I will create a place for you to be safe. I will create a planet for you and the baby to be safe."

"No...I can't-," I turned to Pete. "What have you done?"

"Someone had to put that mutt in his place."

I turned to face the side of the Bridge wall and proceeded to climb it. Pete climbed up the side of the wall to stand beside me. He grabbed my arm, helping me catch my balance.

"You finally have it my way."

"And you finally have it *mine*." I took Fitzray's knife from his hands to hold it beneath his chin. His eyes widened.

"No, that knife-,"

"You used it against my wishes. You killed Fitzray's dragon with this knife and in turn, killed him too. And now...you will be killed by your own revulsion."

"And you will come down with me, like I promised all of your friends."

I struck the dagger through his chest and heard a gasp of disbelief. He glared at me, gritted his teeth, but his breathing did not falter, making me face the possibility that I might have missed his heart. I kissed him and his poison goodbye. And, to my relief, when I pushed him away he did not bounce back, but fell off the Bridge wall and into the oblivion of the universe.

*****

"Chenille! Chenille what's wrong? Wake up."

"Where am I?" I cried, sitting up.

"Easy, everything is ok. We're at my place."

The thick darkness made it impossible to confirm that what he said was true. Lucian lit a candle, which emitted hardly enough light for me to see his face.

"Lucian, it was terrible. Pete came back and you couldn't help me. He killed you," I said through sobs.

"It was just a bad dream," he assured me quietly.

"He wanted to kill my baby."

"Baby?" Lucian shook his head. "What a crazy dream."

My hand flew to my stomach and he caught my sudden movement with astonishment. "I tried to tell you. When we last went to the City, I knew something wasn't right."

Lucian's shoulders tensed as I spoke. If he got to his feet, left, and never came back, I would understand. I told myself to accept his choice, even if it meant never seeing him again.

"Lu...Lucian," I began, hoping he would say something or at least snap out of the trance that made him irresponsive.

"It all makes sense now," he said slowly. "No wonder you were all stressed out." He slowly wrapped his arms around me, offering the comfort I had doubted he would give me.

"I thought you would leave."

"Leave? What makes you think that? A king wouldn't leave his queen," he whispered.

In the silence that enveloped the room, the loud thrum of a pulse rang in my ears.

"Is that the beat of the baby's heart?"

"It is."
"Does that mean…it's a mortal?"
"No. There is a beat of life in its veins. It doesn't mean it's not a vampire."
"Do you think it would overthrow us and claim the throne?"
"What makes you think that?"
"Pete said so. In my dream he said that once old enough, the heir can fight his father for the throne or can overthrow the current rulers by performing a Ceremony."
"No one, not even an heir will take the throne unless we are both killed."
"Do you think the baby is yours?"

He rested his chin on my head thoughtfully. "I don't see why not."
"Goodnight Lu." His acceptance made me smile with relief.
"Goodnight my Queen."

Chapter 25 - Vampire Pregnancy

Bearing a vampire child is not much different from a mortal. The vampire will be extremely protective of his vampress and the baby she bears. Some vampress mothers have died in childbirth, but this is rare. The baby will most likely survive with the care of its father, with hope that the mother will reincarnate within only a couple of years. There are bad side effects from vampire pregnancy such as bad fevers and hallucination.

Chapter 17 - Amour

In celebration, Lucian took me to the City the following day. He showed me around the City, pointing out monuments and statues that basked in spotlights. Construction was fast here, on Catastrophe. What took years to build on Earth only took a couple of months to build here. Amour was recently constructed, now a famous restaurant in the City.

"Where Amour stands today is where the tallest building in the City once stood. If you went there during an eclipse you could have-,"

"Counted the craters on the moon's surface."

"Yes, that's right." He said while holding the restaurant door open for me.

Inside, a dining experience found here, in the City of Lights, was unlike any other. The restaurant was T-shaped with small tables in the front, near the entrance, and larger, longer tables toward the back, closer to the kitchen. The whole west wing was devoted to kitchen space. There were massive columns and marvelous original paintings on the walls from some of the best-known artists on Catastrophe. A waiter attended every table.

The guests consisted of upper class, dressed richly in long gowns and fitted suits. Many women wore necklaces beaded with the shed scales of their dragons. A pianist sat at a grand piano playing soft, atmospheric music.

"How may I assist you tonight?" A waiter asked.

"A table for two."

"Yes, right this way."

He showed us to a table in the far back of the room, large with potpourri scattered over its top.

"This is a bit large for the two of us. A smaller table will do fine."

"Yes sir."

We followed him to another table, which was smaller but just as equally dressed up.

"Here you are." The waiter said as he pulled out my chair.

"Thank you."

"Here are the menus for tonight."

"That will be all."

The waiter nodded and walked off toward the kitchen. I sat quietly to look over the menu at the selection of meals. I did not see anything that suited my appetite, hardly hungry anyway, and stood up.

"Where are you going?" Lucian's eyes flashed up from his menu.

"I have to powder my nose." I bit my tongue. That was something a mortal would say.

"Don't be long."

"I won't."

Before I made it to the other side of the restaurant, a familiar voice struck me - no, *two* familiar voices. There stood my father and Prusaious. They were both dressed to blend in with the rich atmosphere. Quietly, I hid behind a column, the closest thing to hide behind.

"You said she would be here. Where is she?"

"I...I don't know...she's nearby, I just know she's here. I can smell her."

"Find her," my father growled impatiently.

I peered out from behind my hiding spot to see if they were still there. To my relief, they were gone. Hesitant to turn back to get Lucian, I noticed the bathroom was closer and I made my way toward it. Before I could reach my new hiding place, someone grabbed me from behind and my mouth was covered.

My kidnapper dragged me into the kitchen. The chefs were too busy to notice as I passed them. How they did not notice a couple of kidnappers nonchalantly dragging a squealing girl was just astonishing. I wished they were not so oblivious to the world around them and turn around for a moment. I wished they would glance up from cooking their meat or tossing their salad, but they appeared to be in a world of their own. Such a world better have giant pieces of food and gingerbread men running around in lakes of milk and honey. Such a world should better have been more pleasing than such a scene behind them, within their reach.

I stopped moving. A large dragon stood before me and took me from the rough hands of my kidnapper once we were outside. The dragon held me to its body, one of its talons pressed against my mouth so whenever I tried to scream, the dragon's claws pinched my face. I found I could not move at all, despite my attempt to fight the dragon. The dragon flew at extreme speeds, through the City to the Bridge and onward to Earth.

It was dark and I could see nothing once the dragon finally landed. The dragon held me while my kidnappers bound my hands in chains behind my back. They covered my mouth again.

My kidnappers forced me into a room. My eyes pained me, adjusting to the intense light, as one of the chains freed my right hand. The other chain wrapped around a thick column so I could not escape. I was in the dining room of my parent's house. My family members glared at me, all except Tim. He was chained to the column beside me.

"You just disappeared the other night, without even saying goodbye," my father chimed.

"Why? Why do you still hate our species? I want to put an end to this war-,"

"It isn't about the species!"

"Then why do you want me to be a wolf so much? You know that I have the most power of my species...and for you to turn me into a wolf, wouldn't that cause me to be the most powerful and lead you and your wolves-," I began.

"Quiet! I will hear none of that!"

"Why? Because I'm right!"

"Enough! I will find a way to turn you into a wolf."

"Don't waste your time."

"Why not?"

"I have performed the Blood Ceremony already. My transformation is complete and you can't change me now."

"Who did you perform the Blood Ceremony with? Fitzray or Pete?"

"Fitzray is long gone and Pete hasn't come for me yet. You should know that."

"Then who did you complete the Ceremony with? Some poor vampire off the street?"

"No. Lucian."

"You are joking…a vampire from the street would be far better than *him*. He is a reject to both species…no wait, all *three* - the vampires, mortals, *and* wolves. He's hardly superior at all."

"Yes, he is. He is your king now."

"There are no kings on Earth that rule us," my father said.

He walked over to me and brushed my hair away from my neck where the two bite marks still showed, pink and sore. He stumbled back with a growl while Tim let out a sigh of relief.

"And *you*," he hissed turning his head in Tim's direction. "You are a traitor! How dare you try to help her and go against my wishes! I gave you one simple task-,"

"You think turning my own cousin into a wolf by force is *simple*?"

My father snarled. "Throw him over the Bridge."

"No one is throwing anyone over the Bridge!" Prusaious yelled.

"Yeah, if anyone should be thrown over the Bridge it should be *you*." I cried, pointing with my free hand.

"Me?"

"Yeah, you are the traitor! You were working for my father the whole time, weren't you!"

"I wasn't always a traitor. Not until you took Lucian from me!"

"*Me*, take Lucian from *you*? I didn't even know Lucian! He fell for me! He wanted to *help* me!"

She crossed her arms. "Liar!"

"*Liar*?" I growled and took a step toward her, but found the chains still bound me to the column.

"Take her to the dungeon! Lock her up with Tim!"

My father ripped the chains from the columns and led us down into the depths of the cold basement. He tossed us both carelessly into a small cellar and pulled over a metal bar door, locking it. He handed the key to Prusaious.

"Tonight we destroy the Bridge and you will be present to see it fall." My father said.

"Why would you do that?"

"So your species will suffer."

"Because of something *I* did? Your species will suffer just the same. You leave the vampires as they are. This is a family issue, not a reason to continue our war."

"I call the shots here. My species will not suffer."

"Your species won't survive long."

"They will survive long enough for yours to be extinct."

"And then what will you do with me?"

"I don't know. I haven't really thought of that."

They left at once, without another word. Tim and I remained alone, in the darkness.

"Don't worry, I'll get us out of here," he whispered.

"They can't destroy the Bridge, Tim. Catastrophe will be in ruins if they do."

"Then you will have to stop Prusaious…and your own father."

*****

Lucian paced through the restaurant. He scanned the faces of those around him. He shot over to the kitchen and asked every waiter in sight if he had seen the Queen of Catastrophe. He ran off to the bathroom and touched the elbow of a woman who passed him.

"Could you tell me if the Queen is in there?"

"Of course dear," the elder woman replied.

She nodded and walked into the bathroom only to return several minutes later.

"Is she there?"

"No," the woman said sadly, "but you should check outside. Maybe she wanted some fresh air."

After looking again with no hope, he slumped on the edge of the huge fountain that flowed with colored bubbles at the front of the building. He yelled to his guards and they informed him that they had a bigger problem. They claimed explosives covered the Bridge.

*****

A few wolves took me from the dungeon to the Bridge, just as my father promised. The wolves stood in front of me. A distant voice called out a command.

"Go, blow up the Bridge," my father yelled.

Someone lit the fuse that now twisted, snaking its way toward the Bridge and the explosives. My eyes followed it, fearing for my kind, watching the little yellow-orange light burn when suddenly it disappeared. There was not a rumble or a thunderous crash of an explosion that I anticipated. Instead, I saw Prusaious standing where the light had disappeared. A wisp of smoke floated into the air where her boot was, firmly suffocating the small flame.

"What are you doing?" My father roared and marched up to Prusaious angrily.

"Chenille was right. It's not worth killing our own species to try to kill off another."

"What do you suggest we do then?"

"We simply keep Chenille under lock and key."

"What good would that do?"

"With Chenille gone, Lucian won't know what to do."

"I suppose."

"So, he will probably go insane with the thought of what could have happened. And with no rulers, the vampires will fall. They will fall and chaos will rain over them. We could easily beat them in a battle."

"And then what?" I cried.

"And then Catastrophe will be ours. Now, clean the Bridge up and disburse. Make sure Chenille is locked up and leave the rest to me."

Chapter 18 - Control

Lucian stood before Taj' who watched as his mermaid babies splashed in the shallow water of the Frozen Waterfalls.

"I don't understand...it's been days and Chenille is still missing. Did I perform the Blood Ceremony right? What if something happened to her?"

"No," Taj' said quietly. "I don't believe that is so."

"Then why would she just...disappear like that? Do you think someone kidnapped her?"

"Who would do such a thing? There is no reason for someone to take her. But give it some time. It has only been a couple of days."

The snake sighed as Pearl came out from behind the large cave hidden behind the waterfalls and stretched out her arms in the sun. The snake babies coiled around her arms and the little snake, Aura, loosely hung around her neck.

Her once dull blonde hair now curled in golden locks down her back. With all the love surrounding her and new babies to care for, she no longer sat on her rock in the middle of the icy pool before the waterfalls.

"Queen Pearl," Lucian said with a bow.

"No, I am still Princess Pearl," she corrected. "My mother will always be a queen, yet her time was up long ago. She now makes up the waves in the oceans and Earth's sky blue. They call her Mother Nature. She was one of the wisest most beautiful mermaids and had extraordinary powers. She fell in love with my father who was an old phoenix. He became the Father of Time. They both loved Earth so much, but there was no Bridge of Secrecy at that time so they vowed that the day they died they would move to Earth together and become a part of it."

"Is that really true?"

"True as it will ever be."

The little snake babies let out giddy squeaks and slipped from her arms into the shallow water beside their father. Lucian shook his head and closed his eyes.

"I don't know what to do."

He bid farewell to them and went home to his palace. He paced the floor, his eyes resting on the navy cutlass sword that Fitzray had given him several years ago. It hung on the wall above the mantle, showing off its beautiful gold hilt and silver blade. He lifted it from the wall and laid it flat across his hands to examine it. Jasper walked into the room, his head low so he would not hit his head on the ceiling.

"What are you doing Sire?"

"I'm just looking at the sword Fitzray gave me a few years ago." He turned the sword over in his hands thoughtfully.

"Sire…you…you wouldn't."

"How will I go on Jasper, if Chenille does not return?" He said coldly, his fingers running over the slender blade.

"But Master-,"

"I will be your Master no longer Jasper. You would be free from my rule."

"No Sire, I won't let you."

"Leave Jasper."

"I will not."

"Leave!"

The dragon backed up, forced to obey Lucian's command and left the room.

Lucian held the heavy sword in his hands and positioned it right before his chest, testing himself, if he could really seize his last breath.

"Lucian! Let me in!"

He dropped the sword and ran for the door with every bit of hope surfacing upon hearing the familiar voice. Once the door was open, Prusaious trotted inside and threw her arms around his neck. Startled, he stepped back and frowned at the girl who stood before him.

"I don't suppose you have any news regarding Chenille, do you?"

"Oh, I do!"

"What? Tell me!"

"I...don't think I should."

"Tell me!"

"Well you see I have been told that she has...*died*."

"No...no."

"But it will be all right...you will move on...*won't you*?"

He stepped back with Prusaious walking in front of him when his heel hit the sword. Prusaious jumped back at the loud metallic ring and noticed the sword near his feet. She looked at it suspiciously and then at Lucian.

"What...you tried to kill yourself? How could you...all because of Chenille?"

"I didn't try...but I will. I will now if what you say is true," he said through his teeth.

"You only felt sorry for her because Fitzray died and he was your cousin!"

"No, I didn't! I vowed to help her because if I didn't do what I did, if I didn't perform the Ceremony with her...Pete would still be ruling and...who knows what would have happened to her."

"So you felt sorry for her."

"I was protecting her."

"And what about *me*?"

"What *about* you?"

"Did you ever take *my* feelings into consideration?"

"You helped me the way a sister would have. I didn't look at you as anything more."

Her hands tightened to fists at her sides.

"You will regret that."

"You should move on."

"Time is running out for Chenille."

"What? Where is she? Where is my Eternal Mate? She *is* alive isn't she? You...*you* are the one responsible for this!"

She smiled wickedly and touched his face, waiting until his eyes closed and he fell to the floor at her feet. She laughed quietly and took a step back to admire her work.

He stood once she raised her arm and came to her with simple hand gestures like a trained dog. He was her puppet now, loyally obeying all she asked him to do.

The guards, as well as Chenille's friends, became aware of this and devised a plan as soon as they saw Lucian. Calvin walked into the living room while Prusaious was in stitches. She watched Lucian as he balanced plates of food on his head and arms for her.

Calvin stood in front of the fireplace and looked at her. At once, she stopped laughing and all of the plates fell and shattered upon meeting the floor. She carelessly pushed Lucian from the couch once he took a seat beside her and patted it lightly for Calvin to sit instead.

"Sit here," she said quietly. "Have we met before?"

"We have, actually." Calvin sat beside her, expressionless.

"So what is your name again?"

"Eh, Calvin…listen, can I have my friend back?"

She looked over at Lucian and shrugged her shoulders.

"I guess, I mean-," she froze just as he put an icy hand to her face. "I mean…of course you can have him back."

Lucian dropped into the pile of broken glass.

"That's more like it." He whispered and stood up to help Lucian.

"Now, can you tell us where Chenille is?" Calvin whispered.

"I couldn't possibly-,"

"*Please*?" Calvin hissed and neared her ear.

"On Earth."

"Where on Earth?" He pressed, his charm getting through to her.

"She's in the basement of her parent's house." She replied quickly, obedient.

"You have been a great help," he said with a friendly smile.

"You have to hurry though."

"Why?"

"She is terribly malnourished."

"The baby will die for good if she hasn't eaten anything," Lucian said, now fully alert. He shook his head in distress.

Calvin grabbed his shoulder and whispered harshly in his ear. "You get a couple of dragons ready and meet the others outside. Chenille doesn't have much time." He turned to Prusaious. "How much time do you think she has left?"

"I don't know."

"What about Prusaious?" Lucian whispered back.

"I'll take care of her. You have to save Chenille before it's too late."

Lucian ran out the door to where Amelia and Pearl waited for him on the backs of large dragons. Lucian mounted Jasper and Minx stood beside him.

"Let's go!"

Once they lifted off, they heard distant rumbles as if a volcano was erupting, but thought nothing of the loud noise.

"It is good to have you back, Sire."

"It's good to be back."

"It's going to be a long flight," Amelia said.

"Yes, but we don't have much time. We have to make these dragons fly as fast as they can."

"Where is Taj'?"

"He will meet up with us on the other side of the Bridge. He'll direct us to where Chenille is being kept."

The dragons pumped their wings as hard as they could. To get there in time, they needed to fly faster. The tired dragons kept their pace, if not faster, until they reached their maximum speed. Instead of their small, fast strokes they once used to reach their minimum speed, they flew with long, powerful strokes. Once Earth was in clear view, they spiraled down. They flew straight down and once the land was near, swooped up to prevent collision. On land, they broke from their run, skidding to a stop.

Taj' moved in front of Lucian once he slid off Jasper and looked for some way to get into the basement.

"Over here!" he called.

Lucian walked over to him. The barred window created a perfect portal into the basement.

"How do we get inside?"

Taj' wrapped his tail around the bars in front of the window, bending them effortlessly. He then smashed his tail through the glass and looked down at Lucian.

"I will lower you down with my tail. Once you find Chenille, hand her up to me." He curled his tail around Lucian's waist and lowered him down into the basement quickly.

"Over here," a voice called. Lucian found the voice belonged to a blond haired boy. He mentioned that his name was Timothy. "I'm Chenille's cousin."

"Don't worry. I'll get you out of here."

To his surprise the door was not only unlocked, it was broken. But Tim was weak, cut up, and bleeding.

"What happened? Did you do this?"

"Yes. I thought there would be a way out of here. She has…little…time. She hasn't…had blood in…in days. If the baby dies, she might die too."

"Taj' I need you to take someone for me."

"Chenille?"

"No, Timothy, her cousin. Take him to Minx and tell him to fly to Catastrophe as fast as he can to the hospital."

"Ok, where is he?"

"Go up to the window, you will be safe with Taj'." He told Tim. "Taj' hurry, take Chenille now!" He held me up for the snake and his tail curled around my body. "Don't worry about me! Take Chenille to Jasper and tell him to fly! Tell him I told him to fly as fast as he can!"

"Lucian said to fly as fast as you can Jasper! Chenille's life depends on it!" I heard Taj' say as he handed me off to the dragon.

Jasper pressed me to his body with one of his talons and ran at full speed with the other three. He began to flap his wings, each flap steady, and soon rapid strokes hit the air. With one final beat, he lifted up onto his back feet and pushed into the sky, continuing the short strokes.

He held me with two talons pressing me to his soft chest. I could almost hear the strain of his muscles and the hot blood pumping in the veins of his wings. The strokes became longer and soon we passed Minx. The Bridge came into view, but Catastrophe looked like a faded dot from how high we were.

All was well until a huge ball of light came out of nowhere and passed in front of us before our eyes. Jasper roared, but continued to push on. The huge bursts of fire continued to drop like a meteor shower and Jasper banked to avoid collision. He struggled to maintain his fast speed since he had to slow down whenever he saw the blinding light rush toward him.

He roared suddenly and a force pushed us along fast. Catastrophe seemed to be coming toward us within seconds. Jasper still cried out frantically. A giant ball of light had crashed into him and pushed us toward Catastrophe.

He flapped his singed wings once successfully breaking away from the hot meteor and proceeded down toward the planet. He flew through the City of Lights and once he found the hospital, he landed near the building. Being as large as he was, he could not fit through the hospital doors and smashed his head through one of the windows instead.

"Caspian! I need Caspian!"

The nurses gave out frightened cries and ran off at the sight of Jasper.

"No, wait, I need Caspian!"

Two nurses ran forward, dragging Caspian and presented him to Jasper as if to sacrifice him to the dragon.

"The dragon wants *you*," one of the nurses said to the doctor.

He looked up at Jasper confused. "You have the wrong hospital...you see, I am not a veterinarian. Your wings look badly burned but-,"

"No not *me*!" He held me in one of his talons and passed me to Caspian through the broken window.

"She hasn't had blood-,"

"Nurses! I need nurses! Hurry!" He took me from Jasper's claws.

"Wait!" Jasper called.

Caspian ignored him and tended to me. He hooked me up to machines and injected needles into my arms.

"Her cousin is also in the same condition," a nurse yelled.

"Why are you standing here telling me? You know what to do!"

"But, he's a werewolf," she began.

"It doesn't matter, he's her cousin, get him in here," another nurse yelled, defending Caspian's decision.

"Oh no," I heard Caspian mumble.

"Chenille! How is Chenille?"

Lucian came into view, only a blurry figure to me, but I knew it was him.

"Her pulse…the baby is dying. You were too late," he said quietly.

"What do you mean I'm too late?"

"She will be reincarnated if she dies but her baby is going to die. You were too late. I'm sorry Lucian."

Lucian marched up to him and grabbed a fistful of his lab coat angrily. "You are a doctor! You save her!"

"I am sorry, but there is nothing I can do. She needed blood for the baby to get the proper nutrients, but it's been too long."

"No-,"

"There is a slim chance," the doctor's voice faded. "There is *nothing* I can do."

"Are you sure?"

"I am positive."

Lucian walked over to me and placed a hand to my face.

"How much time does she have?"

"Not long. If only you made it here sooner. A day sooner would have made a difference."

"But a few days ago we were in the City. She was ok."

"She was malnourished *then,* Lucian. A few days of not eating are all it takes. The first few weeks are very crucial for development," Caspian explained.

My eyes opened weakly. Lucian kissed me. His poison was sweet.

"Will the baby…be ok?"
"Yes," Caspian lied, "the baby will be just fine."
"I am sorry this had to happen."
"Me too," Lucian whispered.
"I will be reincarnated?"

He nodded and kissed my cheek. "If you die, then yes," he said, though there was a trace of uncertainty in his tone.

"I love you Lu," my voice died and I felt my head fall back weakly. All the sounds around me faded.

Lucian leaned his head against my chest. His breathing rose and fell unevenly. A faded figure, transparent, and almost ghostlike, appeared beside the bed. Beside the figure, I saw a faded image I assumed was my baby.

Something was wrong. The image was fading like a diminishing piece of paper, burning from the bottom to the top. I watched, unable to help my baby. It was dying.

"Fitzray?" I said weakly. The transparent figure, the apparition that stood beside Caspian was more defined now. He seemed so real, but at the same time, so impossible.

"Have you learned about the insanity of this obscure world yet?" After a long pause, he moved closer to me.

"We performed the Ceremony together, remember? Our immortal bond still runs deep in our blood." He said it as if I did not know who he was, but I could not find my voice. I only stared.

"I thought it didn't happen. I thought you would have been reincarnated by now…or would not have been reincarnated at all," I mumbled softly.

"It worked out. We did perform the Ceremony, but reincarnation takes time. I'll be reincarnated soon," he assured me.

"But I performed the Ceremony with Lucian."
"I know."
"But what about our bond?"

"We will be together in other ways, I promise." He looked at me and smiled. "Lucian will take good care of you."

"You were watching me all this time weren't you?"

"Yes." He said quietly.

I glanced over at the image of my baby. It was almost gone.

"My baby," I whispered.

I watched my baby. The last little sliver of its white image faded away. The noises returned to me in a rush. The apparitions faded away. I was still alive.

There was a sudden crash. A distant rumble came from another section of the hospital.

"What was that?" Caspian yelled.

"Fire! Great burning shards of fire have crashed into the hospital-," a nurse cried.

A fiery rock crashed into the room where we were and the force sent Lucian and me across the room, smashing us both into a wall. Lucian rubbed his head and picked me up. He then began to walk over to Caspian who held onto Amelia and Pearl. The floor shook as if caused by an earthquake and I clung tight to Lucian's cape. Through a nearby window, I saw that the fire rocks had stopped falling and the floor ceased its shaking.

Caspian looked around to see if anyone was injured. The fire rocks were doused with water, revealing beautiful pieces of white stone like those that made up the Bridge.

I pulled onto Lucian's cape and he caught my glance and smiled.

"How are you doing?"

"I don't…feel too good."

"Caspian! Where are you?"

"Over here." He said while carefully examining the white stone.

"Come over here!"

"What? What is it?"

"It's Chenille."

I uttered a cry of pain.

"Nurses!"

"Hang on, I'm here. You are going to be just fine."

Chapter 33 - Bonding

Vampires have the strongest bond of any creature to walk the planets. They are powerful and compassionate creatures toward each other. It is unfortunate that some, like me, have not been in a bond before. However, all vampires will find their Eternal Mate and the species will usually be at peace with each other. Will one day come when mortals, vampires, and werewolves are at peace with one another? And if that comes to be the case, what will come of the Bridge? To me, I find that hardly believable. I do not think three completely different species of any kind would ever come together and would certainly not become allies. I believe that the species of werewolves, vampires, and mortals should not unite in any way. But who knows what will come of us all?

Chapter 19 - Supremacy

"Here you are, my Queen." Calvin said and bowed before me with beautiful flowers. I was glad to see him happy, for he had somehow found love with Prusaious, who was at his side. Their companionship served as a little proof that we achieved some peace with the werewolves, if anything at all.

As it turned out, when Pete's planet exploded, it caused the destruction of several other stars surrounding it. This resulted in the fire rocks that fell over the two planets, which were actually fragments of stars. The mortals made such profit with these new priceless rocks that were more valuable than dragon scales.

The wars were over, almost over. The mortals did not slaughter the dragons for their scales, for now at least, and the mortals made a compromise with us. The werewolves were questionable. They would always be questionable as long as I was Queen.

Afterword

There is not much known about vampires. I am not the first to say that their world is strange and complex, but when it comes down to love and Eternal Mates, I take the cake.

By, Pete Silver

I closed my eyes and sighed after reading the afterword of the black journal to myself.

Pete is right. How is it possible to be at peace with all species? The mortals will someday come back to hunt our dragons. And we would fight back. As for the werewolves, they have been our enemy from the start and they always will be. How could they change their minds about us? How could we be so foolish as to trust them? Our world will surely crumble at our feet if we think we can keep this peace, especially since I am the

Queen of Catastrophe. Saneness and reconciliation can scarcely breathe in the air of Catastrophe, I thought.

And with bigger issues to be looked after, one said it was the Bridge of Secrecy that should be watched closely. One individual in particular caught my eye the other day and said, "If you have read the book, may you find the key in saving the Bridge from destruction."

Lucian, my new Eternal Mate, the King of Catastrophe, gathered me into his arms. Breathing a sigh of relief, I found comfort against him.

All of this, only temporary.

*****

Part 3

Return from Ashes

Chapter 20 - Royalty

I was lost in one of Lucian's memory kisses. I saw my past when I had just become a vampress. I was sound asleep, anticipating the weekend morning, when something grabbed my arm and swung me to my feet. I went to utter out a cry when a hand covered my mouth.

"Shh, it's just me."

At the time, Pete and I were close friends so things like this happened often.

"What are you doing here?"

"I've been out of town for a while, so I thought you might want to see me."

"At this hour?"

"Come with me."

"What? No, I'm not going anywhere. It's like two in the morning."

"Just meet me outside, ok?"

He slipped from my room so I could dress into something warmer. I grabbed my scarf and tied it tightly around my neck just as I stepped into the chill of the night. He grabbed my wrist and led me to the backyard.

"Where did you say you were taking me again?"

"I don't know yet." There was aggravation in his tone.

I stumbled over the sprouting sunflowers and the wisteria vines, straining my eyes after him through the pitch-black darkness. He walked past the willow tree and stopped. Once I caught up, he turned and smiled.

"Here," was all he said and fell back onto the ground.

"Pete?" I sat beside him and shook him in panic.

His eyes opened and in one movement swung me over onto the ground beside him and let out a growl.

"What are you doing?"

"You don't get it do you?"

"Get what?"

"I am a vampire."

I laughed. "Vampires don't exist."

He ripped the scarf away from my throat and pressed his fangs to my neck. "You sure about that?"

"You...you wouldn't! You are my friend!"

"It's for your own good, for reasons you wouldn't understand."

"But why?"

"So no one else can have you."

"What is that supposed to mean?"

"You'll find out."

The next morning, I was alone. I managed to make my way inside to the bathroom. Blood ran like water from the wound on my neck. I put a hand to my throat and gazed at the blood on my fingertips that looked appetizing to me now.

I could not let my parents see me like this so I ran off to the Bridge of Secrecy, to Catastrophe, where my brother resided.

Once I was there, a vampire approached me and healed the wound on my neck. A beautiful woman, about my age, walked up to me and smiled.

"You must be new here."

"Yes, I am."

"I am new here too. My name is Amelia."

"I'm Chenille."

That was when my friendship with Amelia began.

I broke away from Lucian, hearing the baby's loud cry from the nursery.

"Fitzray is up."

Lucian and I had some debate with what to call the baby, but in the end, we agreed to name him Fitzray. The memories of him were still strong, especially since I saw his apparition.

I went into the nursery and peeked inside to see him sitting on the rocking chair, his face flushed. His green eyes flooded over with large frightened tears.

"What's the matter?" I said quietly and lifted him up into my arms. Lucian peeked over my shoulder and smiled once the small child looked up at him.

"I almost forgot. There is something I wanted to give Fitzray."

"What?"

Lucian took off the chain he wore around his neck. Hanging loosely from the chain was a large silver key with a red-orange stone in the center of the handle. Two silver snakes wrapped around the key itself with clever artisanship.

"This once belonged to my uncle and later was passed down to Pete…and then to me. But now I think is a good time for Fitzray to have it."

"He is so young though. He is only three."

"That's all right. It will not be a bother to him. It is said that something as valuable as this must be passed down to someone at a very young age."

"Why?"

"I'm not entirely sure, but that is what I was told." He said and placed the key around the baby's neck.

"There is something going on down by the Bridge. Come quickly!" Prusaious called, her figure filling the open doorway.

I held onto Lucian's cape before he could go anywhere. "Please Lu, don't go."

"I have to."

"But Lucian-,"

"Don't trouble yourself more than you already have. Go to the City of Lights. Don't worry about me. I'll be fine."

Before I could say any more, he handed Fitzray back to me and followed Prusaious out.

I followed Lucian's advice and went off to the City, Fitzray in my arms. I strolled through the quiet streets of the city, even when the crowd swallowed me up.

An elderly woman touched my elbow and pulled me off to the side from the swarm of creatures that gathered around me. She wore a dark cape over her shoulders and a mask on her face.

"Lucian is in trouble my Queen," she said in a soft, throaty voice. "You must go to the Bridge of Secrecy at once, but be cautious and keep hold of your child. If you have read the book you shall find the key to save the Bridge and us from total destruction."

That was not the first time someone told me about a book saving us from certain demise.

"What key? And how do you know Lucian-,"

She was gone. If I had not started to run toward the Bridge, it would have been too late.

Chapter 21 - Tetchra

A beautiful lady stood on one of the high walls of the Bridge. She paced along the top of the wall and glared down at all who gathered around to peer up at her in curiosity. She wore a long red dress that came down to her ankles and swished with every step. She held a heavy cape in her petite hands.

"What is the meaning of this?" Lucian yelled above those who spoke.

The woman took a strand of her curled black hair and twisted it around her fingers.

"Are you the King? The King of Catastrophe?"

"I am." He said softly as to not frighten the woman and cause her to fall.

"Then may you be warned King of Catastrophe."

He looked at her long and hard. "What is your name?"

"My name is Tetchra. Get to know it well." She said and jumped down from the wall onto the Bridge.

"What is the problem Tetchra?"

"I'll tell you what the problem is! It's having people like *you* not realize by now that we could be avoiding war."

"I don't understand."

"What is this *thing* I stand on today? Why is it here?"

"To serve the purpose of having the vampires and werewolves cross to Earth to feed and bond with the mortals."

"And now other species are endangered. In making and crossing this bridge, you have allowed them to cross to our world. Why not just make all of the vampires and wolves go over to Earth and stay there?"

"We can't do that. The mortals strictly forbid that and we cannot stay longer than the eclipse of Clesta and Earth's moon."

"But we haven't had an eclipse ever since Pete created his planet and caused the ending of eclipses."

"What are you suggesting?"

"Our little treaty with the mortals is broken. And since that is true...wouldn't it be best if we had two separate worlds?"

"That's impossible. How could we survive without blood from the mortals?"

"What do you mean *survive*? You are immortals. You only need to drink blood for the first year of your life when you become a vampire or werewolf to replenish the blood that was lost. You do not need it anymore. We would be better as a separate world, not two connected."

"We still need the mortals to bond. I will consider the possibilities, but-,"

"Oh, you *will* consider them." She hissed through her teeth. She had pulled out a knife from under her cape.

"Lucian!" The crowd cleared the way to where I saw him and a woman standing on the Bridge.

The old woman was right.

"Do not move Queen." She said, pointing her dagger at Lucian.

"What do you want? Let him be!"

"I want two separate worlds. That is my only wish and you will make it true."

She grabbed Lucian and stabbed him with her dagger. The crowd blocked them from view. I could not be sure if he was dead or not, but that was not my first concern. If that woman killed him, I knew he would reincarnate within a few days. A group of vampires came from behind the woman who had stabbed Lucian. The crowd went into a frenzy of panic and I immediately lost my bearings. A snowy owl flew in front of my face and before I could stop it, Fitzray was missing from my arms.

All fled from the Bridge and I was left alone, in shock, trying to comprehend what had happened. One vampire now walked in front of me. The figure's face was so similar, so strange to encounter again. It was not possible, for all that had happened. Why did this character come forth and reveal the shadowed mask of who he was in the blunt glow of the moon before me? I got back up on my feet and grabbed a fistful of his cape to back him violently against the Bridge wall.

"What have you done? Where is my son? Where have you taken him?"

"I have done nothing!" The figure cried in an innocent plea.

"Yes," I hissed and pulled his cape hood back so I could confirm who I thought he really was, so I could see his whole face.

He opened his mouth to speak, but there came no sound.

"What have you done with my son? Do you want to turn him as cold as you are because if so I can have you banished from this planet and-,"

"No, I did not take your son."

"Liar! You can't expect me to be as gullible as before! I saw your bird fly before my face and he was gone!" I nodded toward the bird that was perched on his shoulder.

"I suppose you did not see the griffin that leapt in front of you then. My bird flew in front of your face to strike at the griffin, and if not for her you could've even been-,"

"So you don't have him then?"

"No."

"How much did you see of what happened on the Bridge?"

"I saw most of what happened. I've seen that lady before and I knew the moment I saw her that she was no good."

"You know her?"

"Well, not personally."

"Tell me everything you know." I said and walked off the Bridge for him to follow. On the way to the palace, he explained everything he saw and heard on the Bridge.

"Two separate worlds?" I mumbled quietly as I entered the large room where the royal thrones were.

"That's what she said."

"What is her name?"

"Her name is Tetchra."

The owl on his shoulder ruffled her feathers and gazed at Valiant who was perched on a scepter. He preened his tattered old feathers and looked at the owl for no longer than a moment, taking no interest in the large bird.

I looked up at the vampire warily. "How do I know you aren't lying to me?"

He smiled. "You don't. But what difference does it make if you know I can help you?"

I laughed. "I have no need for your help. Lucian will be reincarnated within a few days."

"There are two things wrong with your theory."

"Be gone with you. I have no need for this!"

"Lucian will not be reincarnated within a few days. It could be more like months, even years. And secondly, who knows what will come of your son even in a day or so."

"But…I have never heard reincarnation lasting *years*."

"It's possible."

"Then…we have to find him now! Today! We can't let another minute go by!"

"That means you will let me help you?"

"I suppose so."

Not two hours passed and the whole City knew that the Prince of Catastrophe was missing. Many creatures became just as concerned as I was, but that did not keep me from pacing the floor.

"What will happen? What are we going to do? What if we never find him?"

"Relax, even if he was to be taken to Earth, he would only be halfway across the Bridge. By now if someone saw him in the arms of that woman, Tetchra, we would be notified."

"What should I do?"

"There is nothing you *can* do right now. Just leave the hard work to me."

I stood up and clutched a fistful of his cape. "Princess Pearl and Taj'…we can go to them. They can help us!"

Reluctant, he came along with me, at my side like an obedient dog. He scanned the area for any suspicion on our way to the Frozen Waterfalls. He kept his identity hidden, for his own sake, and ignored those who looked at him with suspicion since Lucian was not at my side accompanying me as usual. The civilians probably suspected this hooded figure was a sort of replacement. They bowed their heads politely as I passed, but said nothing.

Once the Frozen Waterfalls were in view, my thoughts raced with the only hope and belief that Pearl could help. My worry would only cease a bit if told that Fitzray was safe. I arrived, panting, already emotionally distressed, and Taj' slithered up to me in alarm.

"Chenille," he said in surprise, "why have you a sorrowful expression and your eyes with tears? And where is the little Prince?"

I breathed out a shaky sigh and sat on one of the large rocks at the edge of the cold pool. Pearl came out of the cave with a bright smile that quickly faded once she saw me.

"They took him away! They took him from me!" I cried.

"Who? Fitzray?"

I nodded. "And where is Lucian?" Taj' inquired quietly with not a trace of a troublesome tone.

"Killed, I think, but will be reincarnated."

"Then who is that?"

He eyed the hooded figure at my side and lifted the tip of his tail before his face. Before I could utter a word, he slid the hood back to unmask him. Silence fell over the pool for a brief moment, until Pete fell to his knees. Pearl was behind me concentrating her power on Pete with fury. Taj' followed through by wrapping his tail around Pete's body like a boa constrictor. He lifted Pete off the ground to study him with his bronze eyes. A forked tongue wavered before the vampire's face.

"Let him down Taj'!"

"He has been such disgrace to you and you tell me to have mercy on him? Have you been poisoned by the venom that fogs your head? Have you forgotten that he committed fratricide? I promised to carry him over the Bridge. What can you say that will possibly change my mind of doing so?"

"He didn't kill Lucian. The woman, Tetchra, I think she killed him...and Pete knows more of her than I do. She could have stolen my baby. Pete is my only hope. Please, spare him for my baby's sake. He could be my only hope."

Taj's chest swelled to nearly twice its normal size and set Pete down, his tail still coiled around his body.

"Perhaps you know where I can go to find him?" I asked, turning to Pearl.

She waved her hand over the pond and waited. The placid water stirred gently like silk, with no more than a quiet swish.

"Go to the Ticktay Mountains which will lead you to the village Nalani. Within that village, you will find my dear friend, Lazuli. She is younger than I am and her powers are stronger. She can tell you the exact route which you will take to find him."

"Must I go, or can I have others go for me?"

"I have already sent a message to Lazuli. She will be expecting you in two weeks."

"Weeks! I don't have that kind of time!"

"We will secure the Bridge. No one comes onto it and no one goes off it. We will take your place when you leave. There is nothing to worry about."

"You will have to do with protecting her since Lucian isn't here." Taj' said and uncoiled his tail to free Pete.

"Leave tonight and you will make good progress by tomorrow morning."

I nodded my head and turned to the snake babies. Aura was looking wide-eyed at a dark butterfly on a nearby branch and once it took off, she snapped at it with her powerful jaws.

"Oh no!" Pearl cried and opened the little snake's mouth to get the butterfly with now tattered wings. "Don't eat dark insects, those are poisonous," she scolded.

Figuring it was a good time to leave, I backed slowly into the woods and headed home so we could be on our way. Pete followed suit.

Chapter 22 - Light the Way

It was nearly midnight when we were on our way, fully packed with Jasper behind us. Minx and Citrus stood at the palace door and watched as we left. I fastened the last saddlebag filled with food and blankets over Jasper's back. The owl and the blue jay were perched on his horns. I threw a heavy wool blanket over Jasper's back, hoping it would offer a bit of warmth from the icy wind.

"You ready yet?"

"Yeah, just one more minute." I secured the Velcro straps together, holding the massive blanket in place over Jasper's cold, scaly figure.

"Done," I said clutching my cape to my chest, "you should be warm now."

"Thank you."

We were on our way at last, headstrong against the winds that picked up speed. All around was nothing but blackness, with no more than a small shimmer of moonlight that poked through the treetops. This darkness continued, making it impossible to tell a gray shadow of a tree from another or hardly anything at all, but soon the City of Lights came into view after an hour of traveling in the dark. I looked over my shoulder at Jasper's bulky shape that moved slowly over the ground behind me.

"Just a little longer to the City," I assured him.

I pulled my cape together even tighter against the cold winds that could chill to the bone. I could see Pete, nearly twenty feet ahead of me, showing no sign of the slightest chill and I felt envious of him. He kept his pace and strutted like a bold warhorse. He paused at the cobblestone streets and looked over his shoulder to me. He waited patiently for my arrival and walked the silent streets at my side.

"We should stop and set up camp as soon as we get out of the City," he said.

"But we haven't even been traveling that long."

"It doesn't matter, if we don't stop now we'll be too tired to get up at dawn tomorrow."

The silence lingered between us. The only sound notable was Jasper's talons on the cobblestone. The stores around us were illuminated only the slightest by the old streetlights. Through the windows, I could see the finest shadows of long gowns and expensive capes, all well protected behind thick glass and bolted doors. One of the very few doors open at night was the blacksmith. He was notorious for staying open for the few customers that need a horseshoe right away or need to pick up a late order of a repaired sword or armor. Next door was the vet, also open late. We were now nearly halfway through the City.

"Have you ever noticed that we have these marvelous buildings, these skyscrapers, but we still have a blacksmith? Why is that?"

"We adapted simple technology like building construction, from Earth, but the planet as a whole is an old world. We prefer the old ways more than trying to catch up with the new. We enjoy candles over the high expense of electricity. We enjoy a sword over a gun with the only reason that it isn't needed here. We don't need to shoot people down since most of the creatures on Catastrophe are immortal. Why would we want chaos to rise because of something that really isn't needed in the first place?"

I nodded in response. "We have taken many things from Earth and used them here."

"Of course, things like clocks and all different foods are here now. I mean, Catastrophe is like a primitive Earth in a way, but with some qualities of modern Earth."

The lights became narrower as we approached the end of the road that signaled the end of the City. Once we were far from the glare of the lights, we would stop to rest.

The moonlight was brighter here and it was easier to avoid thick branches that covered the woody ground.

"Here," Jasper said after a long while and collapsed to the ground.

The City looked as dim as a candle's flame from where we were. I sat down and found Pete immediately settled beside me. He smiled and wrapped me in his cape, holding me for several seconds and then turned to take the heavy saddlebags from Jasper's back.

It was something like that that could be considered inhuman, for one vampire to show strong compassion to his vampress even when her vampire had been killed. Although, Eternal Mates would always be able to still love each other, regardless if a bond was there or not. Pete could love me as much as Lucian did and there would be nothing wrong with that. Of course, Pete was still the one responsible for turning me, after all.

With my final thought, I fell asleep beneath the stars.

Pete pulled me out of slumber early the following morning. My head felt heavy as he lifted me up into his arms to let me continue to sleep. Every bump of the way rocked my body and swayed me into even deeper sleep. For all I knew, it was probably only dawn, since the sun was not even up.

A cool breeze and the warmth of the sun greeted me once my eyes finally opened. I saw Pete's face, bold with no hint of fatigue when he glanced down at me. I pretended to be asleep. My legs were tired and I wanted to take advantage of not having to walk. He mumbled my name beneath his breath and I pretended even harder to appear asleep. He said it louder this time and a slight smile crossed my lips.

He knows I'm awake, I thought to myself, closing my eyes tighter.

A fresh scent filled the air and I opened my eyes at once. We were at the Ticktay Mountains. The mountains themselves were made of gray rock and large portions of shed dragon scales. At their summits was a blizzard or torrential rain, but nothing for us to worry about as we covered the low dirt path that twisted through the range.

I had once heard that cold rain was common during this time of year, but Pete had reassured me that the mountain range was small and would take only a couple of days to travel through.

Pete glanced down at me and said nothing but shifted me uncomfortably in his arms.

"Good morning."

He still said nothing, but I heard Jasper echo my words politely.

"You can put me down if you'd like."

Pete acted as though I had pestered him with an unimportant question and simply scowled, setting me to my feet. I avoided his behavior and stayed beside Jasper, talking to him in a hushed whisper.

"He seems so irritable today. I wonder why."

"I do not know Mistress."

I did not talk to him for the whole day and he did not seem to mind that. I took in the marvelous scenery around me and ran my hands through a small stream. The sun was setting as orange-yellow rays filled the sky with bright pink lining the edge of the horizon. It got lower until there was no more than a sliver of yellow remaining and the dark began to rise.

It was difficult to travel between the cracks and crevasses of the narrow chain of mountains at night, even with the full glow of our moon and the small stars. Eventually we stopped with no more than a word said between us. I took the heavy saddlebags off Jasper as the birds fell asleep on his horns. Once I pushed the bags aside, the dragon nudged me close to his warm body. I leaned my head against his body, felt his breathing rise and fall with short wisps of smoke rising from his nostrils. I closed my eyes and began to nod off when I felt the sickly chill of a hand on my shoulder.

"You read it, didn't you?" A voice hissed.

I turned, unafraid, to see Pete sitting before me. In one of his hands, he held the black book with silver pages. I shivered.

"*Didn't* you?" There was an edge to his voice.

"I did," I whispered back, suddenly regretting that I brought the book with me in the first place.

My words lingered in the air for a long time as he ran his tongue over his fangs in a pleased manner.

"I hardly believed it was you that wrote it," I continued.

"You weren't supposed to read it," he remarked.

"So that's why you were so provoked today."

"This was my journal of my life studying vampires, and being one myself. If anyone powerful enough got their hands on this-,"

"Like you?"

"No, not *me*, but someone on Earth. If they got it, our species could be in big trouble."

"Relax," I said quietly, catching a glimpse of his panic-struck face, "no one will get their hands on this, not when we have it."

He put the book back into one of the saddlebags and looked at me. I leaned back against Jasper's body and felt myself begin to doze off again.

"How much longer until we get out of this mountain range?"

"Not long. We should be in Nalani by tomorrow night."

I turned over onto my side and felt the vampire wrap me in his cape against the chill of the night and then, feeling a sense of security, I fell asleep.

The next day there were clouds stretching for miles up in the sky. A distant rumble of thunder echoed across the mountain range every so often. People traveling in the mountains reported that storms were vile and could last for days at a time. What frightened me most was the claim that the rain here was as cold as ice and could give someone pneumonia overnight if exposed to it.

We traveled on in the gloom of the day without much worry of the storm, since we neared Nalani with every passing minute. I stayed beside Pete and clutched his sleeve like a child whenever I heard a crack of thunder.

"We have to stop and find shelter."

"But we are almost there," I protested.

He shook his head to my defeat. "We don't have a choice. It will rain soon and if we get caught in the storm, we will have no chance of finding shelter."

"Or getting to Nalani," I grumbled.

"We will get there soon enough."

We walked only a little longer and Pete discovered a cave large enough for Jasper and the two of us to fit.

"This is nice," Jasper said as he stepped inside with us.

I slumped angrily beside Pete once he sat down and began to unfasten the saddlebags from Jasper's back. He lit a small fire between us while I was preoccupied with Jasper. I turned my back to Pete and leaned against the dragon with my eyes closed, hoping he would not bother to say anything to me.

"I promise that if it doesn't rain tomorrow, we will go to Nalani."

I rolled over to face him and felt the dragon's hard claw curve itself over my shoulder, pressing me to his soft chest.

"I miss Lucian."

"I do too." Jasper whispered back.

"Well he isn't here, *is* he?" Pete chimed.

"No, but he will come back."

"And what if he doesn't? What would you do then?"

"That isn't even up for discussion. You know as well as I do that he will come back no matter what if he was killed."

"What if we were wrong?"

I was silent but turned to set a steady glare of suspicion over him.

"I know what you are trying to do."

"What?"

"I knew I shouldn't have let you come. I should have never trusted you!"

"What are you talking about?"

"You still want the throne. You still want to be King!"

"Since when was it all about the throne? I wanted you, not so much as to rule."

"And now you are lying!"

"It wasn't all about the throne to me!"
"If it wasn't then why did you kill you own-,"
"Enough!" Jasper yelled. "It is getting too late for this. Say goodnight and go to sleep."
"Fine, whatever." I turned my back to him again while Jasper settled back down.
"Goodnight Chenille."

Chapter 23 - Nalani

I couldn't believe my eyes. Nalani was nothing like I had expected. It was a small rundown village. Few stands sold food and only a couple of old poorly built stores existed. Groups of vampires in long black capes stayed in the shadows and stared at us with hostility in their eyes as we passed. I remained close to Pete, grateful that he decided to leave Jasper back at the cave.

"Where do you think Lazuli is?" I whispered.

"How am I supposed to know?"

A painful, ear-shattering scream sounded from ahead. I froze at the sight of a few vampires trying to hold a beautiful white unicorn. Each held a piece of tattered rope tied in a tight knot around her neck. The rope rubbed off some of her fur, exposing light pink skin, chafing her until she bled. Her eyes were wide and afraid and she reared to try to escape, but was yanked back down.

Pete ran to them and tried to stop what was happening while I still stood frozen in place. I looked at the unicorn's face, saw the beaded sweat on her body and tangled mane, but there was something missing. The one and only thing that could distinct a horse from a unicorn was missing - her horn. There was only a small rigid stub of horn left. It was gone, cut from her forehead.

Too distracted by the image that filled my head, I did not see what transpired between Pete and the other vampires. All I knew was that he was leading the frightened creature toward me now. He loosened the rope around her neck and turned in the direction of the cave.

"We can't stay here."

I looked up when I heard a rumble of thunder. "We have to be quick."

In no time at all, the sky opened up and icy rain came down over us in sheets. I put on my cape hood and found it barely helped, being permeable. Pete took his cape off and tied it over the unicorn's head. My cape was drenched, but my clothes beneath were not as wet. Pete's shirt was soaked and he struggled to move at a quick pace with the weight of his clothes. We managed to reach the cave quickly and took the unicorn inside to where it was warm. She fell to her knees in exhaustion once Pete took off the rope.

"You poor thing," I whispered.

"Oh," the unicorn said, "what did I do to deserve this?"

"What is your name?"

"My name? My name is Lazuli."

"What happened to your horn?"

"They cut it off. Those vampires captured me. I tried to escape but it was no use." She paused, closing her eyes. "I don't have much time to live now."

Pete studied the unicorn quietly. "You're in foal?"

"Yes, but it is too early for it to be born."

"Then you are saying your baby will die?"

"Oh," the unicorn moaned, "I want it to live, but what if it dies too?"

"There is a chance it will live."

"What good will come of my baby unicorn if I give it to the world? I have seen this place, no place for my baby. Just look at what happened to me."

"You can trust us with your baby," I offered.

"How could I trust you?"

"We were sent by Princess Pearl-,"

"She said you were coming. She knew my fate. She sent you for my baby…for its protection, didn't she?"

"Maybe she did, but really I need to know where my son is. She said you could help me and that you are much stronger than she is."

"I would, but I have no power left to offer to you. There is one thing you can do. I know that if you go to the Star Pool, north of here, it can tell you what you need to know. You will need a unicorn to come with you in order for the pool…to work for you." She opened her eyes and then closed them again. "Please…name my foal…Versailles."

Just as soon as the foal was born, Lazuli gasped her last breath. The unicorn's body vanished instantly.

I took off my jacket, wrapped it around the baby, and nestled her in my arms. I sat up against the wall of the cave with nothing to say and simply stared at Pete. He took his wet shirt off and sat close to the small fire. His chest shook with each breath and he uttered a sickening cough.

"Oh no…no…vampires don't get sick."

"Oh they do and when they do, it's usually pretty bad," he reassured me, sarcastically.

His voice was already getting raspy and he coughed loudly again, grabbing a blanket from one of the saddlebags, but it was wet and dripping water. The saddlebags were too close to the mouth of the cave and water had soaked them. His snowy owl flew from Jasper's horn and landed on his shoulder, attempting to spare some warmth to him. Jasper nudged him closer to the fire.

I looked down at the baby unicorn and fingered her short white fur. She was so young, so helpless. The small glass-like horn covered by her forelock was like a stub of porcelain. Pete was already half-asleep against Jasper's hot scales. I leaned back against the rocky cave wall and gazed at the fire for several minutes. My head filled with ease and my thoughts dwindled.

Chapter 24 - The Old Farm

Everyone woke early, eager to travel while the sky was clear of clouds. We traveled nearly all morning in search of warm shelter. Pete uttered a sickening cough. A damp blanket hung over his shoulders. The baby unicorn was sound asleep in my arms. I knew she would need milk eventually or else she would be too weak to survive. I shaded my face from the blazing sun, a figure up ahead catching my attention.

"I think I see something."

As we approached closer, I saw it was a woman. She was elderly with heavy wrinkles below her eyes. She stopped raking the leaves in her garden to look up at us with a kind smile.

"Oh dear," she cried. "Did that awful cough come from one of you?"

Pete coughed harshly in response.

"You must have been traveling for quite a while. You should come inside and I will make some soup for the two of you."

"Oh...really, you are too kind."

"Nonsense, it will be nice to finally have some company." She turned to guide Pete inside and then looked back at me. "You can put your dragon inside the barn. There is a large stall where I used to keep my own dragon...but that was a long time ago."

I smiled and headed toward the barn. It was large, its dark red paint was chipping off, but the doors had locks and it was dry inside. The floorboards were well aged and creaked with every step. Bales of hay were stacked to the ceiling toward the very back. A startled whinny came from nearby once Jasper entered.

We walked together down the long row of stalls and found the largest one at the very end. He stepped inside and found it comfortable enough. The unicorn shifted in my arms, causing me to lose my balance and fall into one of the stable doors.

"Who is there?" A boy, probably fifteen or so, appeared from behind a stack of hay.

"Who are you?" he demanded.

"I am Chenille, Queen of-,"

"I know who you are." He said suddenly, cutting me off.

"Who are you?"

"I am Moran. I work on this farm with my grandmother, Felia. What are you doing here?"

"I have been traveling for days. Thanks to your grandmother's hospitality, we finally have a place to stay for a while." There was a loud banging coming from the stall nearby.

"That is our new horse. She is a wild one, I am sure of it."

I looked down at Versailles as she nudged my arm.

"A newborn unicorn…well I'll be. Here, take this."

He handed me a bottle filled with goat's milk. "It isn't unicorn milk, but it's the next best thing."

I took the bottle with my free hand. "I am going inside."

"I will come with you."

I had to owe it to Felia. She had a beautiful piece of land, a beautiful green pasture outcrop among the mountain range. I stepped inside the small house and immediately felt weak from the heat of the kitchen.

"Your friend is in the shower," Felia said quietly as she carefully stirred the soup.

Moran took the unicorn from my arms and placed her delicately on a chair. She watched him with half-closed eyes as he took the bottle of milk from my hands and poured it into a small pot on the stove. He opened the cupboard, taking out a large white rag and ran it under warm water from the small sink. He looked up at me once he bent down to the unicorn as if asking permission to handle her and then proceeded to wipe her off.

"Have you named her yet?" He asked.

"Versailles."

He said the name quietly to himself. There was a loud creek of old floorboards coming from upstairs. "You can get yourself into a shower now." Felia said, her gaze never moving from the soup.

I hesitated and looked down at Versailles. Moran caught my glance and smiled. "You don't have to worry about a thing. I will take care of Versailles while you are gone."

He is experienced enough, living on a farm and all, I thought.

I went to the stairs and looked back toward Felia.

"Upstairs, first door on the left is the bathroom. And at the end to your right is the guest room," she said, still focusing on the soup.

I turned and walked up the stairs to find the bathroom on the left. The water was either too hot or too cold, but served its purpose to get me clean. I dried myself off and put on a blue robe that I found on the counter beside the sink. I hung the damp towel on the doorknob and went straight to the guest bedroom.

There were two small beds in the tight room, a nightstand between them. A warm fireplace was at the foot of the bed to the right where Versailles and the two birds slept heavily. Pete was in the other bed. His eyes remained closed, but I could tell he was not asleep. He opened his eyes and looked at me once I sat on the edge of the bed. He took my hand and pressed it lightly to the side of his burning face. Felia came into the room with a large bowl of soup and Pete sat up.

"There is more downstairs if you'd like some," she offered.

Moran was sitting at the table, alone, as I expected. His bowl was empty, but the one directly across from him was not. He nodded his head toward it.

"I poured you some."

"Thanks." I sat across from him aware he was watching me like a hawk. "I fed Versailles." He said, breaking the silence. I said nothing.

Felia walked down the stairs so quietly, I had not heard her. She took the empty bowls from the table and looked over at the two of us just staring blankly at each other.

"I have to go and milk the cows. I hope the two of you can tolerate each other while I am gone." She turned to me. "I left some cream for your friend on the counter. It should help ease his cough."

She then left and I turned back to face Moran. "Are you a mortal?" I asked at last.

He shrugged his shoulders. "My grandmother makes medicine. She has a way with herbs. My parents died when I was young and I was placed in her care." He crossed his arms and placed them on the table. "Why do you want to know?"

"Just curious, I guess."

He watched me get the cream and, being overly conscious, I was sure he watched me walk all the way up the stairs. I sat beside Pete and he opened his eyes slowly as I applied the cream to his chest. When I was done, I put the empty bowl on the nightstand and Pete reached out and grabbed my arms, pulling me down so I rested beside him. His breathing was still uneasy and he leaned his head against me as I dozed off.

An icy chill came over me and I shot up in bed. *How long have I been sleeping?*

Pete was stirring in his sleep beside me. My mouth was dry, bidding me to make my way down the stairs to get some water. There were a few water bottles on the counter and I took one. A hand icily grabbed my shoulder.

"Moran?" My voice was barely a whisper.

"Yes," he whispered back.

I turned and rubbed my eyes. In the soft glow from a candle in the far corner of the kitchen, he appeared taller. The water bottle dropped from my hands and the cold liquid spilled over my feet. I fell helplessly, my knees suddenly buckling under me, causing me to clutch onto

Moran for support. Unbearable pain flowed through me and my head pounded with the pain of a severe migraine.

"Chenille, what's the matter?"

He held me up and looked at my desperate face. "Chenille," he said again, "tell me what's wrong."

I could scarcely breathe and held to him as tight as I could manage, even after he put me down on the bed beside the unicorn and the two birds.

"My back," I cried, feeling a burning pain slice down my spine.

"Nothing is there." He assured me. The pain began to ease and turned to numbness.

"You still there?" I squeezed his hand, but could not feel it.

"Yes, I am."

I closed my eyes, trying to decipher if what I was experiencing was a nightmare or reality. My conscious, my instinct, told me I could not stay here another day.

Felia was humming softly in the kitchen the next morning. The smell of fried eggs filled the small room. I looked around in alarm, realizing something was not right.

"Where is Moran?"

A furtive smile played across her lips. "He went to tend to the horses. He should be back soon."

I sat impatiently and stared at the small wooden clock beside the sink. It was nearly noon. Felia handed me a plate of eggs.

"For your friend," she said.

I took it up to the room and found he was still asleep so I placed the plate on the nightstand and made my way downstairs again. The front door opened with a loud slam against the wall and Moran's figure occupied the doorway, his face flushed pale.

"You look shaken."

"She is gone! That wild horse we found the other day is missing!"

"Things happen," Felia replied calmly, shrugging her shoulders.

He ignored her and sat across from me, his head in his hands. "I don't understand. How could I have forgotten to lock the barn?"

He did not talk to me at all that afternoon after that. I gazed at Versailles and stroked her short mane. "The Star Pool, we have to go there soon."

Maybe tonight, I thought.

I went outside and stood on the porch for a long while looking at the mountains. Then I saw Moran coming toward the small house and ran to him.

"What happened last night?" I demanded.

"What are you talking about?" He walked straight by me. I stood in front of him, making him come to a halt.

"What happened last night?"

"*Nothing* happened last night," he breathed.

I could tell he was lying, but I was not going to stay any longer and risk anything else to come over me here. I took a piece of notepaper that was sticking from the nightstand drawer and began to write.

Pete,

I have to leave if I ever hope to find my son. I know you are still terribly ill and it is so that I cannot take you with me any further. You are in kind hands for the time being and I wish you well. I am going to the Star Pool in hopes to find the answers I seek. With all my heart, I beg you to stay here. I will leave Jasper for you so you can find me easier when you are well.

Until we meet again, Chenille.

I placed the letter beside him and put on my cape. Valiant flew to my shoulder and I scooped up Versailles into my arms. With no more than a few bottles of stolen goat milk, I sneaked away from the old farm, hoping Moran would not hear me as I did so.

Chapter 25 - Obsidian

I walked across sun-lit hills with Versailles trailing behind me on small stick legs. We came to a clearing where there were no trees and the only sound to be heard was the sound of running water. Versailles jumped ahead and pawed curiously at the soft ground. Each time she did so there was a splashing noise, but there was no water in sight. I looked down at the grass and saw my own reflection.

"This is water…invisible water."

I dipped my hand down toward the ground to see if the water was actually there and found the chill and wet feel of the invisible element. The sky swirled a dim, eerie overcast and a loud crash echoed in the distance. The unicorn's ears pricked forward in alert and then she cowered behind my legs for protection. I lifted her into my arms. There was a loud rumble of thunder and lightning cracked across the sky. The immensely strong winds pushed me back and my cape whipped in the air behind me as though a helicopter was about to land.

Then a shape, a large distorted shape with a rigid outline, rose from behind the mountains, blocking whatever sunlight that shone through the black clouds. Then there was a sound of metal against metal, or even a train coming to a screeching stop, but a thousand times worse. I screamed, my ears pulsating from the deafening noise. I fell to my knees and huddled over the petrified unicorn until it was silent again.

Her rapid pulse thrummed against my body as I looked up at the coal black sky. Versailles had her head pressed to my chest and her small horn stabbed me, but barely concerned me. Once I mustered up the courage to stand on shaky legs and look around, the ground began to quake. I looked back, heard the deafening noise again and saw the shape shimmer with vibrant colors. The color exploded in a wave of unbearable heat. It was raining fire.

With nowhere to run to, I held my breath and jumped into what I thought would be the invisible water, but it was no longer there. The fire singed my back and my cape was suddenly ablaze. I threw it off and turned. The hills, it seemed, were steeper and I could not climb them. There was nowhere to escape.

The fire stopped falling and the black shape advanced. It swooped down from the mountains and the screech came again. I huddled over the unicorn and felt the heat overcome me. Once I turned, the black shape stood over me like a fifty story building. I looked over to see that Valiant was gone. There was a loud hiss and I could not move.

"No," was all I managed to say before I fainted.

The air around me was hot and suffocating and I stayed where I was, in a shallow puddle of water. Versailles was nudging me awake. She was all right. I sat up and froze. The black shape stood, appearing gray against the starry sky. It sensed I was awake and moved closer. It bent over to see me with its dark slits for eyes and suddenly burst into flames with a horrible cry. I backed up quickly with Versailles beside me. Valiant flew onto my shoulder, his feathers tight against his body, watching in horror. The shape took form of a bird, a large bird unfathomable to existence. Fire covered its body from head to tail. Only its eyes were untouched by the flame. The two coal black eyes stared at me for a long time.

"Who are you?" The dark voice asked.

"I am Chenille."

"Chenille what?"

"Chenille Noir, Queen of Catastrophe."

The coal black eyes studied me more closely. "What business do you have here?"

"The Star Pool…," I breathed and gazed down at the invisible water that now reflected the night sky and all of the diamond stars.

"You are looking at it," he remarked.

"I need answers. I need to find my son!"

He looked down at the pool and back to me. "The Star Pool is dangerous. It may show you your deepest desires or your deepest fears."

"I have a unicorn with me."

The bird laughed. "Do what you must, but I will warn you that if you use my Star Pool, you shall do whatever I please for as long as I request."

"I don't have that kind of time."

He shrugged. "Your choice to make."

"Who are you anyway?"

"I am Obsidian, the great guard of the Star Pool, the last of the giant phoenixes."

Valiant flew from my shoulder and turned into his phoenix form to bow at the feet of the great bird.

"I must use the Star Pool."

"Not tonight."

"But why?"

"Because that is what I say."

I turned away. "Then I will just have to leave."

"You can't do that either. You are prohibited to leave until I say."

Escaping was an impossible task. Over a weeks' time passed by and I begged to use the Star Pool every night and each time received the same dreadful answer.

"Come with me." He said one night.

Versailles and Valiant stayed by the Star Pool and waited for me while I traveled with the phoenix.

"I have no more goat milk to give to Versailles and without it she will die."

"Teach her to graze like a unicorn mother would."

"And what about me? What will I eat?"

"What would you like?"

I shrugged. "I don't know."

"The nearest village is maybe fifty miles or so away and there is no way that I would leave the Star Pool unguarded for that long to travel there."

"Couldn't I go?"

Obsidian stopped walking and poked me sharply with his beak. "You must think I have feathers for brains," he hissed. "You shouldn't possibly think I am stupid."

I continued to walk and he flew in front of me like a fiery bullet. "You are foolish."

I folded my arms impatiently. "Why did you take me out here anyway?"

"I took you out here so you would take your mind off of the Star Pool."

"How could I? My son's life is on the line and I don't know where he is! I need to use the Star Pool! Don't you understand?" I cried.

He looked down at me gravely. "Follow me then." He went back to the Star Pool and I followed close behind. "Fine. Have your friend test the powers of the Star Pool." He nodded toward Valiant.

The little bird walked up to the water and glanced up at Obsidian. "Think of what you want most."

Valiant looked down at the water and it shimmered with many colors. In the distance there was fire lighting the sky. There were dozens of phoenix-like birds flying above the pool. Valiant looked back at me and then flew straight for his dream in the distance, when he smashed into something and burst into flames. It was as if a force field separated the dream from reality.

"Valiant! Oh what did you do? Bring him back!" I screamed to Obsidian.

The bird shook his head. "This is what the Star Pool does. The Star Pool revealed his dream and he went for it. Once he realizes it is a dream, he might return. Or he might not."

I went to put my hand into the water when the bird's beak snapped at me.

"Do you not understand? Do you want to turn out like your friend and many others that have attempted to try the Star Pool's power? Its power is so great it haunts dreams making the good and the bad. It plays a big role in dreams and it is so that if one is having a dream, they must realize it is not reality for them to escape from it. Those that struggle with this often remember their dream as one they never forget...as a nightmare that haunts them."

"Why would a unicorn recommend for me to come here if it is so dangerous then?"

The bird shrugged his shoulders. I thought back to a dream I once had. "I had a dream, it was horrible. It expressed both my fears and desires. There was a glass wall in the dream-,"

"Did you break through?"

"I did. It shattered at my feet."

He looked at me calmly. "You had broken through the barrier between your desires and fears. Which side won?"

"My fears won."

He looked away. "Don't tell me I didn't warn you. You broke through the barrier in your dream…but who knows what could happen to you. All I can say is don't forget that what you see may be a vision and if so it is real. If you get overwhelmed by your fears, you may not be able to tell what a dream is and what reality is."

I hesitated briefly and went for the water. The colors shifted and all the stars began to move in the reflection. I saw a young woman in a red dress and heavy black cape - Tetchra. She held Fitzray in her arms, a smirk on her face. Hundreds of creatures passed her on the Bridge, all going to Earth. The stars revolved faster and faster until horror filled my eyes. The worst was going to happen, I knew. The sights and sounds became so real I screamed as loud as I could, but nothing changed. It became worse.

I heard a voice echo my own. Pete appeared and pushed me aside, pulling me away from the pool. There was the screech of metal and Obsidian erupted in a fiery blaze, causing fire to cascade around the pool, preventing escape.

"Nobody touches anyone near the pool without my consent!"

A golden beak shot from the fire and hit Pete with a mighty force. Beside me came a cry.

"Mama!" It was Versailles.

She stood close to the Star Pool and Obsidian pushed her closer toward the center where the deepest water was. I ran to her, knee-deep in water, and spread out my arms.

"Why are you doing this?"

"Don't you see? The reason to have a unicorn at the Star Pool is so you can pay me for using it."

"You can't have Versailles!"

"I think it is too late for that," the bird replied.

I looked over to see the unicorn on her side in the water. There was a voice close to my ear. "She isn't going to make it. Her pulse is dropping...pulse is dropping," the voice said.

A hand touched my shoulder, pulling me from the pool. The phoenix let out a scream and a wall of fire rose up and blocked my view. I faced Pete, felt metal scrape across my back and fell to the ground. My body was suddenly bound to the ground by twigs. That did not make any sense. The voice came again calling my name, a voice I knew so well, calling out to me. I tried to call back and it became quieter and quieter still. A soft humming filled my ears, like muffled words I could not understand.

"Chenille, come to me. Listen to my voice. Listen to the words I speak. Open your eyes and decide what is true, Chenille."

My head, now in a complete daze, felt heavy and delusional.

Chapter 26 - Unmasked

The wind blew lightly over frozen, dewy grass. I woke with warmth pressed to my face. A figure hunched over me with its face pressed to mine, when suddenly the warmth departed and the chill stuck fast. I met dark eyes filled with relief.

"Your visions are over at last. I was afraid you would get lost in your own head, but I brought you back," Pete whispered.

I shifted uncomfortably with a searing pain flowing down my spine.

"A griffin came out of nowhere," he continued, "and it scratched you. It's gone now."

He looked down at me and smiled a dazzling smile.

"You were never like this…never like this on your planet."

"I was enraged for all the wrong reasons and if I could go back, trust me, I would."

"Were you angry with me?"

"No, not at all. I was going through the phase of every vampire's life, back on my planet. I had stopped drinking blood and was drawn to yours. I was fed up with jealousy, but I would go back and I would have treated you better than what I did."

"But you can't change it."

"You are right. I am still your Eternal Mate though and if a day came when you chose me instead of Lucian, we would be impenetrable. Our bond could split universes."

I closed my eyes. "That would never happen."

He smiled again, his gaze shifting to Versailles who ran over to us on unsteady legs.

"Mama," she said, rubbing her head against my arm.

I looked from the corner of my eye where Obsidian stood nearby. A large crow bowed before him and placed a large chunk of bread at his feet.

"For the great firebird," it cried.

The crow turned and looked at me with its beady little eyes and took a hop forward. One wing drooped to the ground and it struggled with its balance. Obsidian gobbled down the bread and walked up to the crow.

"Many thanks for the generous donation," the phoenix replied.

Pete got to his feet and held out a hand. Grabbing it, I felt my legs wobble, but he kept me steady. The crow still stared at me and tilted its head back, letting out a cry. Its body became a black blur and formed into a woman with a red dress and heavy cape. It was Tetchra.

She looked at me and whispered words. These words made me dizzy and weak.

"It is a spell...the one mortals used to sing when under threat of a vampire attack," Pete whispered in disbelief.

A shout came from the distance and I looked weakly in the direction from which it came.

No, why has Moran followed? He shouldn't have come, I thought.

Moran seemed to be walking in slow motion as my thoughts lost clarity. His body seemed to change completely. He was taller and stronger. His eyes became lighter. He turned into the vampire I knew and loved. Moran was really Lucian all this time.

He stood alert, aware of the shape shifter's spell-like lullaby. He ran toward me, put out a hand and began to speak. The words he yelled twisted Tetchra's words and made them different, altering what she said to sound like nonsense, like a jumbled mess.

She stopped at once, her gaze angrily settled over Lucian as she changed into a large black horse. Before she could move, Jasper landed and blocked her escape. Quickly she transformed into a black butterfly with tattered wings and flew, dodging each vicious swipe of Jasper's claws.

Lucian ran to me and placed a hand to my pale face. "I am going after Tetchra. I have stayed hidden from her for a while and now I must go and find our son." He said.

"Pete and I can help you-," I began.

"No! I don't want you to get hurt, you are too weak. Go back to the palace where I know you will be safe." He looked over to see the black butterfly flying higher away from Jasper.

"I have to go. Please go back to the palace. I will end this."

With a swish of his cape, he ran to Jasper and together they were off. I slumped in front of Pete and waited for Versailles to come over to me.

"If only we knew where Tetchra was going, we could beat her there," Pete said.

I ran my fingers through the unicorn's short mane and froze once Obsidian landed before us.

"There is a blizzard coming this way. I must retreat to the mountains. As for you, there is a small house that will offer you shelter a mile or so west of here."

He bid his farewells to us and flew up on flaming orange-gold wings. Pete led the way in the direction the phoenix had told us to go and Versailles pranced beside me.

"How long did you know that Moran was really Lucian?"

"I didn't know at all."

"When did you leave the house?"

"As soon as I got your letter."

"You sound a lot better."

"I get over colds pretty fast."

The dirt pathway became darker and dismal as the storm clouds raced over our heads. Pete's snowy owl looked back toward me with golden eyes, searching the empty space on my shoulder for Valiant. Sadly, she turned and rose to the sky with a sharp cry. She broke through to a clearing where a small, decrepit house barely stood.

"Here we are." I heard Pete mumble.

I watched from the small window to the calm landscape outside. It was motionless like time itself was frozen. Beneath my crossed legs I saw grass breaking through decayed floors. Versailles kept her head down, looking around with scared eyes, aware of the storm that was to come. Pete looked around uneasily at the ceiling that was on a dangerous slant and then followed my gaze outside. He knew the ceiling would not hold as I did and was probably pondering the outcomes we would have to face if it did not. I said nothing, not to interrupt his thoughts. He sat beside me, eyed the window again, and rested his head in his hands.

"If you were Tetchra, where would you run to?"

"I don't know what her intentions are, do I? Her intentions would relate to where she was going."

"What does she want from us?"

"I don't know," I whispered helplessly.

The house began to shake. The cold air seeped through the cracks in the walls and covered the floor with a light sprinkle of snow. Hail pelted the roof, the wind blowing even harder.

"Stay close to me."

Versailles cowered under my arm, pressing her head into my side. The wind blew to the extent of the door flying open, revealing the dark chill of a monster we hoped we would not have to encounter. The snow found its way in and piled up quickly. My Eternal Mate held me close, my head spinning for a moment, and then I remembered something.

"If you have read the book you shall find the key to save the Bridge and us from destruction."

"What are you talking about?"

"An old woman told me that if I have read the book I will save the Bridge."

"What is that supposed to mean?"

"Well, what is the *book*?"

"That can be anything. You expect *me* to know?"

"The book…*your book perhaps*?"

"My book. You mean my journal?"

"Yeah, do you have it with you?"

He stuck a hand into his cape pocket and pulled out the small black book with silver lettering on its cover.

"Ok, now to find a key. Did you ever mention a key?"

"I don't think so."

He began to flip through the pages shaking his head and paused once he reached the last page. On the inside of the back cover there was a tab indicating a sort of secret compartment that I had never noticed before. He fingered the tab as he bit his lip and shifted his gaze toward the ceiling that let out a loud cracking noise. The roof was crumbling under the harsh pressure of hard packed snow and ice. Without warning, he stood, pulled me to my feet and threw me. I flew into glass, an icy chill embraced my body and I slammed into wet snow. The only sound I could hear was a cry of disparity.

"Mama! Mama! Ma-," And then I could hear nothing but the loud smash of the snow bringing the roof to its end.

The snow covered me in a blanket, leaving me numb and alone. There was nothing else in the blackness of the winter night but the smooth glow of the silver lettering of Pete's black book beneath Clesta's beam of orange light.

*****

When I realized I was awake, I sat up aching with cold. Versailles was beside me, wedged under my cape. I strained my eyes through the snow and spotted a patch of black on the ground. It was the book. I picked it up, placed it in my pocket and reluctantly turned to face the house. Its roof had collapsed and nothing was standing. There was only a pile of debris. Pete was not within sight. His snowy owl swooped down from the pile of broken wood and landed gracefully on my shoulder.

I turned to the sky where heat filled the air, turning the falling snowflakes to rain. Obsidian landed before me. The deep snow melted around him.

"I heard a crash-," he paused and looked startled at the fallen house. "Are you all right?"

"Yes, but I can't seem to find my friend, Obsidian."

The phoenix walked around the house and searched under everything, but shook his head. I brushed the snow from my pants and stared at the bird.

"We shouldn't stay here. Please, take me to shelter."

Obsidian bowed his head and flew above me, scanning the ground below. I walked with Versailles who played in the falling snow. I failed to realize that I was standing on a pond, only a sheet of ice separating me from the water below. A deafening noise made me jump and then the ice under my feet split into billions of cracks.

"Look out," a musical voice cried. An icy blue blur flew past me and before I could react, I was laying in a bank of snow. Someone shook me conscious, a kind voice calling for me to wake. I rubbed my eyes. A mermaid sat before me. Her tail consisted of light blue scales. Her aquamarine eyes sparkled when she saw my eyes open.

"Oh I am so sorry. The ice was breaking…I…I had to push you…I didn't mean it, honestly," she stuttered nervously.

"You saved me. That is nothing to be sorry for."

"But still-," she began.

"What is your name?"

"My name is Willow."

"I am sure you know my name, right?"

"Oh, of course! You are Queen Chenille Noir."

"You may call me Chenille."

"Oh, what can I do to repay you for my mistake?"

"It wasn't a mistake Willow," I paused and looked down at the water, "but can you contact a friend of mine?"

"Yes. What is your friend's name?"

"Princess Pearl."

"Oh yes, yes I know her." She smiled and went over to the water, gazed deeply into its calm, icy surface and gestured to me.

Pearl's face appeared in the water, like a reflection, clearly distressed. She rubbed the little snake Aura on her neck.

"Chenille," she said, startled. "What a surprise! How is your journey going?"

"It could be better. How is it at the Bridge?"

"Uh...fine I guess." There was shouting in the background.

"You *guess*? What's going on over there?"

"Everything is under control. Don't worry about a thing!"

A blue dragon's face filled the picture, pushing Pearl aside. "Minx! What is going on there?"

"Someone was spotted on the Bridge!" Pearl jabbed him with her elbow and her face appeared on the water's surface again.

"But everything is fine, so don't worry."

"I am coming for you Mistress!" Minx cried, flapping his wings. "Where are you?"

"I am just a little west of the Star Pool."

"I will be there in a few hours, stay where you are!"

The water shimmered for a few seconds and Pearl's face faded into a ripple of water. I looked up at Obsidian with a hard frown. "I need you to do me a favor."

The bird bowed his head before me and studied me. "And what will that be?"

"I will stay here and wait for Minx, but Versailles cannot come. It's too dangerous for her. I need you to take her to my palace and then meet me at the Bridge. I have a plan."

Chapter 27 - Lock and Key

Minx ascended away from the Star Pool as soon as we said our goodbyes to Willow. Obsidian grabbed Versailles in his talons and rose with us. We went in different directions, but I knew I would see the great bird again.

"I missed you Minx." I said, hugging the dragon's neck.

"I missed you as well Mistress."

The storm began to clear. The sun broke out, casting its warm rays over the snowy landscape. Pete's snowy owl rested on one of Minx's horns where Valiant would have been. I told Minx about the journey and about all that happened.

"I wonder where Lucian is," I whispered.

"If I knew I would tell you."

"He wasn't on the Bridge then?"

"No he was not."

The glare of the sun was gone in an instant, as if a cloud had passed over us. I looked up, expecting to see a dark storm cloud, but instead saw a creature. Its wings fully extended had to be over eighteen feet each and had huge silver claws as big as my hands. Minx let out a frightened roar and turned from the creature. It had to be the largest, most powerful dragon I ever encountered. It caught up to us with only a single wing beat. A huge black-blue head with a row of dagger teeth stared me square in the face. A small blue flame flicked at the back of his throat, causing Minx to swerve aside, just missing the fire. The dragon flew low and grabbed Minx's tail, its claws raking his scales as if they were thin and fragile as paper. It was after me.

"Get out of here Minx!"

Minx twisted around and sunk his teeth into the dragon's soft blue chest. The dragon fell, lost altitude and then regained its balance, staring a deadly glare at its target. I focused at the sun that leaked across the sky and then heard a yell. There was a dark figure on the dragon's back.

Not something, but someone is after me, I thought.

"Just keep flying Minx."

I shot a glance back to his tail. Loose scales hung in a bloody mess down to the very arrow tip.

The snowy owl had flown off in an explosion of feathers. The dragon came for us again reaching out with its talons to capture us in a grip we would never escape.

"Try and shake him off!"

Minx obeyed and started to glide from side to side in a crisscross pattern, but the dragon was not intimidated by our game and flew on. I looked behind me, but it had vanished.

"Where is he?"

To my dismay, the dragon hovered above us. The dragon dropped, its talons sinking into Minx's wings and blew hot fire over his body. Minx shrieked with fright more than pain and I cowered over him and grabbed hold of his neck to steady myself. A hand reached down from the dragon, grabbed a fistful of my shirt and forcefully turned me over to face him. Tears welled in my eyes and I choked them back at the sight of my own Eternal Mate.

"Pete, how could you? Let Minx go!"

"Give me the book!" He yelled.

How could I trust him? It could be Tetchra for all I know.

"Give me the book," he repeated.

Grabbing his hand, I sunk my fangs into it. Pete ripped away and nearly lost his balance. He grabbed onto his dragon's neck and it let go of Minx instantly. The dragon was at our side once again, but this time Pete made no motion for me.

"Remember when you told me there is a key to save the Bridge if you have read the book? Well? Remember when we found the tab at the back of my book? There is a lock in there. That lock with Fitzray's key together makes a bond between a mortal and a vampire by force. There is only one key and two locks, but with that, a mortal could control a vampire under his or her own will. Don't you get it? That is what Tetchra wants."

I looked away, still uneasy. "That's why she went after Lucian on the Bridge. She thought he had the key. She looked for it and found a vampire she could easily control herself even without the lock and key, Fitzray."

Everything made sense now. It was all falling into place. I shook my head and glared at him. "Now, give me the book."

I shook my head and kicked Minx's side, sending him spiraling down out of reach. Quickly he caught up to us and clung to my shoulder. I could not move and watched helplessly as the dragons snapped at each other.

"You will either hand it to me or I will take it from you."

I laughed, his grip tightened. "You may have underestimated me in the past, but don't *ever* do it again," he hissed darkly. "Vampires always get what they want." He hissed again and I noticed his sickly glowing poison was beginning to form. "I am no exception."

"You had poison all this time...I thought you used it all."

"Vampires never lose their poison. We all have to keep our vampresses in line, don't we?"

I struggled with his hand on my shoulder and froze, now face to face with him. "Remember what my poison did to you. Remember how it felt, how it paralyzed you. If you don't want that to happen, just give me my book."

He reached out with his free hand and laughed, grabbing the book from my cape pocket. Once pulling it away, I grabbed the book, locking my arms. The poison began to drip onto my hands, making me fight even harder. He neared my neck and still I tried to keep hold of the book.

"Don't you dare! If Lucian finds out he'll-,"

"He'll *what*? He isn't even near as strong as I am and never will be. He's a *half-mortal*. What could *he* do?"

"He will have your head!"

I pulled the book from him and threw it. His jaw dropped and then tightened in an angry fix. His dragon was after me in an instant and chased us all the way down. A claw ripped through the air, sending Minx and me in different directions. The dragon landed with one claw pinning me to the ground. He gawked, snorting smoke from his nostrils and looked to Pete at his side.

"That's enough Mullein."

The dragon released me and pulled me to my feet with one of his claws. Hundreds of vampires crossed the Bridge by force. The closest figure I saw to us was Tetchra. The book was at her feet. At first, she did not even know it was there, but at last, she smiled and picked it up. A silver chain hung against the back cover.

"What's this?"

She opened the book, flipped to the last page and pulled out a large silver lock embedded with rubies. In the bundle of dark blankets nestled in her arms, she pulled out a key. It was the key Lucian had given to Fitzray, I knew. She placed the key in the lock, a wicked smile crossing her face.

"Perfect fit."

She put the lock away and tossed the book carelessly, turning back to the Bridge. Minx stumbled to retrieve the book for me.

"I got the book Mistress." He handed me the book.

A fiery heat filled the air, making it unbelievably muggy.

"After her!" I cried, pointing toward Tetchra.

In a rush, Tetchra turned and scurried across the Bridge. A distant roar filled my ears. Jasper descended, given strict directions by Lucian. Together they were after the shape shifter. With incredible skill they spiraled down and with fire splitting at her feet, Jasper's claws extended out to the bundle of blankets. Together they turned around and tried again when they failed, each time unable to recapture the Prince of Catastrophe.

The sun was already setting on the horizon and Earth's moon and Clesta shone together over the Bridge.

Lucian was gaining on Tetchra, but now she was almost halfway across the Bridge and nearly out of sight.

"Go Mullein! Help Lucian!"

The dragon roared and took off to take his place alongside Jasper, but then I saw Mullein turn around and fly back to us at once. A blinding light was approaching. A terrible heat no one could endure was approaching the Bridge.

"What are you doing? Go and help Lucian!"

"I can't! There was something above us. Whatever it is, it's coming down!"

I looked to the Bridge where a mass of orange flame hovered. The phoenix had arrived.

Obsidian hovered above the Bridge of Secrecy, above Tetchra. I smiled at the sight of my secret weapon, but found it disturbing that Tetchra was also smiling. I studied the phoenix closer and stepped back with my mouth agape. He tossed his head back in pain and struggled to keep himself airborne.

"What is happening out there?"

"The food the crow gave him…there must have been poison in it." Pete said in disbelief. "Tetchra poisoned him."

Obsidian flapped his wings in all hope to keep flying. I wanted to go out and help him, but I knew such a task was impossible. In all my horror, the masked woman's words came alive and the phoenix fell. With wings outstretched and a final cry, he collapsed, falling out of the sky.

The white stone that was once the Bridge of Secrecy flew up to the stars. Smoke filled the air and, in astonishment, no one spoke. It did not take long for the smoke to thin, but when it did, I wished it had not. The bridge that had once linked the worlds together was gone, with no more than a few stones as its remains. The phoenix's body had turned to ash, had fallen with the stones, and too was gone.

I did not see Tetchra or Lucian and could only assume they had gone down with the bridge. If that was true, then the Prince of Catastrophe was gone as well. I stood on the broken ledge that was once the beginning of the bridge, and I jumped. I nearly dropped when I felt something grab me and held me back. Pete stood behind me, still grabbing my arm, said not a word to me, just looked out toward the empty space as I did. The immortal creatures wept and fled from the scene as I fell to my knees and wept the same beneath the darkened sky, a deathly chill in the air.

There was a sound like gunfire ringing out, becoming louder until the sky exploded with a vast orange glow. Clesta had shattered in the sky, its pieces rained over Catastrophe until the only light was from the stars in the blackness.

"Our species, all of Catastrophe has suffered a terrible loss." Pete said to me late that night.

"I did everything...everything...and I overlooked the simple things."

"You did everything you *could*," the vampire said, taking a seat before me.

"How will we survive? The Bridge is gone."

"We don't need blood. After your first year as a vampire or werewolf, you don't need it anymore."

I shook my head. "What about those vampires that were led over the bridge?"

"That is up to Tetchra, I'm afraid."

"I lost Lucian...the Bridge, Clesta, and Fitzray. What else do I have Pete?"

"Remember what I told you? Our power could create universes. We could *create* a new moon. I could help you get your son and all of those vampires back."

I straightened up and shook my head. "With all that you have done to me in the past, no forgiveness could ever make me perform a Ceremony with you."

"Tell you what. If Lucian reincarnates I will remain your Eternal Mate, and he will no longer exist. But if there is a slim chance that he was unharmed during that...incident, you will still be his and things would remain no different between you."

He could be King. As far as he is concerned, I have total power right now. This is what he has been waiting for. Regardless if he will help me or not, that is a risk I will have to take.

I looked at him closely. He had the complexion of any vampire, but he was the strongest vampire to walk the planets. With his power, he was beyond my control already.

"I will think it through tonight."

I left the room and walked down to the large sitting area. Pearl, Amelia, and Prusaious all looked at me. I sat down thoughtfully before them and sighed.

"Pete wants me to perform the Ceremony."

"Did you agree to it?" Pearl asked quickly.

"I don't know. He wants to be King, but he promised me a bunch of good things."

"You will be stronger when united with your Eternal Mate," Amelia added.

"He is unpredictable," Prusaious said quietly. "He does want to be King, but is that the only reason he wants to perform the Ceremony?"

"I don't know."

"Say no!"

"No, say yes. You will be stronger when you perform the Ceremony with him."

"Catastrophe will be better off with a king."

"Enough!" I stood up in frustration.

"This is for you to choose, Chenille. However, if there is a chance that you do agree, beware of the phases. They will be the most dangerous of any set of phases to happen," Prusaious warned.

"Phases? What are phases?"

"A phase is a time when an Eternal Mate goes through emotional stages. The first one is love. The second is protection and the third is trust. The love phase is the shortest. You will know it is present right away. Protection is huge since you will be vulnerable during the time of the

Ceremony. He will guard you and kill anyone who comes too close, no matter who it is. That phase could last weeks. And the trust phase is the most dangerous. Your Eternal Mate will prove he can be trusted, but that will vary upon the individual. If you watch for the phases, you shouldn't be alarmed if something you don't expect happens."

"Thank you. I will be in the library if anyone needs me."

I rushed from the room to the palace library and tried to take in everything, tried to make up my mind. I stayed there for hours until it was nearly midnight and I had made up my mind. I walked up to my room to find Pete was not there.

Perhaps he forgot. I thought and hoped that was true.

After waiting for what seemed like forever, I turned to the burning candle on the bedside table and just as I was about to blow it out, a shadow flashed across the wall and I turned hastily. By turning too fast, I had ended up in Pete's grasp and had kissed him even before I realized it happened. He stepped back, almost shocked, and then smiled.

I knew he thought my answer to the Ceremony was yes, but he was wrong. I shook my head, but before I could contradict what I knew he was thinking, my eyes were heavy and I was propped up against a pillow on the bed. His poison already set in and I felt weak.

"I knew you would see to it," Pete whispered.

Chapter 28 - Misconstrue

I needed to come up with something, needed to stop this, but it wasn't easy when I felt weak. It was like trying to devise a plan half-asleep. I did not even know the Ceremony even started, all I knew was that I wanted to close my eyes and disregard the whole thing. I was asleep within only minutes. The heavy poison had quite an affect. But there was a pain that woke me in an instant.

"You have to end it," Pete whispered.

"End what? We didn't even say any words."

"I already said what needed to be said. You don't have to say a word, my sweet."

"What do you want me to do?"

"You follow your instinct."

"No…no!" I stood up, shaky on my legs and he was on his feet before I could stumble away. "This is all a misunderstanding…all a mistake."

"Oh," he whispered quietly, "I know you are just nervous, but it's going to be ok. You will be ok, love."

The love phase has already started. There is no way I am going to get out of it now.

I backed up to the wall and slid down against it, falling to my knees. He sat before me.

"Don't make me perform the Ceremony, please."

"I'm not. It has already started."

"This was all just a mistake."

"But just get it all over with. Just have a taste of blood. Have the blood of a king!"

"It tasted horrible last time. How could I ever forgive you for what you've done? How could you ever deserve the right to be King?"

"I was a horrid creature in the past. I wanted you to myself-,"

"You had me to yourself when you created that planet. You were still horrid."

"But I knew there would be someone willing to take you back. And it did happen. You knew how I wanted you to myself and Lucian captured you and brought you back to Catastrophe. Imagine how I felt when I saw you, only months later, holding my cousin's child. You don't understand. I am your Eternal Mate. No one else should have had you, but I let you slip through my fingers twice." His voice rose in sudden anger. "The least you owe me is a Ceremony. I could have killed them both easily, but I decided not to. Now is the time I have been waiting for. With all of my anger came regret. And now," he breathed, "I will not let you slip again."

"It was never about being King?"

"It was *about* getting back what was rightfully mine and refraining myself for failing again."

I rested my head on his shoulder, clutching his cape in my hands.

"I do love you," he said, "and if you love me you will understand what I am asking. With a Ceremony I can never lose you again."

"No. You won't be like the others...I can't do that again. You can't make me. You haven't changed."

"You are going to have a very angry vampire on your hands after this phase is over."

"So? What if we *said* we performed the Ceremony? Would it make a difference?"

"For me it would," Pete grumbled.

"But for now...at least until I am ready, if I ever will be ready, can you respect my wishes?"

"I'll go easy on you now, but just because I'm still at ease with this phase. If I lash out at you later, you know why."

*****

The clock on the bedside table read twelve o' clock midnight. I felt the weight of a cape on my arm, nothing out of the ordinary.

"You awake?" I was startled to hear Pete's voice behind me.

"What happened?"

"What *didn't* happen?"

I sat up. "We slept through a whole day?"

"I guess so."

I got up and walked over to the French doors that led to the balcony.

"Where are you going?" He was immediately behind me.

"I'm getting some fresh air."

"I will come with you."

The crisp winter air filled my nose as I turned my gaze toward the night sky. I shook my head in astonishment. A huge blue moon lit up the sky. Pete smiled beside me. It looked as though Clesta had been glued back together. Cracks covered the new moon's surface.

"What's all this?"

Pete laughed. "You wanted a moon, didn't you?" I could still tell he was being nice because his first phase was not over.

"It's beautiful."

"Let's go have a closer look."

Together we went outside and began our walk through the calm, silent streets.

"What should we call our moon?"

"I don't know. I have never named a moon before."

"Verneil was the name of the planet I created."

"I didn't know that."

"No one knew it but me."

"It would make a good name for a moon," I offered.

"Yes, it would."

Silence hung in the crisp air between us for a moment and I turned to look down at the lake that led to the reservoir.

"This Ceremony may not have been completed but it was started. The phases are going to continue you know."

I stopped in my tracks recalling the last phase - trust. I knew that was what he was implying.

I wanted to run. I did not want to stick around to find out what trust game he would play. However, I did not run. I simply stayed a step or so ahead of him while we walked. His footsteps stopped short and he put a hand to my shoulder.

"You seem uneasy about something," he mumbled. "But don't worry. You will trust me completely by the end of tonight."

Before I realized my feet no longer touched the ground, I was already in water. My head shot up through the surface and, in panic, I yelled, hearing no reply. There was a rumble of thunder and a flash. Cold rain started to fall. I swam, hoping to find the edge of the lake, but each time it seemed I did not swim far enough. The light flashed again and I swam faster. I swam beneath the water, in complete darkness and it suddenly became light. The water was clear as if sunlight had cast its rays over it. I felt an energy run through me, a prickling to my skin. There was a rumble and then nothing.

There was warmth where I sat before the fireplace. A cold voice hissed to me. "I told you so."

I laughed to myself. "You're just like your brother, saving me from the cold depths of water."

I could hear there was an edge coming back to his voice. "So why didn't you want to perform the Ceremony with me again?"

Chapter 29 - Ally Conformation

The snow and ice mercilessly bombarded the window in an icy blast. The storm continued on, with black clouds hiding the blue of the sky as though it were late night. I stood to warm my hands near the fireplace when I heard the soft clopping of Versailles's small silver hooves on the wood floor. She lay at my feet and looked at me with wild blue eyes, waiting for me to say something.

"Has Pete left already?" I asked the unicorn, my fingers running through her mane for a moment.

Today Pete will be leaving to meet up with Taj' and some werewolf allies. They have to figure out something. There has to be a way to get to Earth to save our vampires, there just has to be.

I heard chatter coming from the sitting room. *They must be leaving. Prusaious is going too. I almost forgot.*

Citrus, who let out a small flame for my attention, sparked a nearby book, setting it up in flames. I grabbed anything I could and began to suffocate the fire that burned at the edges of the book.

"Oh, Pete is going to kill me," I said aloud.

Versailles hid behind my legs and peered at Citrus as I flipped through the book. "This is his journal." I said, glancing angrily at Citrus.

Some of the pages were partially burned, others were only faded at their edges. Even the silver lettering on the cover seemed to have lost its metallic glow.

"Bad girl Citrus!"

I tapped her lightly on her nose to show my disapproval and placed the book down on the nightstand. The dragon lowered her head and curled up like a dog before the fire. Her scales reflected the flames and glowed dark orange. They reminded me of Clesta.

"That's it!" I ran from the room down the stairs and snatched a cape from a coat rack near the large mahogany doors.

"The weather is horrible outside Mistress." I turned to see Minx. He walked to my side and swiveled his head in front of the doors.

"I need to say goodbye to Pete," I protested.

"I can't let you go out there."

"I will only be a second." I scurried behind him and grabbed the handle, swinging myself into the storm.

I strained my eyes through the fast moving snow and saw a large black shape sticking out from the blurry mess. Pete was there with Prusaious, putting heavy equipment on Mullein's head and wings to help him fly against the storm.

"Pete!" I called. He looked my way, and Meleve, his snowy owl, flew to me and perched on my arm. I trudged through the snow to him and held onto Mullein for support against the wind.

"What are you doing here? Get back inside before you freeze!"

"Pete, I know how to get to Earth!"

"How?" Prusaious cut in while tying a heavy blanket over Mullein's back.

"We build another Bridge."

"It will take too long." Prusaious shouted over the wind.

"Besides, what do we make a bridge with?"

I buried my foot through the layers of snow and at last picked up what looked like a piece of orange glass.

"Do you know what this is?"

"One of the shattered remains of Clesta." Pete said simply.

"Yes, one of billions of pieces. We can make the bridge with Clesta's fallen pieces."

"It will take years."

"But what other choice do you have? You can't ride dragons-,"

"We will figure out what we can do by consulting with our allies. I will figure out what is best. *Trust* me."

"Goodbye Pete. Bye Prusaious."

"I will only be a couple days." He said leaning toward my ear. "Watch Meleve for me while I'm gone."

I adjusted his fur-lined cape and looked back to Minx who called me. When he turned to kiss me, I turned away, pretending I had not noticed and walked off to the palace. Mullein let out a roar and they were gone, swallowed up by the icy monster.

I walked casually inside, the color returning to my face. Minx looked at me impatiently, but I did not pay him any attention. I walked up to the library and sat in the large chair positioned before four large windows, overlooking the woodlands behind the palace. Today there was nothing but swirling white, so the heavy red curtains were not pulled over with a tassel as usual; instead they hid the snowy landscape from view. I heard a heavy wing flap and soft tapping. Minx rounded the corner of the hallway and stepped into the dark library.

"Something is wrong. What is the matter?"

"I almost performed the Ceremony with him. I made up my mind that it would be best if it wasn't done, but somehow I feel it's still haunting me, like it should've been done."

"But Mistress, you looked so happy these past couple of days-,"

"It's all because of the poison, Minx. Because of the strong poison I once loved, I feel weakened to it. I feel weak now in so many ways. I did not want this to happen. I don't want to feel weak and powerless to *him*!" I began to pick at the arm of the old, fraying chair. "Ceremony or not, I feel guilty."

"You are not powerless." The dragon walked up to me and rested his heavy head in my lap.

"But he is in charge…it's up to him to decide what is best and how we can get to Earth. All of those vampires, including Fitzray's life now depend on him, not me…all because we pretended that this Ceremony really happened and he's *King* now."

"Surely you have some power left. You are a queen, remember?"

I shook my head. "If I am so much of a queen, why couldn't I go with them?"

"It's dangerous enough for them to go and if anything happens-," Minx began.

"I am too weak to go, that's why."

"No." Minx raised his head, flicking out his tongue.

"His poison weakened me to an advantage."

"You may only be weak, but physically weak. You can still make decisions."

"Yes, but it's up to Pete to tell whether my decisions are considerable or not. I recommended we build a new bridge from Clesta's pieces. He said he would think about it, but he said *he* will figure out what's best."

"And he will." Minx said. "He *is King* of Catastrophe now. He is not just making decisions for you. Mind that, it is about what is best for all of us as a whole."

I looked to the snowy owl at my side whose eyes half-closed gazed over us in deep amber. I looked back at Minx, fingered his light scales and placed the palm of my hand to the notch-like horn on his nose.

Minx is right. I shouldn't worry. After all, Pete promised me he would fix everything.

I opened my eyes slowly. My dragon was still as stone, his great head before my face. "Do you remember when you were young? Do you remember everything that happened on the Bridge of Secrecy and in the tallest building of the City?"

"I do remember. I remember all that you remember."

"I don't understand Minx. Why did you choose me over Fitzray? After all, he *was* the one that took care of you as an egg."

"Have you forgotten that he gave me to you?"

"No, I know, but that was after the fact. Weren't you supposed to be his dragon?"

"He had Moonscale before my egg was given to him by my father. And when he did have me, he could have given me to anyone."

"And when you hatched, you peeped when I spoke."

"He had made the decision that I was yours before I hatched."

"How did you know?"

"I sensed it. I heard him talking to Moonscale through my shell. He had said so himself."

"You mean a lot to me Minx."

"And you to me, Mistress. A dragon will always be at the side of their Master."

"How is that possible? I mean, what if we are separated like when I was going to Nalani or the Star Pool?"

He stood, arching his neck to look down at me. "I will show you. Stay here, I will return."

When he came back, he looked at me, calmly placing something into one of my hands. It was a necklace of a silver dragon holding onto a copper marble. The dragon looked exactly like Minx. I took the silver chain and clasped it around my neck.

"This is beautiful Minx."

"It is not just for beauty, Mistress. If you rub it when you are feeling doubt and weakness falls upon you, I shall give you strength when you need it. It is a pure gift of heart. You mustn't lose it, for it is one of a kind."

"Why haven't I seen other dragon owners wear a necklace like this?"

"A Dragon's Soul necklace is invisible to all but the Master of the dragon. If it were there for all to see, it would be stolen. You see, in the copper marble a small fire burns, and the dragon around it consists of my own scales. That is a part of me. It contains a part of my soul to connect to you. That is why they call the necklace a Dragon's Soul. If someone were to hold the necklace and it did not belong to him or her, or if it was destroyed, the dragon would suffer. The dragon would become savage and cruel and may even kill its Master."

"What if something happens?"

"No one can see it. And if someone could, you would probably be under threat and I would be there."

"If it's invisible can someone still feel it around your neck?"

The dragon nodded his head slowly.

"The chain Pete always wears…could that be his Dragon's Soul?"

"It could be, but the silver dragon will always be invisible to a stranger's eyes."

I sat back and held onto the silver dragon. "You must have made this when I was gone."

"That's when I missed you most." My dragon replied humbly.

Chapter 30 - Poison Kiss

When I woke, two healers gazed down over me, closely examining me.

"You are weak from Pete's poison." One healer confirmed. "You should try this berry juice. It should help rid the poison's affect on you."

The healer handed me a bottle of berry juice that was thick and dark blue in color.

"Be sure to drink *all* of it because if you were to have any more poison, you could become paralyzed."

The door shot open and Pete stood in the doorway, snow covered and cold.

"Out." He said quietly, almost as if to himself. When he noticed the healers had not heard, he said it even louder and they ran from the room like mice.

"How did the meeting go?" I began to sip the berry juice once he had taken a seat before me on the large bed.

"Not bad at all."

"What did you find out?"

"We can't use dragons to cross to Earth. It's too risky."

"So what are we going to do? How will we get there?"

He moved closer, seeming not to have heard me. I shoved the bottle in his face at once. "What are you doing?"

He purred, looking at me through the bottle and instantly moved away as though I had snapped him out of his thoughts.

"Focus," I hissed, "how are we getting to Earth?"

"Like I said, I took your plan into consideration. The Allies agreed it would be best to make another bridge, but they argued it would take too long."

"How long do you think?"

"They claimed it would take years, years of hard labor and finding pieces of our orange moon."

I put the bottle on the nightstand beside his journal and at once he moved closer, pressing me to the headboard.

Paralysis, I thought and looked back at the empty bottle.

He kissed my cheek, the icy poison stinging as it ran down the side of my face. I was shaking, terrified for what would happen if it hit my lips. He put a hand to my shoulder, trying to get my attention while I looked away.

I fingered the silver dragon around my neck and Minx burst through the door and pulled me from his grip instantly. Mullein was beside Pete just as fast. The dragons stared at each other the way Pete and I were. Minx gathered me in his claws and flew through the broken door, down the stairs to the front doors of the palace. I opened it and he flew out, closing it behind him with his tail.

The storm was still bad, but not vicious as it was nearly a week ago. It was just bad enough to hide Mullein from our sight until he got close enough and smashed into Minx. I tried to hold on, but helplessly fell out of Minx's talons and landed into snow.

Pete was in front of me before I could blink and helped me up to my feet. He looked at me passionately and drew me toward his sickening poison. I fingered his neck, following the chain he wore until I felt something hard in my hands. I traced it quickly to confirm it was his Dragon's Soul and snapped it from his neck, proceeding to throw it into the snow. He was after it just as I expected and I ran for the palace, Minx close behind me. I rubbed the copper marble of my own Dragon's Soul and tucked it under my cape, feeling my strength return.

Pete stormed in, Mullein growling beside him.

"What's with you today?" He growled at my comment and launched forward, sweeping me off my feet. "You seem so angry."

"Of course I am. You avoided me when I left for the meeting and now you are avoiding me again."

"Your poison weakens me. I felt so weak I told the healers and they said I could be paralyzed if I had any more of it."

"Why didn't you tell me?"

"What would it matter? You are a vampire. You will always have poison."

"Not all the time, only when I want."

"And the paralysis-,"

"You drank the berry juice, didn't you?" I nodded my head. "Then you should be fine."

My eyes flicked away, trying to avoid his now softening face.

"You should have told me you were afraid."

Slowly I got to my feet and he grabbed my arm to steady me.

"So we will build a bridge. And then what?"

"We save the vampires and find Tetchra."

"And then?" I looked up at him hesitantly.

"And then, we rule together."

"What about Lucian?"

"You already know the deal. If he isn't reincarnated, then the both of you will rule together like none of this ever happened."

I held onto Pete, my legs becoming weak again. "I am sure you didn't think you would be the *King of Catastrophe*."

"Oh no," he said with a smile. "I knew." And he sealed what he said with a poison kiss.

*****

Chapter 31 - Woken

My life flashed before my eyes in the form of a monotonous nightmare.

How long have I been dreaming? I turned, startled by the brightness of a candle on the nightstand.

"What are you doing up?"

Pete looked at me for a moment and then continued to pace quietly as though he had not heard me.

"Thinking," he whispered. "I am thinking."

"Thinking of what?"

"The new bridge, that's what. Why is it taking so long to build? We are just over halfway across."

"Well…it has taken a *bit* of a while-," I began.

"It's been nearly *five years* Chenille."

"Yes, it's been years…years that Fitzray has been raised by that woman, that shape shifter."

Even though I had said it countless times, I woke up screaming from horrible nightmares in Pete's embrace, and I could not condone it. It was my fault that Fitzray was gone.

"Chenille."

Pete enveloped me until it felt like he was crushing me, which somehow offered me comfort and security.

"You *promised* me," I began.

"I haven't broken that promise yet, have I? If the Bridge had not been destroyed, you and I both know we wouldn't be having this conversation. Fitzray would be here, behind palace walls with us."

He grew angry and rushed to the window to peer into the black night. I pushed away the heavy blankets, my gaze turning back to Pete. I could see he was looking out toward the bridge.

"I can't stop thinking about it all."

"I know you can't, but we are going to get to Earth. I don't care what I have to do to get there."

"But...when we *do* get there, what do you think will happen?"

"We will find Tetchra and your son and free the captives there."

"And do you know how you are going to do all of that?"

"I have some ideas."

"What kind of ideas?"

He sighed. "I am done thinking for the night. I didn't mean to wake you. I promise you, I have a plan." With his final words, he blew out the candle and I fell asleep.

*****

Chapter 32 - The Lost Boy

"Happy Birthday Fitzray!"

The boy opened his eyes to see a smiling woman and a girl both standing next to a large white cake. Banners and balloons surrounded them. The girl, Violet, walked up to him and put a wrapped gift in his hands. The woman beside her was his caretaker since Tetchra was almost never home.

"Hurry and blow out the candles. Then you can open your gift."

"Yes Ms. Brown," Fitzray mumbled.

"How old are you now, eight? You are really growing up." Violet said taking a seat beside him once he blew out the candles.

"Yeah, but you're a teenager." He smiled, opening his present. "It's a book," he said disappointed.

"Yeah, but this book has all kinds of creatures in it."

"Creatures like those on Catastrophe? Like vampires?" He flipped through the pages.

"No, there is none of that." Ms. Brown lowered her voice. "You know that kind of stuff is forbidden here."

"Oh." He put the book on the table and looked up hopefully at her. "Why?"

"Ever since Earth broke away from Catastrophe, nothing has been the same. We don't like too much information to be given to the vampires if they were to escape-," she stopped herself and shook her head. "Nothing like that would happen anyway," she corrected quickly.

"Why did Earth break away?"

"Oh, I have said too much already, Fitzray."

He frowned and walked to the back door. "No one tells me anything," he mumbled.

"Where are you going?"

"I am going outside to ride Hickory."

"Fitzray just be-," Violet began. He slammed the door angrily behind him and walked off toward the stable.

"Hello Hickory. Want to go for a nice long ride in the mountains?"

The pony looked at him long and hard, waiting to be let out of his stable. "I'll take that as a yes." He led the pony away and grabbed his saddle. Hickory stayed still while the boy worked and then turned to see what he was doing. "Now for the bridle."

The pony's ears pinned back at sight of the leather bridle. He hated the bit, especially in Fitzray's inexperienced hands. The pony put up a good fight but in the end found nothing in his mouth and pricked his ears forward as the boy mounted.

"I don't understand Hickory. No one tells me anything."

He gave the pony a gentle pat on the neck and he started to trot.

"Why are there all these secrets? Why am I so different?"

"Hey Fitz!" It was Violet.

She came up beside him on her big brown mare and smiled.

"Leave me alone." He kicked his pony's sides and they sped off toward the mountains, where they stayed until dark.

"Just in time for dinner," Ms. Brown said quietly as he walked into the kitchen later that evening.

"I am not hungry. I am going to bed."

"Don't you want to wait up for Jeff?"

"No, I am too tired." He looked at the table and noticed a dark figure sitting in one of the chairs. The figure stared at him. He knew this was Tetchra's vampire.

"Goodnight Ms. Brown."

"Goodnight Fitzray."

Tetchra's vampire said nothing.

Fitzray sat on his bed, looked out the window to see a blob of glowing orange in the distance. It was getting larger each day. He smiled to himself. "One day I will find my parents, maybe soon."

* * * * *

I leaned against the white horse fence and called my unicorn. Versailles came to me, her silky white mane flowing behind her. She greeted me with a neigh.

"I will be going to Earth soon."

"Will I come?" The unicorn asked, her mouth unmoving as her thoughts transpired into words.

"It's too dangerous for you to come."

She snorted, her ears pinned back as Pete's stallion came over.

"Pete is calling for you," she said.

"What do you want Pete?"

"Come inside, I need to speak to you," he called from the palace.

"I'll come back soon Versailles."

I stepped into the library where Pete waited. He stood facing one of the windows, looking out into the bright, cloudless day and quickly closed the curtains upon my arrival.

"We are going to jump the bridge."

"Jump? What do you mean?"

"I mean we will *leap* over to Earth."

"How is that possible? We can't possibly jump that far."

"I didn't say *we* as in the two of us. I mean the unicorn and the stallion. They will jump it and we will be riding."

"Are you insane? How-," I began.

"I know it's possible. The new bridge is nearly completed, but with that gap I know they could make it across." He turned to face me.

"And what if we do make it there? What will we do?"

"I have talked with the wolves. They promised to help us."

"Help how?"

"They will help us find Tetchra. And we will find Fitzray. But we need help. As soon as the mortals find out vampires have crossed the new bridge, they will declare war."

"And how long do you think we could pull off being hidden?"

"It's simple." He walked slowly toward me. "You will cover as a mortal, and I will be your vampire. No one should suspect a thing just as long as you blend in."

"And if word breaks loose?"

"I will take care of whatever happens when it happens. You need to trust in what I'm doing."

"So there is more to your plan?"

"Of course," he smiled, "this is just the beginning."

"When will we cross?"

"I will let you know."

His voice was low as he pressed a hand to my face, leaning slowly to my ear.

"You must promise me."

"I promise."

He whispered, firmness forming in the back of his throat. "You mustn't tell a soul of this."

*****

Chapter 33 - Masterpiece

Fitzray pressed his nose to the hot glass, trying to get a good look at the diamond rings and necklaces displayed behind it. A jeweler was examining the old round statue Tetchra had inherited years ago.

"Ms. Brown can we *go* yet," he whined impatiently.

"Just a little while longer child," she replied quietly.

"I see it is mostly silver...but I see flecks of gold and a bit of platinum." The jeweler said as he ran his hands over its surface. "It will go for quite a bit of money."

Ms. Brown smiled. "Oh Tetchra will be pleased. Thank you." She turned and held tight to Fitzray's wrist. "Come along now, let's go home."

The walk was short from town to the house, but Fitzray could not stop staring at the egg-shaped statue that refracted every glint of light in its facets.

"Oh your mama is going to be so happy, Fitzray."

"She's not my mama," he mumbled.

They had no resemblance, he knew. She was hardly ever home. And he had no father.

"Go upstairs and wait for dinner, I'll call you when it's ready."

Ms. Brown put the statue on its stand, a bronze eagle claw base, and walked off to the kitchen. Fitzray walked over to the statue and picked it up. He sunk to his knees from the weight and it hit the floor. Quickly, he put it back on its stand and found pieces were falling off from the new crack. More and more pieces fell, revealing a thin white inner layer. The white layer cracked and Fitzray held it in his hands again. There was a small hole in the layer and peering from it was a bright orange eye.

"A monster," Fitzray said quietly.

He rushed into his room and placed the statue on his bed while he rushed around to find his new book. A scaly head popped up from the top of the statue, covered in silver scales. Gold lined its orange eyes. The sides of the statue broke and two thin wings stretched out. Its claws raked at the shell before its chest and it scrambled onto the bed.

Fitzray looked from the pages to the creature. "A dragon," he read, "is in the serpent family. It has wings and similar characteristics of a snake, but with legs. When it is a year old, it can breathe fire." He stopped reading to look at the creature again and noticed the shell scattered on his bed.

"Uh oh…I'll be back. *Stay.*"

He gathered the shell remains and put it on the eagle claw stand as though nothing had happened and returned to the dragon.

"What am I going to name you?"

The dragon climbed onto his lap and blinked its orange eyes. "Serpentine," it hissed.

"You can talk!"

"Yes." It said.

"Are you a boy or a girl dragon?"

"Boy," it said.

"Fitzray!"

"Stay here Serpentine. No one can find out about you."

"What is the meaning of this?" Tetchra's words echoed through the house. "Why did you do this Fitzray? This is my priceless statue, ruined!"

The boy cast his green eyes down to the floor and said nothing.

"Did you hear me? What do you have to say for yourself?"

He stayed silent and ignored her.

"What am I going to do with you Fitzray?" She paused. "Oh, you selfish boy!"

He scrambled up the stairs away from Tetchra as she raged after him, but she stopped. Her vampire held her wrist.

"Let the boy go."

"Unhand me you fool!"

He disobeyed and in doing so, Tetchra lashed out, her fists pounded against him. Fitzray could hear her rage from his bedroom and her vampire tolerated it.

"I can't stay here Serpentine. We have to go somewhere else." He looked out his window to the orange dot in the distance. "I don't know where I will go, but I can't stay here. I have to find my real parents. Will you come with me?"

"Yes," Serpentine hissed, "I will."

"How dare you disobey me? You are a foolish vampire, you are."

"What do you have against the boy?"

"He destroyed my statue. Do you know what I had to do to get it?"

"I don't want to know."

She hit him and he stepped back unharmed, forced to redeem himself because his eyes were glazed. He was bound by lock and key.

*****

Chapter 34 - Over the Bridge

"Are you ready?"
"Ready as I'll ever be."
"You know the plan?"
"Yes, I do."
"Good. Let's go. We are more than halfway across. It won't be a long stretch."

All I could hear was the hard pounding of the horses' hooves on the bridge. I held onto Versailles's mane as she ran faster. We approached the end of the bridge. Her nostrils began to flare and sweat formed over her body.

"We're almost there. You wait until you get to the edge. Then you pull her up and she'll jump it." Pete yelled to me.

I looked ahead and waited for the gap. I felt one of her hooves slip against the edge and she hesitated for a fraction of a second to jump at all, but she needed the force to push her forward to make it all the way over. I looked over to see Pete holding onto his black stallion's mane, bent forward, nearly leaning against the horse's neck. I realized the gap was closing, and the ground rose up from under us. The horses landed half-running, slipping against the mud. They slowed to keep their balance. I loosened my grip from Versailles's mane and stroked her neck softly.

"How are we going to disguise Versailles?"

"We're not. She is going to have to jump back over. My stallion can stay. He will jump back over tomorrow evening."

"Can she rest a while?"

"That's too risky. Just let her catch her breath."

I dismounted and stood by her side, waiting for her breathing to slow. Pete led his stallion away and I followed him, looking back every now and again to watch as Versailles made her way back over the bridge.

The sun was rising, an orange halo glowing around it, the sky once gray turning blue. I walked the busy streets with Pete. There was a frenzy of people around every corner. I did not know where we were going. The people crowded even closer and I lost track of where Pete was and stood on my toes to look for the stallion, but did not see him either.

Pete where are you? I thought.

People stopped, eyed me wearily and spoke hushed to each other. I kept looking, searching desperately for a hint that he was near, but heard nothing.

"Vampire! Loose Vampire!" Someone shouted.

I looked around hopefully, but I did not even see Pete. Someone grabbed my hands and people screamed.

"Where is your mortal?" The person demanded.

"*I'm* the mortal you fool!"

"Is that so? Where is your vampire then?"

"I lost him in the crowd."

"*Sure* you did. Clear the way! Loose vampire coming through!"

Pete where are you? I need you. I'm in trouble! I thought, but there was no reply, as I expected.

Someone tied my hands together and pulled me onto a high platform.

"Vampire bidding starts at twenty-five dollars. Twenty-five dollars for this fine vampire," a man chimed, gesturing to me. "Do I hear twenty-five dollars?"

"Twenty-five!"

"Twenty-seven!"

"Thirty-seven! Do I hear forty? Forty! Do I hear forty-five?"

"One hundred and ten dollars!" someone cried.

"One twenty!"

"One fifty."

There was a long pause. "One fifty. Do I hear one sixty? One sixty? Once, twice? Sold!"

The mortal came to the man, gave him the money and pulled me from the platform. He was only a teenager.

"What's your name?"

"Chenille. What is your name?"

"My name is Jeff."

"Where are we going Jeff?"
"To my house," he said.

He put me in his car, and drove away from the town. I watched the trees pass in silence until it made me feel sick and I closed my eyes. He pulled up to a small house, smartly decorated with a nice plot of land. He opened the door but I refused to move. I was feeling sicker than ever.

"You feel all right?"

I shook my head. "I feel awful."

"Come inside. That car ride was probably long for you."

He led me inside the quiet house. "Is anyone else here?"

"Yeah, the nanny who takes care of the kids."

I moaned, feeling sicker still.

"This is my room. Sit down, relax."

"Jeff? Are you home? Come here, come quickly!"

"Don't go anywhere." He closed the door behind him.

I plopped down on the bed and listened to the conversation on the other side of the bedroom door.

"How am I supposed to know where he is?"

"I thought you might have seen him."

"The pony is gone." A girl's voice cut in. "And Mom is going to be home any minute."

I felt myself begin to nod off, the voices dying out as I tried to focus my energy on retracing my steps, wondering where Pete had gone.

I heard a door open and a flurry of voices, one rising above the rest. "He's gone? What do you mean *gone*?"

The voice slowly died away like the others. After a few minutes, I began to wake from sleep from the voices again. They were close, but it was hard to hear them. They were still muffled from behind the door.

"Look, I got a vampire."

"Will you look at that? Who would have known?"

"Known what?"

"I like your taste in vampires."

"Can I have the lock and key Mom?"

"No, not yet Jeff. You can have patience. I need my vampire to become acquainted with yours, but I will need that to be done in the basement. Keep her away from him for a while, ok?"

"All right, I'll try my best."

"Now vampire, there is something I need you to do for me. It is a serious task that only you can perform." Tetchra said to her vampire.

"What does it involve?"

"Let's just say...things are going to get interesting around here."

The door clicked shut and my eyes opened slowly. Jeff sat on the floor, his eyes closed.

I reached for my Dragon's Soul around my neck, held it in one of my hands and felt its warmth, lulling me to sleep again. When I woke, my wrists were cold from the chains that bound them. I was in darkness, my back to the hardness of a wall. I called for anyone that could hear, but no one, nothing responded. I pulled on the chains confused, until I heard footsteps. Afraid to speak now that someone had heard me, I settled down. The figure stopped to light candles scattered around in the darkness. Each one had a different aroma, making it hard to breathe in, surfacing a lingering headache and dizziness to cloud my head. The figure came close, taking slow, loud steps and stopped just before me.

"You will be mortal again."

"No! No, you can't make me mortal!"

"No? Not even a mortal with fangs?"

The figure smiled and looked at me, the dim light shining on his face. "Lucian?"

He smiled and held me in an embrace that nearly crushed me. I looked at him and smiled as he went to kiss me, but Pete's voice filled my head.

What are you doing?

Lucian is alive. The bond between us is broken just as you promised years ago.

"No." Pete appeared from behind Lucian and let out a growl, as if materializing out of nowhere. "He works for Tetchra. He's under control, I know he is."

"That's not for you to conclude. He might not be under control at all," I cried.

Tetchra was there, grabbed hold of Pete and the darkness swallowed them up before I could warn him.

"Pete! Lucian, help him!"

"Why would I do that?"

A low laugh echoed through the basement and he held up a small bottle filled with black liquid. It glowed slightly where the dim light did not reflect over it.

"What is that?"

"If you take an Eternal Mate's blood and poison, bring it to a boil and feed it to his vampress, she will become a mortal. Temporarily, of course. It doesn't really turn you into a mortal, but it does prevent reincarnation for a while."

He dangled the bottle in front of my face, the liquid swaying from side to side.

"Being temporary, it may last only a couple of minutes, making a quick death vital."

"And if you aren't killed by the end of the couple of minutes?"

"Well, you would become immortal again, in the sense that you will have the ability to reincarnate. I will assure that impossibility to you though, so you don't have to worry about that."

He put the bottle to his mouth, pulling off the cork with his teeth and tilted my chin up.

"This should hurt you more than it hurts me."

"What are you doing to my vampire?" Jeff came running over. Lucian turned, knocked him to the ground in one swift movement and looked back at me. He pressed the small bottle to my lips, held my chin and forced it down.

"Step two," he mumbled taking the sword from under his cape.

I pulled my legs off the ground, tucking my knees beneath my chin and kicked out toward his hands, sending the sword across the room.

He dove after it, but Jeff was already on his feet, the sword in his hands. He forced it upward, slicing across Lucian's chest but not deep enough to do any damage. I slid down against the wall and screamed.

*****

"How much longer Serpentine? I am so tired of walking."

"Just a little longer…there!"

"What? What is it?"

"Well, you want information about vampires, don't you?"

"Yeah."

"Well this is a library. It has all sorts of information. I am sure you can find a book on vampires there."

"Will you watch Hickory for me while I'm gone?"

"I will."

Fitzray walked into the library. It was quiet inside, with only a few people searching for books. There were shelves filled with old books from the carpet to the ceiling. A ladder was on a track to access the high books. He browsed through the shelves looking over Greek Mythology to fantasy stories and then found a big book with detailed pictures and descriptions of all kinds of creatures. Although vampires were not mythical or fantasized creatures, that subject was still close by. He read about different phoenixes and dragons and several stories about vampires, but found another creature that caught his eye. It was a glass swan, the species type was unknown, and the only one on record was called Phantilla.

"She was known for being allies with the vampires and aided in several wars. She was last seen helping dragons escape from Earth before they were slaughtered for their scales. Some say that she holds great power over the stars and many suspect that she is a star herself. No one can say for sure where she has gone or if she will ever appear again," Fitzray read to himself.

He did not know how fast the time passed while reading in the library and he rushed out to find Serpentine and Hickory just where he had left them.

"I found out there is a swan made of glass. Her name is Phantilla. People think she is a star, like an *actual* star."

"Did you find anything about vampires in there?"

"Yeah, I did."

"Did you find out who your parents are?"

"No. There weren't any family trees in those books."

"We will just have to find that information elsewhere."

"Where are we going to go now Serpentine?"

"Wherever the road leads."

They stopped walking at the sight of a wolf in their path. It was big and snarled at them; its hairs on its back stood on end.

"Nice wolf. I…I am Fitzray."

"Fitzray?" The wolf inquired, surprised.

The boy nodded nervously. The wolf began to change into a figure - a girl.

"Werewolf," Serpentine said uneasily.

"My name is Prusaious. Do not be afraid, I can get you to your mother and father. I know who they are."

"How can we trust you?"

"What if I brought another vampire with me? Would that make you feel better?"

"Maybe."

"Calvin!" The werewolf girl cried.

A vampire with striking orange eyes came over in a hurry. He opened his mouth in astonishment.

"Fitzray." He smiled. "I am Calvin. I bet you don't remember me. I knew you in your past life."

"Past life?" Fitzray asked with confusion.

"Don't worry about it." He shook his head. "I can't believe it's really you."

"Yeah, me either." The werewolf girl chimed. "Come on. Let's get you back to Catastrophe."

*****

Chapter 35 - Torn

"Chenille? Chenille, Baby, wake up."

My eyes opened and I hissed. "Stay back, I'm warning you!"

I sank back. It was Pete, just Pete. He sat hunched on the middle compartment between two front seats, his head in his hands. I looked around. I was in a car, positioned uncomfortably on the back seats.

"What happened to me? Am I a mortal?"

He shushed me and sat in the small space between the front and back seats. "You are going to be ok. You are going to be ok." He said it more to himself then to me.

"What happened?"

"We got away," he whispered.

"Lucian…What did you do to Lucian?" I sat up in alarm.

"Nothing, nothing, relax." He pressed me down into my uncomfortable position again.

"Listen to me. I am going to take you somewhere where you can rest and get better."

"Get better? What's wrong with me?"

"You are just really, really weak. But you are going to get stronger. We just have to take it easy."

He kissed my cheek. His face was wet. My breathing began to quicken as I thought of the worst. I ran my hand against his face and held it to the light emitted by the headlights of a passing car. I caught my breath. There was not any black liquid on my fingertips. He was not bleeding. Just to calm my thoughts I heard the pounding of rain on the car roof and sighed.

"Why are you so shaken? What's wrong?"

"Nothing is wrong."

He slid into the front seat, grasped the steering wheel and began to drive.

"How did you get me out of there? How did you find me?"

"I heard you scream and I came and got you."
"What did you do to Lucian?"

He didn't answer. "What-," I began.

"This looks like a nice place."

He pulled up to a hotel. I did not even bother to read the sign. The rain blocked everything from view anyway. The car stopped and he got out, opening my door. He pressed me to his chest, carried me to the entrance and stumbled to the front desk.

"Room for two," he said quickly.

The woman eyed him suspiciously and nodded to me. "What's wrong with her?"

"She is very tired."

"Room forty-five. Here are your keys."

He walked around the hotel, searching for the room and at last, he found it.

"Here we go. Here," he placed me on the bed, and locked the door.

I sat up and flicked on the lamp beside me. Pete took off his cape in a rush, turned his back to me and sidestepped to the bathroom.

"You ok?"

"Yeah, fine."

I got up, not convinced by his words and peered through the open doorway. His shirt was a tattered wet mess on the floor. His back was to me.

"Get back to bed baby."

"Are you ok?" I asked again.

"I am fine. Now go, I'll be right there."

I walked over to him and stood at his side. He put a hand to my arm and moved me over so I stood in front of him, my back to his chest. I looked up to him and he gave me a smile.

"What are you doing in here?"

I stepped back and felt something wet seep through my shirt and turned. His chest was a mass of bloody scratches, some deeper than others oozing black blood.

"What happened?"

"It's not bad," he said quietly.

"Not *bad*?"

"Considering I wasn't the one with the sword, I think so."

"What happened?" I breathed.

"Don't worry about it. Just go back to bed and I'll get cleaned up."

"Oh I feel so weak," I sat down on the toilet seat cover and looked up at him. "You will have to carry me."

He smiled. "Fine."

I put up a hand. "You should get cleaned up first," I insisted, wanting to see his scratches.

He turned on the faucet and I watched quietly. He ran his hands beneath the water and turned, gathered me up in his arms and practically threw me onto the bed.

"Don't move," he teased.

He walked back into the bathroom, stayed there for several minutes and came back out. Without the bloody mess, I could see every scratch and its depth, each one worse than the last.

"They look really bad."

"It's nothing, just a couple of scratches."

I ran my fingers over them slowly. "You should heal them."

"It will take too much energy, besides, they're not that deep."

"So tell me."

"Tell you what?"

"Tell me what you did to Lucian."

"You won't leave me alone about that."

"Nope. You're going to hear my voice in your *dreams*."

"I didn't kill him. I just scratched him up as bad as he scratched me. Fair?"

"You wanted to kill him, didn't you? You didn't want to see him ever again."

"That's right, but I didn't kill him."

"He's not the same Lucian I knew."

"Of course he's not. He has been bound by the lock and key." He looked at me more sternly. "Remember when I told you how bad things would turn out if my book fell into the wrong hands?"

"You didn't *tell me*. You threatened me that if I didn't give it back you would bite me."

"Still, I had a reason for doing that."

"How are your scratches doing?"

"Don't even feel them," he whispered.

"It feels so nice to have a vacation from being royalty, don't you agree?"

He was quiet. I could only feel him breathing on my neck.

"Hmm? Oh, yeah, really nice."

He kissed me, careful not to let any poison set on his lips so I would not be any weaker than I was.

"Good night baby," he whispered, but I had not heard, I was already in a deep sleep.

*****

"We are going to rest here for the night." Prusaious said quietly.

Fitzray followed her to a small house. He was so tired he could barely stay awake. There were people in the house, all crowded around a table talking hushed to each other. They stopped as he entered and all looked from him to Prusaious and back.

"The Prince of Catastrophe," someone whispered.

"Come to me child." Fitzray looked up at the woman who spoke to him from across the table. She wore a mask. A heavy black cape hung over her shoulders.

"Who are you?"

The woman took the mask from her face and set it on the table.

"I am Verna, your great-great grandmother. I knew I would have the honor of meeting you one day."

"You know my parents?" His eyes lit up.

She laughed quietly. "Yes, I do. And I will bring you to them, on Catastrophe."

"How will we get there?"

"We will send for our dragons and fly across! We will do so soon, but quietly. No one can know we have gone. No one can know you are with us."

*****

Chapter 36 - Out of Mind

I woke up with pain flowing over me. Pete looked down at me, his eyes set in a menacing glare over my body. Gashes covered my arms. I sat up confused and he held my shoulders.

"What are you doing?"

He did not seem to hear, just stared blankly and pressed his fangs to my throat. I jumped from the covers, landed roughly on the floor and felt his presence behind me. I rose to my feet, but he grabbed my shoulder and pressed me to the wall before I could escape. His breath settled over me in a dizzy scent. His scratches were worse, bleeding again. He drank something I could not identify, to ease his pain, I assumed. But in doing so, I could tell he wasn't in his right mind. He did not even see me cowering at his feet, breathing heavy in fear. I looked over to the light in the bathroom, a beacon.

I slipped away again, rushing toward the light. There was water running, a coldness beneath my feet and I turned, finding him right behind me and ran from the bathroom. I kept running, felt the floor tremble beneath me and turned around. Pete was sprawled across the floor, blood mixed with water by his head that had hit the tile. I shook him, called out, but he would not wake. His mouth opened slightly though his eyes remained closed. I screamed into the halls for help, any help, and returned to his side, sunk to my knees.

"Please wake up…please." I whispered, crouched over him at his bedside. My fingers traced the edge of the white bandage on his head when I finally had a chance to see him again.

"He hasn't woken up yet?" A nurse asked me. She noted some things down on an old clipboard. "The doctor will be in to see you in a moment."

I held onto the sheets that covered him and took a shaky breath. *Even though he won't be reincarnated, he may never be the same vampire again. He might not speak or think the same. Oh, why did this happen? What did you do? How am I supposed to get Fitzray back now?* I thought.

"We called your parents. They should be here soon." A voice said.

I turned around, only saw the glint of golden eyes and a lab coat and then turned back to Pete.

How is that possible? I never said anything about my parents. How could they have contacted them?

"There you are." My father's voice hit me like a bullet, making me turn to face him as if he had just shot me.

"We came as soon as we heard the news." Timothy was standing beside him.

"What happened?"

"I am not entirely sure."

"Will he be staying overnight?"

"I don't know."

"I'll go find that nurse. She'll find out for us." Tim said and walked out of the room. I wanted to stop him. How could he leave me alone with my father and trust him for a mere second?

"You know," my father began, "if he does stay overnight, you are welcome to come and visit for a couple of days."

"I don't think-," I started.

"Oh why not? It's your mother's birthday today. I'm sure she'd be glad to see you after all that time away from home. It will be a big family party."

"Yeah," I mumbled, "like old times."

"Oh what do you have to lose? Do you even have a place to stay tonight?"

"No."

"Then you *will* come." My father insisted.

Tim came back into the room and I looked up at him hopefully. *Oh, I hope he can leave. If we could just get out of here, we'd have a chance.*

"Well?"

"I couldn't find the nurse."

I looked back down. "He is free to go. He can go now." I looked up. It was the doctor with the golden eyes. Just as I leapt to my feet, he turned out of the room into the hallway and out of sight.

"Well that's good news. You can both come."

"I'll go get a wheelchair," Tim said.

Once he returned, they both carried Pete from the bed and into the wheelchair to the car. I did not object. I could not just leave Pete with them and I could not carry him along with me. There was no way for me to escape, so I sat beside Pete. Tim sat in the front beside my father. I closed my eyes and listened as Tim changed the radio stations to find one that would tune in. The trees rolled by in a green blur for miles and miles road after road. At last, the car came to a slow as it turned onto a small cul-de-sac and stopped at the very end where dozens of cars filled the driveway.

"Come on inside Chenille." Tim put out a hand to help me out of the car. As long as he was with me, at least I had some protection.

I stood, waited for them to get Pete out of the car and walked into the house. The party stopped once I entered, the volume of the music turned down and my werewolf family stared. I rushed behind Tim and my father up the large staircase to the small guest bedroom.

"Can you give me a moment with him?"

"Sure. We will be downstairs."

Once they left I sat on the bed beside Pete.

"That doctor, I swear that was Lucian, I am sure of it. How else could my father find out so quickly? It must be Tetchra. She's probably involved in this and she knows where we are. What do I do Pete? What do I do?"

He was quiet, did not even make the slightest movement at my words. I held his shoulders, shook him violently, but he did not flinch. I clung to his tattered shirt, shook him again – nothing.

In defeat, I stepped out of the room, closed the door behind me and walked down the stairs. Everyone looked at me, no music played.

"The Queen of Catastrophe!" My father said.
"So she isn't a wolf, is she?" My Uncle asked boldly.
"No, not part of the pack," my father said.
"And now look at the King."
"The King? He's the King? I thought Lucian was."
"He *was*. He's not anymore."
"What happened?"
"I don't know what happened."
"What happened to Lucian, Chenille?" One of my family members yelled to me.
"Yes, what happened to Lucian?" My mother asked, shoving her way through the large family.
"Not you too mom," I whispered. They all began to shout, demanding answers from me.
"I don't know where Lucian is."
"Why are you here?"
"I'm here to save my species."
"Who is ruling Catastrophe then?"
"Lord of the Sea and his wife, for now while I'm gone."

Everyone looked at each other, confused. "You mean the snake?"
"Yes."
"He is the one that killed Zaire!"
"You let that traitor be a ruler? How could you do that to the pack?"
"I didn't come here to argue with you."
"Oh? Then why don't you go and never return back to Earth?"
"What do you want from me?"
"We want you to leave. We like Earth as it is. The vampires are controlled by the mortals, and we aren't bothered."
"You selfish creatures. Your heads are filled with arrogance!"
"So is yours! Do you even know if the vampires enjoy it the way it is? I don't see them rebelling."
"They *can't* rebel, that's why they are under control."
"Yeah, just about every one of them has a lock around their neck and the mortals have the keys around theirs. It is

impossible for you to free them. That is the mortals' choice," Tim said.

"We will go to war then."

"With your own kind?"

"I say if you don't get off this planet in a week, the wolves will join the mortals in the war against you!" My Uncle raged.

There was a cheer of agreement.

"How could you do that to me?"

"You aren't part of the pack," my Aunt said bluntly.

"Get off our planet!"

"I am sorry Chenille," my father said, "but you are no longer welcome here."

The family let out a growl as I backed up the stairs. They changed, one by one, into a wolf of a different color and snarled, chasing after me in a wild pack up the stairs. I ran into the guest room, a shadow slipping past me as I closed and locked the door. There was a beautiful wolf with dark brown eyes before me. Her fur was white, tipped with a silver shine.

"I am sorry this had to happen," she said.

"Mom? Oh mom, how could that happen? Look at what they've done to you!"

"I am sorry they have done this." She looked at her paws. "I didn't want them to, but your father, he insisted. Still, I didn't want to be a wolf, but it seems I didn't have a choice, no more than you had."

"When did this happen?"

"Long ago, sweetheart, when you left for Catastrophe."

I took a step back. Claws raked against the door. Piece by piece they were breaking it apart. A wolf's eye appeared through one of the holes in the door.

"What are you waiting for? Get her!" My father yelled through to my mother.

I stepped back cautiously once my mother took a step forward. "You have to get out of here. Just go out the window onto the roof. You will follow that down to the back of the house. You can jump from there."

I turned to Pete. "I need to get him up."

"He's unconscious."
"It's too risky for me to drag him onto the roof."
"He can't stay here though. The pack will tear him up."
"What do I do?"
"I know. Go ahead. I'll keep him in the closet until the pack passes by, then I'll take him to the front door. You can take him from there."
"All right."
"Go!"

I opened the window, balanced myself on the roof and walked, following the long stretch of shingles. I heard a slam of the door's demise and walked faster. The wolves came fast, piling onto the roof and one by one came dashing to where I was. I jumped off the roof and hit the ground all at once, not even thinking. The wolves watched, indecisive whether to jump after me or not.

I ran to the front where my mother was. She held Pete by his shirt in her mouth.
"Run Chenille, they will be after you again."
"I am sorry this had to happen."
"Me too Chenille. Now go. Good luck."

I held Pete by his arms and began to walk backwards, away from the house.
"Goodbye," my mother called, "Good-," her voice was cut short. I heard a cry, a howl, and turned.

My father was there, his claws digging into her.
"Mother!"
"Don't worry about me Chenille. Go before the pack gets you!"
"You know what we do to traitors in this pack?" My father yelled.

I held onto Pete's arms tighter and ran faster, dragging him with me. My father's voice was the only thing I heard. "Your fate will be the same Chenille. You are a traitor to this pack!"

Chapter 37 - For and Against

I ran for hours, only to stop when the moon was high like a big white marble in the sky. That night I stayed awake, unable to sleep, only to stare at my Eternal Mate. His breathing was slow and I knew he might never wake. Now and again, I shook him, but each time there was the same dead response.

The sun was beginning to rise and I closed my eyes, tired from the sleepless night. There was a sound beside me, the slightest noise. I was surprised I had heard it at all.

"Pete?"

There was no response and I turned, shaking my head. The noise came again and I turned to face him. I pressed my ear to his chest, heard nothing but the sound of his breathing. I whispered his name again and waited until I felt the slightest tremor of vibration coming from his throat. I sat up and shook his shoulders knowing he could hear me.

"Pete, wake up! Wake up!"

His eyes refused to open.

"Pete *please*," I begged.

"Chenille? Oh...what happened?" He asked in a low, drunken voice.

"You hit your head and we went to the hospital. I swear Lucian was there."

"Is that so?" He opened his eyes and slowly sat up against the trunk of the tree behind him.

"And then my father came and he took us to his home and my family got out of hand!"

"What happened?"

"He killed my mother Pete! He killed her!" Tears began to form in my eyes, my throat closing.

"Who? Who killed her?"

"My *father*."

"Oh, I wish I was awake. I wish I could've helped you."
"There was nothing either of us could have done."

He let out a sigh and touched his head where the white bandage was and began to unwrap it.

"They want us to get off of Earth. They threatened to go to war and to join the mortals against us."

He threw the white bandage to the ground and held my face.

"If we must go to war, we will."

"But why? Is that the only way we can get our captives back?"

"I am afraid so. It's the only way we can get Tetchra."

"And Fitzray."

"Actually, I didn't see Fitzray in the house. I heard he is missing."

"Missing? How can that be? He could be anywhere with anyone!"

He shushed me, drawing me close. "We will find him and we will free the captives. We will go back to Catastrophe and build our army, finish our bridge and wait. When they attack, we will be ready."

"What about the locks? How will we free the captives?"

"I don't know yet, but there has to be a way."

"What do we do now?"

"We rest for now. Later we will go home and prepare for war."

Pete woke me hours later from my nap beneath a shady tree. A cool breeze coursed through my body.

"The wolves are coming. We have to leave."

"How are we going to get across?"

"Trust me, we'll get across."

At the edge of the bridge the orange stone was so far away, it seemed. I looked down, regretting doing so. There was an edge of white; only a couple of stones remained from the Bridge of Secrecy. I placed my foot on one of the stones and looked over as far as I could manage. The stars hung in their place like tiny diamonds that made the new bridge glow. There were shapes in the distance flying to the other edge of the bridge where we needed to go. They were dragons, I could tell, carrying aboard figures.

"If only we could get across like them." I looked over at Pete who was concentrating. He rubbed the back of his neck, irritated. He was whispering to himself, being so secretive, I could barely read his lips. He looked up from his concentration to me and smiled slyly.

"We will get across." He put out his arm and waited for something. He looked straight ahead and let out a whistle as though he could see something I could not. Then, I did see something. A small dot of white became larger as it neared. It was his snowy owl Meleve and Mullein following close behind.

"*That's* how we will get across."

"Do you want me to get Minx?"

"No need to."

The snowy owl landed on his outstretched arm, turned her head around to face me and blinked her amber eyes. Mullein landed behind Pete and stood at command for him. He climbed up onto the dragon, held onto his wing to pull himself up and put out a hand for me. I looked at the dragon that towered over me, and took a step back.

"You aren't *scared* are you?"

"Of course not." I took his hand and pulled myself onto the heavy built muscle.

The dragon ran forward and flapped his wings, glided over the gap effortlessly and landed harshly on the bridge.

"We'll walk from here."

"But why can't we fly?"

"We can't be spotted. It would be too risky."

I could not believe all of the commotion that took place in the palace that night. Pete had left me at once so I could see Versailles while he tended to the demands placed over him. I could tell they were planning for war. Everyone was waiting for it to happen. I only saw

Versailles for a moment to see how she was. It was too late to bother her with stories.

I returned to the palace that was surprisingly quiet as I entered. There were low voices coming from the dining hall, echoing down the dim-lit corridors. I followed the sound to the door, took a breath and opened it. The muttering stopped and everyone looked in my direction and stood up in respect.

"Come here Chenille. We were just going to start our feast," Pete said.

I took a seat, disturbed by the uncomfortable silence. Everyone stopped talking of the plans for war and simply ate quietly as though nothing was going on. I looked up from my plate after several moments, losing my appetite suddenly. I could not bear the silence, the secret plans they were keeping from me, though I had every right to know.

"Is something wrong?"

"No, just not feeling so well," I said and took a sip of water.

"Maybe it'd be best if you went up to bed," another vampire recommended.

I rose from my seat delicately, curved my fingers over the back of it and calmly pushed it forward.

"Yes, get some rest. I will see you as soon as this important business is taken care of."

I turned away, said nothing like Pete would have done to me and walked away. I ran to the bedroom angrily, hoping they had all heard my loud pounding on my way up the stairs. I slammed the door shut, pressed my back against it and sighed heavily. Just as I was walking to the closet there was a knock and the door opened when I said nothing.

"What's with all the noise?"

I ignored him, simply walked to the bed and threw my jacket onto a nearby chair.

"If you think we are keeping the plans from you, you're wrong." I shook my head, disregarding his pointless words. "Let me make it up to you," he whispered. He exhaled deeply, the smell of meats and spices wafting around him.

"I don't want your poison," I hissed.

"No?"

I shook my head again.

"Why not?"

"I feel too weak."

"You will always be weak. Every time you perform a Ceremony, you become weak and it takes time to get strong. You have performed it two times. Each time it made you weaker than the last."

"I don't want to be weak."

"You will have to stay on bed rest then."

I moved away and pulled back the heavy quilt on the bed.

"This could be the last time you taste my poison in a long time," he insisted.

"Why do you say that?"

"You can be reincarnated. I won't since I am too strong for that. I was born a full-blood vampire."

"Then why would *this* be the *last time*?"

"In the morning the gap on the bridge will be filled with the remaining pieces. We are going to war tomorrow and if you are killed-,"

There was a knock on the door, interrupting him. "King Pete, you must tell us the remaining plans. There is little time for us to prepare."

"There is always a knock at the door," I mumbled.

He got up slowly. "I will be back, hopefully before you are asleep."

"Of course," I grumbled, "you go make the war plans *Your Majesty*."

*****

Chapter 38 - Tintinnabulation

More than three servants helped me put on all of the armor I had to wear. There was layer after layer of clothing. My hair had to be up and out of the way while I fought and a heavy metal choker was mandatorily around every vampire's neck. A vampire came up to me, handed me a sword and a knife.

"When you see a lock around a captive's neck, you take the knife and place it behind the chain and pull it towards you. The chain will break. You will take the remaining lock and throw it over the bridge, understood?"

"Yes, understood."

He took my sword and put it in its place, at my hip.

"The gap of the bridge is closed and mortals are already beginning to cross. You will go outside where the others are waiting. It may seem empty of vampires out there but I assure you, there are reinforcements being sent."

I followed his orders and went to join the others. I could not see Pete, since he was probably in the front. More and more vampires began to crowd around me noisily and waited for the coming of the mortals.

"Here they come! Send the dragons!"

Ten dragons flew overhead to find their place on the low bridge walls. They stood in position and breathed fire, covering the bridge in thick smoke.

"Send out the snake!"

Taj' came slithering to where we waited. Diamond armor covered his body, protecting his tough skin.

"Are you ready Taj'?"

"Yes I am."

"Where is Pearl?"

"She is at home, my friend. She is with the children to keep them safe in case of invasion."

"Good luck Taj'."

"Good luck to you as well. We have all waited long enough for this."

"Even you?"

"Yes, they took my green-eyed friend."

He looked ahead boldly and blinked his copper eyes. Versailles charged ahead, flying past me in a blur with her head down, her horn exposed. She ran to the bridge and everyone followed.

"Charge!"

That was the command everyone obeyed. I tried to stay near Taj' once we were on the bridge in the midst of the smoke, but found it impossible. I did not see one mortal, not even one, until the smoke cleared to a thin fog, revealing the hundreds that were crossing. I wanted to look back to see how many vampires were on the bridge but I knew I could not look behind me now that everything was happening ahead of me.

I saw a captive at last and ran to her. She let out a hiss as I grabbed her necklace and sliced my knife through it. She fell onto the bridge and looked up at me with a new glint in her eyes. She was free. At once, she rose to her feet and asked for my sword. Hesitantly, I gave it to her and she rushed forward, showing me she was fighting *for* us. She too began to free other vampires who, in turn, freed others. The confusion was just beginning to start.

The sides continued to clash and more mortals came onto the bridge with their vampires. Dragons swooped down, spitting out fire and gathering captive vampires in their arms for the locks around their necks to be broken. I moved up further on the orange bridge, waiting for another captive to pass me. I looked around and spotted Pete, sword to sword with another vampire, trying to break the lock around his neck. Fire exploded nearby and smoke filled the air around me. Nothing was visible again. I could only see the faint shimmer of a horn. Versailles was close. She reared and came down on a werewolf. She looked around and spotted me through the smoke.

"Come on!"

I held onto her mane and pulled myself up onto her back. She raced across the bridge until she saw a captive and got close enough to slice the chain from her neck with her horn. She picked up the lock in her mouth and turned her neck to me so I could throw it over the bridge. She ran again and reared at the sight of a vampire with a sword. Helplessly, I fell and a blast of fire ascended in front of me like a wall. A dragon flew above, high over the bridge and went into a spiraling drop down toward me.

"Chenille!"

There came a yell, a desperate warning for me to get out of the way, but I did not hear. I stood, frozen with fear as the fast dragon came bounding toward me. It swooped down, let out a roar and wrapped its talons around my body. I yelled to anyone that could hear, which was no one really, and tried to pry myself loose as it flew higher and higher. It lifted me up to its scorching chest and a rough hand grabbed me from the dragon's claws and yanked me up onto its back. I tried to get a good look at the rider but he pressed me against the dragon's neck. The dragon's spikes dug into my armor. A small bottle filled with black liquid hovered above my face.

"Lucian, what...what are you doing?"

"I am obeying my master's command."

"Will you listen to yourself? You sound like a dragon."

He laughed. "This time I will not fail. I will get you this time."

"It was you in the hospital, wasn't it?"

"Yes it was. Now stop distracting me."

He held the bottle above me, pulled off its top. I looked at him knowing I needed to free him now. I wrapped my arms around his neck, kissed him, tried to find the small clasp on the chain that bound him to Tetchra. He held the bottle higher, trying to resist me. I held onto the chain, held it tight so I could choke him if I had to. I tried to find the clasp, fingered for it blindly. He let out a growl and bit my arm in his attempt to make me let go. Still I hung on and fingered the clasp, working with it until there were two pieces of chain in my hands instead of one. The lock fell.

"You freed me Chenille." He mumbled, the trance leaving his face.

The bottle dropped from his hands and fell. It did not break, but simply spilled. It spilled all over the white dragon's wing. The acidic-like poison burned the very flesh of the dragon's thin, leathery wing and he breathed fire on it to burn it off, but simply crashed in doing so. I was able to break my fall, but watched helplessly as Lucian fell onto hard paving stones. His own dragon trampled him, fleeing away in panic.

I sat up from my recovered fall and looked around me for Lucian. He was a long walk from where I had fallen, on his side, barely breathing at all. Deep gashes were on his body from where his dragon's claws had struck him.

"Lucian?"

I rolled him over onto his back to find he was not breathing anymore. His mouth and eyes stayed closed. A stream of blood ran from his neck - it was broken, I was almost sure. I said his name again repeatedly, knowing the chances of him responding were slim to none. I shook him even though his body had lost all its warmth and there was stillness to him that was not believable. I held onto his hand even though I knew I would never feel the security of his fingers gripping my own. Still, Jasper did not return.

Freed captives walked by me, barely noticing me in the middle of the road or the terrible scene upon it. A loud, familiar voice came to me and I looked up to see the licorice black snake staring down at me with great disparity.

"Come," he said quietly, "let us leave this place. This is a place of great sorrow where many have come to their last breath. Come with me Chenille, I will take you back home away from this place." Taj' said, nudging his great head against my body so I looked away from the terrible sight set out before me.

He picked me up with his tail and set me against

his armored back only to slither onward to the palace. I watched as healers came up to the cold body and picked it up, lifeless I knew, and placed it in the talons of a dragon that carried it off to the palace where they would examine it.

I entered the palace unsure if the war was even over. Vampires were crowded inside, many with wounds or broken armor that dug into their skin. It was not anything like the palace it used to be but instead served more as a hospital. Healers ran around checking for the most severe cases compared to minor scratches.

One healer led me through the halls to a room where it was quiet and there was little commotion. Lucian's body was in that room on a sofa. They covered his body up to his chin with a white sheet to shield my eyes from what they had already seen. I placed my hand over his body and took a shaky breath, no different from before. A healer came over to me.

"I am sorry for your loss Queen Chenille, but he will not be reincarnated."

"But...but why? We performed a Ceremony."

"He has never been reincarnated and never will be. He is and will always be part mortal, even with a Ceremony."

"He is never coming back?" I whispered.

The healer shook her head slowly. His body moved slightly beneath my touch like sand slipping away from the shore to the ocean. His body began to fade and blow away like smoke from a dying fire in the woods.

"You must leave," the healer said calmly.

I gazed over his body, cold and still for one last time before I turned away from it forever. I walked to the door, took a shaky breath and closed it behind me. Pete knew where I was. He was standing there, waiting for me.

"You are at his death bed and here I stand. I don't see a hint of worry for me on your face. Look, I have come back for you in one piece." He clenched his jaw angrily. "And yet you care more for a dead half-mortal."

Without thinking, I raised my hand, felt it smack hard against his face, and heard the harsh sound of the slap. There was a red imprint on his cheek. Slight astonishment and wild fury built up in his dark eyes. I held my wrist, damaged for what I had just done to it and he said nothing, nothing at all. I walked on to lock myself in the bedroom, to keep him away, but I knew he would not let me get away with that. Any moment, I knew, he would appear and pry open the locked door. I knew I could not let him get away with that. I wanted to escape him before he could get me, before he could make me regret what I just did.

I ran for the bedroom, beat him there and hid myself beneath the bed trying to figure out what to do, what my next move would be. I heard the loud footsteps, the closet door open and slam shut. The steps came closer until I could see his shoes from under the bed skirt. I slid from underneath the bed as he lifted the bed skirt and I let out a sigh of relief. There was silence, not even a tap of his shoes and he was over me. He had leapt across the bed and landed right on me, preventing escape.

I uttered a scream, wriggled in his grasp, unsure if anyone would hear me. I could not let him win.

"No stop!" I cried.

He let out a harsh growl in frustration and sliced his fangs against my neck. I shrieked, hoping for someone to hear, and held my hands against his neck. I could not start to beg or cry now. This was my punishment.

He held my hands away from his neck. I balled my hand into a fist that pounded against him, forcing him to sit up. He touched the left side if his face, now bruised as I slipped from under his grip. I backed up, holding my neck, and crawled to the open door. He sat bent over, his hand still to his face and watched me, waiting to leap again. I had done it, made it to the door in one piece and stood up. Slowly, he rose to his feet and before he could jump, I did, and tumbled down the stairs. I lost control of my body and it took total impact from each roll from one stair to the next.

"The Queen," a nearby servant yelled.

A healer came, picked me up and was joined by

several others who carried me into a room. They were talking, checking over my bruised body, sticking me with needles, wrapping bandages over wounds. They called for me to wake, and I felt almost numb when I did. The chandelier above me was bright and I looked over my arms. Most of the bruises and wounds that the healers tended to were covered. I looked to the healers to thank them, but they had left the room.

Pete opened the door and stood at the side of the coffee table on which I remained. He was quiet, looked me up and down with a mumble to himself. He put a hand on the table beside my shoulder and leaned over me so his gaze rested over my face. His lips turned darker before me, covered in the thick black color of his poison. He neared closer, breathing the scent of the sweet smelling poison over me.

"I was a fool to have not given you my poison the other night. I didn't know you would become so disobedient if I hadn't."

"I hardly consider that...an apology."

"I'll give you an apology."

He neared closer, the black poison beginning to drip. I grabbed for my Dragon's Soul, clutched it in my hand and called desperately for Minx. On cue he came, crashing through a window and landing into the room.

He ran over and breathed a jet of flame in Pete's direction, but he moved out of the way and was gone before the fire trapped him. Minx picked me up gently and flew back through the broken window.

"Where do you want to go?"

"Take me to the bridge. I must see the damage done."

"Yes, of course Mistress."

*****

Chapter 39 - Glass and Gold

Fitzray looked out to the bridge and tugged on his great-great grandmother's sleeve.

"Why are all of those wolves coming over the bridge?"

"The ally wolves are coming home. The war is over." She said simply.

A pair of wolves approached them quietly. A gray-haired one walked up to Fitzray and gave him a smile.

"Hello dear boy," she said in a harsh, throaty voice.

"Hi."

"I know who you are. I know who your parents are too."

"My parents?"

"Yes, dear boy. I could take them to you if you'd like."

"But what about the others?" He turned to face them, but they were not there.

"They left you in my care. I will take you further to find your parents."

Hickory gave a startled snort at sight of the wolf and fled away. "Oh no, my pony!"

The gray-haired wolf turned to the wolf beside her. "Bring it back to me," she said softly. Once the wolf beside her was out of sight, she turned back to Fitzray.

"We'd best be on our way now."

"Where are we going?"

"Why, we are going to the bridge of course."

"It's not that far from here, is it?"

"Actually, it's only a couple of minutes from here. See, there it is."

He looked over at the bridge where a group of wolves crossed. "Who is that person standing all alone on the bridge?"

The wolf said nothing, but a smile crossed her ugly face. She stopped walking once she got on the bridge to stare at the person, transfixed, and refused to go on. A group of wolves headed straight for the lone woman.

I glanced down at a corpse, just near my feet, and pointed my chin up to look away. I saw at least a dozen wolves were heading in my direction. The leader of them was a wolf with chocolate brown fur. He walked right to me, stood on his hind legs to match my height and his body began to change. I stepped back cautiously, shrinking in the presence of my father.

"Hello Chenille." He put a casual hand to my shoulder with a friendly smile. I could not say anything, too afraid to speak, the past visions of my mother running through my head. "Do you see that child over there?" I turned in the direction where he pointed. My eyes widened.

"Fitzray?" I said quietly. I looked at my father with a glare.

How dare he take him to a place like this? This place is a place of war. Fresh blood and carcasses still cover the bridge.

I noticed my father's hand was in the form of a fist before my face. He held my Dragon's Soul in his hand.

"How is that possible?" I looked at him in confusion. "You...you can't even see it. How did you know about my Dragon's Soul?"

My father smiled. "Almost every vampire I found had a Dragon's Soul around his neck. Why shouldn't *you*?"

I tried to get it back from him, but he threw it, sent it sailing over the bridge. Minx was there in an instant, caught the necklace before it fell. He held it in his mouth through his teeth, his eyes burning with rage.

"Minx...it isn't what it looks like. Please Minx."

I knew my begging could not help me here. His nostrils flared and I shot a desperate glance at the werewolves to see a smile on all of their faces.

"This is how you planned it all along? To find me on the bridge while the werewolf allies crossed?"

"You didn't think *we* were going to kill you ourselves, did you? That much publicity would be too much for the pack if word got out that we *killed the Queen*." He paused to laugh. "Why, we would never be able to go back to Earth if that happened. But I want revenge. The whole pack wants revenge, so we put our heads together. Nothing said *we* would get in trouble if it was your own dragon that killed you."

The dragon took a step closer and dropped the Dragon's Soul onto the bridge.

"Minx, listen to me! It's not my fault!" The dragon refused to hear me and let out a harsh growl, his teeth showing in fine pointed rows. My father turned to Fitzray.

"You see," he said, "dragons will never be a problem to you, just as long as you belong to *our* pack."

"You wouldn't dare!"

A wall of fire rose up, blinding me. The wolves dove aside. I could not tell if Fitzray was hit or not. I crawled on my knees to pick up the necklace and fumbled with it to put it around my neck. The dragon looked down at me, growled, eyeing the Dragon's Soul. Even with it on, there was no difference. I held the copper ball in my hands, felt the small silver dragon molded around it and dug my fingernails into it. He did not even notice. He simply took flight on his white wings, thin and light as cotton sheets, and let out a blast of fire in my direction. I cried out, shielding my face with my hands and heard something.

A loud, clear note rang in my ears and the heat of the flame subsided. Everything was still as though someone froze the bridge in time. I looked up, felt the air still and saw a glass swan on one of the bridge walls. She had a beak of gold with dark black eyes. She took a step, blinked her eyes and lowered her head in a bow.

"Greetings," she said triumphantly. "I am Phantilla."

"Hello Phantilla." I stood up shaking. "You saved me."

"Timing is everything you know."

"How did you know I was in trouble?"

"I have a way of knowing. I can see almost everything from where I perch."

"I don't suppose we have met."

"No. I have been in hiding these past couple of years, but I have returned. Do you hear? Phantilla has returned," she yelled, spreading out her wings.

I turned to look back to Minx. "What are you going to do about my dragon?"

"His Dragon's Soul was broken by the wolf, wasn't it?"

I nodded. "Yes, I didn't mean for it to happen."

"I am sure you didn't. Here is what I shall do. Take whomever you want from the bridge with you to be safe. I will try to mend this dragon back together. All I need is his Dragon's Soul."

I took the necklace from my neck and handed it to her. She placed it beside her feet on the bridge wall.

The fire regained heat again and Minx's wings began to quiver, his eyes blinked. "You must leave quickly," she called.

I ran to find Fitzray and gathered him up into my arms. Startled, I saw a small dragon crawl from under his jacket and looked up at me. He looked over, spotted Phantilla and flew to her.

The dragon bowed his head and began to change. He turned to a deep shiny yellow color and became muscular like a lion. His body was now pure gold in color.

"I want to help you," the dragon said.

"What about the boy?"

"I can still visit him, can't I?"

Phantilla looked at him displeased. "I do not tolerate selfishness."

"But I want to work with you Phantilla!"

"No," the swan shook her head, "you will stay with the boy. He needs you more than I do."

"But you have such an awfully busy job," he protested.

"Yes, and I will continue to do it on my own as I have for those hundreds of years and more to come."

The dragon bowed his head in defeat and glided to my shoulder.

"I will send your dragon back to you when he is cured," the glass swan called.

"Thank you Phantilla."

I made my way off the bridge, Fitzray asleep in my arms. I would go straight to the palace and would not stop until I was there. He began to wake and opened his green eyes to look up at me.

"Look," Serpentine said, "you finally found your Mama."

"My Mama?" He rubbed at his eyes to wake himself.

He did not say anything more so I stopped to set him down. He held my hand and walked, just stared up at me and said nothing. We walked silently on the palace grounds until he finally spoke up. "Where are we going?"

"We are going to see Versailles."

"Who's Versailles?"

"You'll see."

The unicorn let out a neigh once she spotted us coming. Fitzray let go of my hand and raced forward.

"Hickory!"

He ran up to a chestnut colored pony tied to a fence post. "You know this pony?"

"Yeah, this is Hickory. I took him with me from Earth."

"Aren't you a beauty?"

I ran my fingers through his tangled forelock and took off his saddle quietly. Fitzray brought him into the paddock to meet Versailles and handed his bridle to me once they were securely inside. I put the saddle and bridle away, listening to the sound of the playful neighs not too far away. Fitzray scrambled out of the paddock once I returned and stood to watch the pony and the unicorn play.

"They look happy," Serpentine said.

Fitzray held my hand again as we began to walk back toward the palace. "What is Dad like? Is he home?"

"Well, he's not home and I don't expect him to be home for some time," I replied quietly.

"Why is that? Is he working?"

"Actually I think she is trying to say that your father will not be coming back."

"Why? Did he die?"

I flicked the little dragon's snout for saying what he did.

"What was he like?"

"Well," I began, "he was tall with black hair and golden eyes. He had the most wonderful smile and he loved me…loved us all very much, especially you."

"I wish I could have met him."

"You did know him until you turned three."

I stopped walking to show him the palace entrance. He looked around, his eyes growing wide and he stared directly ahead toward the front doors. Pete stood there looking over his shoulder at me and he turned his bruised face back to the entrance again. Fitzray broke loose and darted to where he stood to look up at him in awe.

"Father," was all he needed to say.

The vampire looked at me in disgust, back down at him and walked into the palace angrily. If you had not known any better, Pete probably would have looked like how I had described Lucian, without gold eyes. Fitzray stood where he was, confused as I rushed up to him.

"He isn't my father, is he?"

"No, he is not. He is a foolish, egotistical man."

I led him inside and he yawned. It was getting late.

"Let's get you to bed." I brought him into one of the guest rooms. He rested on the bed, closing his eyes. Before I could even get him washed up before he went to bed, he was already asleep. Serpentine settled down beside him, curled up like a cat.

I kissed his forehead, gave a pat to the golden dragon and closed the door, leaving it open just a crack. I stood for a moment, smiled to myself and turned to see Pete leaning nonchalantly against the railing.

"I see you've gotten your son back," he said rather coldly.

"You don't sound too enthusiastic about that."

He said nothing. "Why did you act like that earlier? He thought you were his father and you acted as if he had just stabbed you in the chest. I thought you supported me in finding him."

"He is not my child and I am not his father."

"So that gives you the right to push him aside like that?"

"I helped you free the captives and get your son, now you want me to show *compassion*?" He sighed heavily and smiled slyly. "Oh, I get it. You want me to be more like Lucian don't you? Well, here's the fact sweetheart, Lucian is *dead. Lucian* will not reincarnate. And if you think I will just warm up to you and sooth your worried little head that maybe he will return, I won't, because *he isn't coming back*."

"What kind of Eternal Mate are you? If you think I am some vampress you can just use your poison on and drink blood whenever you want, you are wrong."

He strode up to me in several steps. "And so are you. *I* may do as I like." He grabbed my shoulder with a smile.

"Mama, what's going on?" Fitzray called, opening the door to peak out into the hallway. Pete immediately let my shoulder free and stepped back.

"Nothing, everyone is just very tired from a long day."

I led him back inside his room to tuck him in again. After I assured him that there would be no more arguing, I went to the bedroom where Pete laid against a stack of pillows on the bed. He got up quickly and stared, waiting for me to say something.

"You still haven't apologized." I pointed to the large stitches on my neck.

"Neither have you." He pointed to the blue-black bruise on the left side of his face.

"Do you see what you have done?"

"Yeah, but why did you have to do that to me?"

"I had to do *that* because you did this to *me. You* apologize." I said still pointing to the stitches.

"Let me see what I can do."

He walked up to me, placed his fingers against the stitches and I felt them come apart, until there was a single piece of thread in his hands. He pressed his lips where the stitches had been.

"I am sorry," he whispered.

I felt the wound begin to reopen itself, no longer bound by the thread and I slipped away, shaking my head. I walked backwards out the bedroom door and down the stairs, through the sitting room, dining room, and kitchen where a dark corridor led to a wood door.

Pete was still following me, just as I hoped and I

opened the door, went down the brick stairs into the chilled darkness of the dungeon. Prisoners were once kept in the dungeon, in the past, but now there were none. I opened one of the heavy metal bar doors and stepped inside the chamber with a lit torch I found near the entrance. I waited for Pete to come and at last, he appeared and angrily stepped forth. He held me, his poison dripping painfully against the raw flesh on my neck. I slowly wrapped my arm around him, tilted the torch so his cape caught fire and he backed off to swat at it. I made my escape, closing over the heavy metal door as he ran for it and held the bars in his hands.

He held the metal bars tighter and growled as I began to walk away off to bed where I could finally sleep and rest my aching head. I started to walk up the stairs to the bedroom when I heard a knock at the palace door. Once opening the door, three figures stumbled in. Prusaious, Calvin, and an elder woman all looked at me, exhausted.

"We…we got away from the wolves," Calvin breathed.

"What happened to you guys?"

"Werewolves, there was a group of werewolves that attacked us, but we got away."

"Sit down, make yourself comfortable."

They took a seat and rubbed their eyes. I looked over to the elder woman. "Who are you?"

"My name is Verna. I was Luna Silver's mother." She placed her mask down on the coffee table.

"You are the woman who told me about Lucian on the bridge."

"Yes, I warned you about that and told you about the book."

"How did you know?"

"I can see the future just before it happens, that's how I knew."

"How is Pete doing?" Prusaious asked.

"He's well…acting pretty aggressive lately. So aggressive I had to lock him in the dungeon."

"Oh really?"

"Yeah, you know, it's all about blood and poison. I don't know why, but he's usually not as aggressive as he has been lately."

"Some Eternal Mates have the tendency to get especially aggressive before a lunar eclipse."

"Why is that?"

"The lunar eclipse has a very strong affect on a vampress and an Eternal Mate will guard her until it's over. Many have said the mood of their Eternal Mate is so aggressive that it is worse than any phase."

"What will it do to the vampress?"

"If a vampress sees the lunar eclipse, she could change, maybe come to hate her Eternal Mate completely."

"I never knew that could happen."

"That is why you must release him immediately. I don't know how close the eclipse is, no one knows, but if you don't let him out, your life could change as you know it."

I stayed where I was, hesitant to go back down into the dungeon.

"I will go and let him out if you want," Calvin offered.

"Ok, just be careful."

He stood, made his way to the dungeon, leaving us in the sitting room.

Verna's eyes grew wide and she let out a gasp. "The eclipse is coming…now, it's coming now!"

I felt something come over me, like a trance, and walked toward the door.

"Chenille!" Prusaious launched, tried to stop me, but I was already outside.

"Pete is coming!"

I continued to walk and as soon as I was out of the palace, I looked up and saw Minx standing before me, his great head blocking my view. I looked up at him dazed.

"Chenille!" There came the harsh shout from Pete who dragged me back into the palace.

"Did she see the eclipse?"

"I'm not sure. She was outside, but her dragon was blocking the way."

"Say something Chenille."

I stared blankly, still in a trance and at last closed my eyes.

"Help her onto the couch, quickly now."

"Everyone upstairs, let them be."

My name was said repeatedly, even when my eyes had opened. I shook with every bit of energy leaving me and still nothing happened. It was as if I was reincarnating, as if a part of me had died.

"You saw the eclipse…and I couldn't stop you."

"She didn't see the eclipse, stupid vampire."

He looked over his shoulder to see a swan made of glass.

"What did you say?"

"She didn't see the eclipse, fool!"

"How do you know?"

"I was standing right there!"

"Is she going to be all right?"

The swan swayed her head from side to side as though unsure of what to say. "I don't know. I am not a healer. Besides, I just came here to drop off a dragon."

"What should I do?"

"You're the King of Catastrophe. What are you asking a star for?" She blinked her beady black eyes.

"If you aren't going to help me, leave."

"I have to go somewhere anyway."

"Oh? Where?"

"That isn't any of your business, but if you *must* know, I am going to Earth."

"What for?"

"There is a big party on Earth tonight. I can't be late."

"Fine, we don't need you here."

"Good." The swan turned up her golden beak and walked away swaggering.

He turned back to me, saw that I was gasping. I coughed and continued to gasp as Pete grabbed his knife from his belt and cut the tight cape from my neck. The cape was choking me. He cut it off, allowing air to pass and gather in my lungs again. His hands became bloody from the wound still dripping from the side of my neck. My eyes opened and I sat up in alarm. I saw the knife and the blood on his hands, and pushed myself against the couch to make the space between us larger.

"I...I can't trust you for two seconds," I said through gasps.

"Your cape was choking you and the wound on your neck-," he paused to touch my neck. I backed away, putting a hand to my wound to shield it from him.

"I...I can't. I can't trust you."

He looked at me and backed away calmly, putting his hands up in innocence. He opened his hand and let the knife drop onto the floor. My head was heavy, half-delusional and he whispered to me.

"How'd you like to go to a party? You could me my little doll tonight. Dress up in something pretty for me."

"A party? What about Fitzray?" I asked, now light headed.

"The night is still young. We'd make it home before he wakes up."

He pulled me to my feet, helped me climb the stairs that seemed like a mountain to me. My servants put an indigo dress on me with a feathered mask to hide me from the mortals. Before I knew it, Pete was holding me close and we were on Earth.

There were hundreds of people all talking to one another, some wearing masks, others without. I looked around, still dizzy, looked to the roof, a dome made of colored glass. For a moment, the room and its stature of mahogany and marble dazzled me. Several people approached us and began to talk, though I did not engage myself in conversation, too confused to say a thing. I saw her - the glass swan, Phantilla, again. I heard laughter coming from the people behind me, still talking to Pete and felt something dripping from the corner of my mouth. Still, I kept my eyes on the star.

There was a sound, a traumatic sound, and the sound of gunfire rang. The peoples' voices faded from my mind and I could only see one person, one not screaming or running toward the entrance like the others. Tetchra.

She held a sleek gun in her hands pointed at the star who continued to scream from her beak of gold. There was a crack branching from the center of her chest spreading until she burst into an eruption of glass. Pete was there. I did not even see him run. He just appeared behind Tetchra, holding her to his body with his arm, half-crushing her to death. He threw the gun to me and commanded me to shoot. I looked down at the weapon. I had never used one, nor would I ever have considered killing someone with it, nevertheless.

"Shoot her!" The command came again.

I held up the weapon and pointed it at her. The star had shattered, collapsed in, and became a black hole in the middle of the building, sucking everything in its path to never escape, not even light.

I hesitated, fingering the trigger and lowered my arm. I could feel Pete's icy glare, but he lowered his head. He understood. Once he looked up, the black hole was near and he tossed Tetchra aside into the darkness, where she belonged, where she could never escape. Startled, my finger pressed down, like a reflex, and the bullet shot up to the glass roof. It too shattered and fell as if Phantilla herself was falling over the innocent.

I let out a gasp, heard the sound of laughter again and the voices returned to me. There was poison over my lips and I wiped it away in front of Pete and the people who had gathered to watch.

"Look at the way she yelped, like it was actually happening to her."

"Yes, it was amazing. I've never seen such a thing."

"What happened? What did you do to me Pete?"

He smiled a wicked smile, sly and wonderful. "Mind control. It worked, didn't it?"

"You tell me," I growled.

I could tell he was taken back, but would not show it in front of the spontaneous crowd.

"This is why you wanted to come? So I could be your puppet and you could show off your little trick?"

He gave me half a smile as though my question

was obvious and stupid.

"It's like I'm chained to you…I am your puppet. Well, you know what? I am cutting my strings. I am breaking free."

"How do you think you are going to do that? You need me to bring you back to Catastrophe."

"I don't *need* you. I'll walk home."

"Then go, I will stay here and *enjoy* myself."

I turned to him as the masked figures began to talk amongst themselves.

"I honestly regret performing the Ceremony with you." I needed to say it, just so I could hear the frightened gasps from the others.

The masked figures were silent and Pete turned away from them to glower in my direction.

"How *dare* you say that to me?" He walked up to me, lowered his voice and the crowd nonchalantly backed away.

"It seems like your group is gone."

"You have one chance to take back what you said."

"Or what?"

"Or you will regret to have said that."

There was something bubbling up inside me and I wanted to strike him while I could, but something held me back.

"You just keep one thing in mind." He licked his lips. "I am the strongest in the world…strongest in the world," his voice faded and my thoughts were gone. Was it a dream again? Was it reality? I could not tell the difference if I wanted. "And I can *control* you."

No. It was mind control. I took a step away to let my head clear, but he held me in place.

He can make me do anything…anything to his advantage and I wouldn't know. I wouldn't even feel it. Being under his control would seem like a dream to me, but he is weak, vulnerable every time he does so.

He wrapped his cape around me still gasping, and in a flash, the voices were gone, and the people vanished. We were in the palace again. He crumbled, toppled over himself, and sat hunched on the wood floor beside the bed.

"Help me."

"You got yourself in this mess, you help yourself."

He stood up on shaky legs, held onto the bedpost and called after me as I made my way down the stairs. I broke into a jog, out into the dawn. The sun was just breaking the horizon now. I knew where I had to go. I needed to seek help and advice.

I ran through the empty City of Lights to the Frozen Waterfalls. Taj' had just slithered from the cave with Pearl to begin their normal routine. I stood at the water's edge and waited for them to come over to me.

"Look who's up early!"

"Yeah, I know. Listen, I have a favor to ask of you."

"Anything, my friend, you name it."

"I need you to watch Fitzray for me."

"Where are you going?"

"I'm going away from here. I need to get away from Pete. He'll have me killed by the end of the week."

"Where will you go?"

"I have heard that at the other pole of Catastrophe, the aristocrats reside. I could start a new life there, maybe even marry."

"Oh, Pete will have you killed all right," the snake mumbled. "If he caught you-," the snake began.

"No, he *won't* catch me. He is only my Eternal Mate. That does not mean I can't marry. That doesn't mean I can't have a life I choose. Not everyone loves their Eternal Mate, so there are exceptions."

"There aren't any exceptions with *him*."

"Yeah, if he found out, he'd-,"

"No, don't even go there. I just want to get away."

"And if you do decide to marry or just find a good guy, he'd find you and tear him to pieces."

"He wouldn't find me."

"Oh, he would."

"It would be wrong if you left. If you found someone, put his life in jeopardy, at the end of the day, the only one you'd have to blame is yourself."

"That *wouldn't* happen."

"It *would* Chenille! And when it does, don't expect us to help you."

Taj' shook his large head. "You are making a mistake, but I will let that be redeemed by you."

"I have already made my mistake."

"We will take your boy into our care for now, and when you come to your senses, we will be here."

I turned away. The plans I had for the night ran through my mind. When I stepped into the palace, the only noise came from the soft steps of my bare feet on the polished floor as I walked briskly up the stairs. My stomach twisted inside. Fright began to eat me from the inside out. My hands were twitching by the time I had to open the bedroom door. I could not even imagine all of the possibilities that could happen once I walked through that door. I could not imagine what would happen if he found out what I was planning.

The door opened a crack, just enough for me to poke my head in to see what was going on. Pete was on the bed. Not much had changed in being gone for nearly an hour. I sneaked into the room, acted as casual and calm as though I had never left, but I knew he was eyeing me with suspicion. I knew he had been *waiting*.

I was afraid to sit on the bed beside him, so I stood and waited for him to say something.

"You didn't help me."

"I know…I was a little angry, but I'm ok now."

"I knew you'd come running back, you always do."

I gave him a bit of a nervous smile.

"You must be tired."

I nodded slowly. "I am."

I leaned against the door and he watched me, my every move, until he grew tired and turned his back to me and fell asleep.

I could not take it. I could not wait until the night; I needed to leave as soon as possible. I got up quickly and left only with the clothes on my back. I could not make my disappearance seem planned. I would only leave with Versailles, the only evidence of a broken gate behind me. I would ride her bareback. This escape could not seem planned at all.

It would take me five days to reach the other pole since Versailles could get me there in record time. There was only one thing left to do. I grabbed a knife, my only weapon, and cut off a bit of my hair.

I walked with the unicorn quickly to the front of the palace. As we passed Minx, whom was sleeping, I quietly sent him my regards, placing my lock of hair beside him. He would know I was safe.

"Where are we going to go?"

The unicorn stopped, waiting for my reply as I gathered her mane in my hands.

"We will go to the North. That's where all of the wealthy reside."

"Like who?"

"Well, there are creatures of royalty there. There are princes, princesses and kings."

"But I thought you were the Queen."

"I am, but there are royals who exist on the other continents of Catastrophe. And between you and me, I am not going to be the Queen of Catastrophe anymore, well, at least not while we are visiting the North."

"Are you going to change your name?"

"I might have to."

"What will it be?"

"I don't know yet, I'll have to think of one."

*****

Chapter 40 - Alias

I sat at the end of a long table, isolated from the coming travelers who stumbled into the restaurant. The wealthy-looking came to sit at the table where I was, and I buried my nose into the menu, looked at the expensive meals, trying to blend in.

The group of people began to talk noisily around me as though I was the seat cushion on the chair I sat on. I looked up to the man that was now speaking, his voice rich with the heavy accent only heard in the northern parts of Catastrophe. He was dressed well in a uniform suit, showing a high rank, maybe a general. A boy about his age, young, maybe in his early twenties sat beside him. I could only assume this was his brother due to the similar, handsome features they both shared. I listened to him as he spoke to the girl beside him.

"Wouldn't you like to go see a play," he asked her.

"Oh I have seen dozens of plays. To see another, I would simply find it unbearable to sit through."

"You know there are others that aren't as wealthy as you and would love to see a play. Wouldn't you miss?"

I looked up, unsure if he was even referring to me. Surprised that he was, I flushed.

"What's your name Miss?"

"Me?" I asked, still unsure if he was talking to me. He nodded his head.

"I'm Annabel Richards," I said quietly.

"Would you like to go to a play?"

"Well, yes. That sounds nice. I would love to."

The man smiled at the girl beside him and looked at me. "I am William. This is my brother Sebastian. And this is Catherine."

He gazed over Catherine. I gave them a smile and just as I turned to see a platter rich with meat and bread, my stomach gave me a sickly launch. I felt sick to my stomach for no apparent reason. Even sipping at the edge of my glass of icy water intimidated me.

"Are you all right?" William asked quietly, his voice low and calm.

"No. I don't know what has come of me."

I stood up, feeling sick. William stood up, put an arm around my neck and held my waist. How tiny it looked against his hands that held me upright.

"Let's get you some fresh air." He peered back to the table. "It wouldn't be a problem if Sebastian took you, would it Miss Annabel?"

"No, I don't think that would be a problem."

Sebastian stood up quickly, took his brother's place and began to walk me out. Once I caught my breath and my stomach settled, I looked up at him and moved away.

"I never knew how different people are in the North."

"It's very different here. Are you visiting?"

"Yes. I do not have a place to stay. Where is the nearest hotel?"

"Not far, maybe a couple blocks down." He paused. "If you are feeling better, maybe you'd like to go to that play."

"I thought your brother was joking."

"No, he meant it. You want to go?"

"No promises, I don't know how my stomach will handle it," I joked, feeling uneasy under the pressure of the gaze from the aristocrat.

My stomach twisted and I looked over to my unicorn. She was occupied eating some hay, but once she sensed my pain, she came over.

"I think I should go before I cause you any trouble."

"You're not going to ride feeling like *that* are you?"

"I'll manage." I mounted upon the unicorn's back, holding a fist under my ribs.

"But wouldn't you prefer-," he began.

"It was nice to meet you. Please give my regards to the others." And before he could utter another word, Versailles ran off.

I went straight to the hotel to rest for the night. I

walked in quickly, boarded Versailles in one of the public stalls nearby and waited at the front desk. The receptionist was fumbling with the room keys, clearly distressed while dozens of people waited on line. I was feeling even worse, so I held my breath and wheeled around, spotting William, Sebastian, and Catherine also waiting there. I hoped that they would not notice me. It was just a coincidence.

I was next, grabbed my key and was off before they noticed me. Walking down the hallway, I knew I was almost out of the woods but no, not just yet. I made a run for it, not expecting to see a woman turning a corner with a cart piled with white sheets and towels. I made it out of the way, but it was long enough that they could have seen my face. I did not even turn back to the exasperated maid who simply uttered a loud, obnoxious sigh as I passed.

Once I made it safely to my room, I sighed with relief and put my back to the door. I made it. I gave myself a rest before I entered and turned my head to eye the door beside me. Sebastian stood there, leaning casually against the door, pretending to figure out how to unlock it. He caught my glimpse, held his breath. He was good.

"Annabel?" He said it uncertainly. He did not know it was me so I still had a chance. He mumbled my name again, confirming it was me, probably since I had not moved and just stood arched over to protect my painful stomach.

"You're hurt, you must be." He walked over, which was only a couple of steps from where I sat.

"No, no I'm not. I'm just sick."

"You should rest then."

"I was just about to but…but-,"

"But what?"

"I just…I can't…I feel so," my voice drifted off as my back slid against the door.

"Give me the key, I'll help you inside." He picked up the keys that I had placed beside me.

"I don't need your help."

"You don't?"

"No, just leave me alone."

"All right, if that's what you want."

He walked slowly to his door, checked back at me slyly to see if I had changed my mind, opened his door very slowly, and I called to him for help. Of course he still had my keys anyway. He helped me inside and sat on the edge of the bed, making himself feel welcome.

"Are you a vampire?"

"What makes you think that?"

"A lot of things…especially since vampires can get strange ailments."

"Oh are you a doctor now?"

"No, but do you need blood? Is that it?" He asked rather quickly, hope in his voice.

"Why are you so interested in that?"

"I'm curious. You don't find many vampires here in the North."

"Ok." I sighed, making myself comfortable against the pillows.

"Do you need blood?"

"Are you offering?"

He was quiet and nodded his head after a long while. "Why? I couldn't possibly do that to a common traveler. What kind of a person would I be? That would be cruel of me. No one deserves to get bit by one of us. Not unless you…wanted to be. Not unless…you wanted to be a vampire." A glint appeared in his eyes. "But even if I wanted, I couldn't turn you into one. I am a vampress. You need a vampire for that kind of thing."

"I am just offering then, just to you."

"I couldn't possibly."

"Would it make you feel better?"

"I don't think so and I don't want you to find out."

"*I* do."

"I can't help you then."

He smiled, got as close as he could to me without making me feel self-conscious.

"Are you a mortal?"

"No, I'm an immortal, but more than ever…more than ever," he edged himself a bit closer, "I want to be a vampire."

"No you don't. You really don't."

He rubbed his hands against his neck, emphasizing its length and smooth texture. He rubbed even harder so the blue-purple veins stood out against the red surface.

"Leave," I snapped, "I'm not going to hurt you…that's all I would be doing. If you want to be a vampire, go find another. All I would do is cause you pain." I wished he would leave now that he barged in as if he knew me. It was too much.

He paused from harshly rubbing his skin. "You're in denial."

"Leave," I said again.

"You are fighting your instinct."

I put up my hands to stop him from getting any closer. "I normally wouldn't but I don't know what's causing me to feel sick like this. If it is a bad disease or something, you would get it." I said, hoping he would forget the whole idea. He moved away a fraction of an inch. "But I'll make you a deal then."

"What?"

"Once I get better, and I mean fully recovered from this illness, then I won't fight you, deal?" I lied.

"Fine, you promise?"

"Yeah, but I'll let you say if you want to call it off."

"So what do you need now?"

"I need to rest. Leave me to sleep."

He stood up, made sure I didn't need anything, and once I knew he was gone I sat back on the bed to think. Gone at last. I knew I couldn't do what I had promised, I just needed to make sure it didn't happen, even if that meant staying sick for my whole visit. Still, I needed a plan. I sat up, eyes closed, thinking of a plan, one that would keep me from going out of my mind, and to keep him safe. I wondered if I should leave the hotel altogether, but I knew this was a safe place and to leave really wouldn't do me any good. There was also the rain, now pounding hard against the windows. I heard the door reopen and Sebastian ran over to sit back on the bed.

Startled, I jumped, my reflex of Pete always coming into the room and surprising me with some poison or an ambush. I bit him, not deep, just a mere scratch, but that was all he needed, accident or not.

"Look at what you made me do!"

"That doesn't bother me." A smile crossed the immortal's face. I knew he had planned this.

"Get out of here before my…instinct kicks in." A bit of blood dropped onto my lips, and I knew it was too late for him. He didn't say anything for a long ten minutes, but simply let sighed, stretching out his hand like a tease, waiting, trying to lure me into a trap like a mouse.

"You are such a fool," I said. He grabbed my hand and held it to the scratch, just waiting for me to crack.

"Let me go!"

"I'm trying to help you!"

"No you're not!"

I could hear the pounding of his heart. He was an immortal with a heart that would always beat, a near impossible occurrence, but I knew of the wonders it could do for any vampire. It almost mesmerized me in a calming hypnotic tone and I couldn't help but sit back and feel myself become calm.

"I am not bad," he whispered waving his bloodied hand before my eyes.

There was a distant slam. A door opened and then the sound came again, closer.

"What was that?" I sat up. It was Pete, I was almost positive. I turned back to Sebastian, recalling there were few vampires in the North. If Pete saw him like this, it would be a clear sign that I was a vampire. Quickly, I tore a piece of silk from my dress and wrapped it around his hand, covering the blood that would tempt me no longer.

"What are you doing?"

The door slammed open from across the hall and I cowered beside Sebastian.

"What's wrong?" He put a hand to my shoulder and moved closer.

The door flew open, nearly off its hinges and Pete

stood in the doorway, his face full of rage. He inhaled deeply and took a step forward while waving a candle around. Sebastian stood up and walked over to Pete with his hand to his side.

"Get out of here!"

Pete acted as though he didn't say anything. "I know you're here Chenille," he whispered, "I know you're here."

"You've picked the wrong room. There is no one here named Chenille. Now go."

"I know she's here."

"She *isn't here*."

The vampire turned away and walked out of the room. By the time Sebastian returned to me, I was feeling deathly ill, worse than before.

"He's gone, don't worry."

He took his place beside me and put the bandaged hand to my forehead. "You have a fever."

I held onto his hand, pulled it away from my head and turned my back to him.

"Look at what you've done. You made it worse!"

"I can get you better. I know at William's palace, there are some of the best healers. I'll take you there."

He began to pick me up, even though I started to yell and wiggle free from his grasp. "I don't want to see healers! They can't help me! They don't know what's wrong!"

"Hey, don't say that. *You* don't know what's wrong."

"Let me go!"

"No, I'm going to help you."

"No." The pulse filled my ears again like a song, like a spell, and I couldn't fight it.

He ran out into the rain, put me into a buggy and held me, letting the rapid pulse do its job to keep me in a calm state, making me not realize what was happening for a while until we arrived at the palace. He took me inside, half-delirious, to the healers. The three of them crowded around me, took my temperature and put some ice on my head.

"Look at these bruises," one of them remarked, gently touching my arm.

"I tripped and fell," I mumbled.

"She said her stomach hurt."

"It could be a virus."

One of the healers led Sebastian away to talk to him while the healers tended to me. I would be calm for only a short while if he was gone, the rhythmic beating of his pulse subsiding as he moved away.

"You will be fine Annabel," he said once he returned.

"What's wrong with me?"

"Well…you could have a virus, or a disease, but they're not sure."

"That's it?"

"Well, there is one more thing."

"What? Tell me, what's wrong with me?"

"It's just a possibility," he said quickly.

I waited for him to give me further information.

"Are you going to tell me or not?"

"I can negotiate."

"Don't tell me you want me to bite you." He didn't say anything. "Tell the healers to leave."

"They're already gone."

I gestured for him to come closer and began to take the strand of silk from his hand. Once I pressed my lips to his wound, he began to speak even though I would not dare let myself go any further.

"They think it's either a cold or virus-," he began.

"Get on with it."

"And they think…possibly…that you are pregnant."

"What?"

"I said-,"

"No, I know what you said. That is impossible." I sprung to my feet, tossed the bag of ice from my head as if I had never been sick.

"They said that's what they assume."

I backed away, mumbled to myself. "I have to go," I said quietly, finally finding an excuse to leave.

"No, no you can't."

"Nowhere is safe for me now."
"You…you can stay here or-,"
"No, you don't understand." I knew Pete would find me now. It would be easy to find me if what the healers suspected was true, even though I was sure it was not. Regardless, I could use that to my advantage. I could get away from this immortal.

I turned away, walked briskly to the front door. He followed but stopped short once I opened the door. Pete stood there, his eyes black, filled with rage. The smell of his poison knocked me out cold.

I couldn't even tell where I was when I woke. "Where am I?"
"Don't even recognize your own home?" He spoke darkly as if he was a different person.

I looked around, looked out a nearby window. "No."
"Remember my old planet?"
"No! You took me back here! How could you?"
"I am tired of having to hunt you down. At least now I can keep an eye on you," he hissed.

He inhaled a breath of air and looked at me sternly. He paced slowly, then stopped, and just stood where he was.
"Do you think I'm stupid? Do you honestly think I wouldn't find you?"
"No." I sobbed.
"Why did you run away?"
"I just couldn't take your belligerence."
"What am I going to do with you?" He lifted me up, pressed me close to his body. "I am sorry."
"Put me down."
"Didn't you hear what I said?" He asked, an edge in his tone.
"What you say means nothing now. It's too late for apologies."
"How can I make it up to you?"
"You can't."
"There has to be something."

"No, nothing will change my mind. I don't want anything to do with you."

He started to laugh. "I'm sure you don't."

"Just take me back to Catastrophe."

"We are already on Catastrophe."

"I thought you said-,"

"I lied. That's what I do."

"Then just leave me be."

"I can't, not after you pulled that little escape of yours. You're going to be stuck with me until I figure out what to do with you."

"You must be angry."

"Yes, but that's nothing that can't be handled."

"What do you mean?"

"I have my ways," he purred.

"Put me down."

"Why? So you can run away again?" He put me down gently and I backed away slowly. My eyes began to fill up again.

"I do regret performing the Ceremony with you." I spat, watching as he tensed at my words. Even though a Ceremony had never transpired between us, I knew he wished it would have.

"I didn't want to hear that from you once and now you say it *again*?"

"It was the *biggest* mistake I ever made," I continued.

"If you value being in the shape you're in now, don't say another word."

"And I do hate you. Nothing can change my mind about that."

"Hold your tongue," he said a bit louder.

"And one more thing-,"

"I swear if you say another word-,"

"Pete I-,"

"If I *ever* find out that you go back to the North without me and see that immortal again I will make you regret ever meeting me. Do I make myself clear?"

I looked down at the floor. My chest became heavy with fear.

"Did you hear me?"
"Yes…I…I promise."
"Come here. Don't be so afraid."

I looked up, but did not dare move from where I was.

"Fine, have it your way. I'll be right back," he grumbled.

He turned, left the room where I was. The space around me turned black and before I knew it, I was outside. Versailles stood proudly before me. Confused, I simply stared and then noticed a long piece of silk tied in her mane. I slipped it from her mane quickly and found there was a piece of paper attached to it. I looked around, only allowing the unicorn's inquisitive glance to settle on the paper once I unraveled it.

Dear Annabel,

Please come to my brother's palace this weekend. There is going to be a ball and I would like it if you could attend.

-Sebastian

I crumbled the note in my hands, held it like that for a moment, and then unraveled it with a smile, hardly considering how he got the note to me. Regardless, I knew there would be no harm in going to a ball. I heard footsteps and quickly held the crumpled paper in my hand behind my back nervously.

"Would you like me to take your horse back down to the barn?"

My gaze rested over the stable girl. "Yes, thank you."

I walked back into the palace to sit on one of the couches in the sitting room. Sinking into comfort, I sighed and hoped I would not be bothered for the rest of the afternoon.

"There you are."

Agitated, I lodged the piece of paper under one of the cushions and closed my eyes as though I had been taking a nap. I heard a soft laugh and I clutched my wrist, afraid he had suspected I was faking. I could feel a ghostly presence sitting before me, suspecting there was a steady fixed stare looking over me.

"Chenille, are you asleep?"

After silence enveloped the room, he picked me up and set me down on the old, large leather chair in front of the fireplace. I could tell he was tense, focused in some other direction, probably near the couch. That wretched piece of paper was most likely showing itself just a bit from the cushion and I knew against the black color of the couch, even the slightest speck of white would be evident.

"Oh Chenille look at the fool I have become." He whispered, almost to himself.

I opened my eyes to slits, enough to see him. He was watching the flames in the fireplace. He watched them dance and pop and he continued, unafraid of their power. He simply listened to the fire's story of cracking and popping and then looked back down at me. I looked at him for a second, pretended I had just woken up and scurried down to the floor, moving up near the fire to put my back to him.

"You still don't forgive me."

"There is no need to. If not now then some other time you will be *demanding* that I accept an apology from you," I grumbled.

He slid beside me, swift as a snake to put a hand to my head and hold it in place against his chest for several long minutes. I could tell he was wiping away some poison that fell on my shoulder. It had burned a small hole through my shirt, but he wiped it away before it could do any harm.

"Your neck looks so scarred…so scarred to me."

As he looked closer to examine my neck, I felt him pull his head away, suddenly becoming stiff.

"I don't like the smell of that immortal." His gaze shifted to the couch. "He has imprinted fear…such a fear I can tell you feel it in your bones…because of *me*. He fears me too, but you fear me even more *now*."

I did not say anything. I was too busy holding my breath. His fingers curved around my shoulders and at once, I felt him relax, his thumbs kneading into my shoulder blades. I remained quiet, enjoying his calm state of mind for once. I knew even the slightest hint of my discomfort would start up something with him. He inhaled deeply. The fire became intensely hot and uncomfortable. I shifted uneasily and sat up straighter.

"I am going to-,"

"You are staying *here*." He interrupted, holding my shoulders tightly. I did not want to get him angry again and slumped back down, feeling him slowly creep closer toward my neck.

"Hello Mistress." It was Minx. I smiled relieved.

"I have been looking for you." I lied.

"Yes…there was something I have been meaning to tell you."

"What is it Minx?" His face was turning solemn.

"Citrus and Mullein have flown away without a say of where they were going."

"You know the dragons are able to fly freely to and from the palace."

"Yes but they flew away several days ago. They still haven't returned."

"There is nothing we can do." Pete grumbled, tracing his fingers against my neck.

"But that's not all. Prusaious heard…she said she heard from a couple of wolves that two dragons were captured and further sold to the leader of the werewolves."

"My father. I should have known."

"I will get them back." Pete offered.

"You?"

"Mullein is my best dragon. I'm not going to lose him to those damn-," he started.

"Ok, don't get yourself all worked up. I am sure you of all people could get them back. When will you leave?" I tried to make my voice not sound desperate.

"Tonight," he said. "So I'll be back in a couple of days."

"You can take Minx if you want."

"Maybe I will. Now, go upstairs will you? I have to talk to him privately."

I got up and walked out of the room as he told me. This would be perfect. He would go for a few days to get the dragons back and I would get to go to the ball without him knowing. He would not suspect a thing.

I made my way into the kitchen, put on a pot of tea for myself as a little inside celebration that he was leaving. I tried my best to conceal my happiness of him leaving, but it would be difficult. I was already feeling a thrill. There was a low voice in my ear and I turned. He was there, unmoved. Now almost positive I knew he could feel what I was feeling, I shrunk back into fear again.

"I am leaving now."

"Now?" There was a tremble in my voice.

"Yes, right now. I will return in a few days." He drew himself close and lowered his voice so only I could hear.

"You remember what I told you. If I find out you go up to the North again I swear I'll-,"

"Pete, I am not going to the North-,"

"I'll kill you," he finished.

His face stayed in its stern shape for only a few seconds and his jaw then softened. He kissed me, began to wrap his cape around me, but backed away hastily as if it had occurred to him that I was not going with him. He reached from around his neck and took off the heavy chain he always wore. He held it in his hands, wrapped it around his fingers and then clipped it around my neck. It was cold. It probably always was without a chance of ever getting warm.

"Now I will know what you are feeling while I am gone. And now I will know if I have to come back early for any reason." He smiled, his fangs showing slightly. "Goodbye."

I swallowed hard, feeling my plan had just slipped down the drain. I swear he knew it too. I tended to the tea now, almost feeling that deep inside he was laughing for his own enjoyment. I never quite knew how clever and manipulative he really was, but I knew now, I would *always* know now.

"Goodbye." I looked up. He was not there. I was alone at last. I felt the loneliness settle in quickly, but not the way I had wanted a few minutes ago.

Chapter 41 - Preparations

That night I spent alone was long and loathsome. I still felt apprehension from longing to go to the ball. No chain would bind my own free will, not even *his*. I tried to take it off, but there was no clasp. I only caught my fingers in the links, helplessly. I knew I shouldn't have been so paranoid about it, but I couldn't help but wonder if it was only a piece of metal to hang there only for my subconscious to scare me. After all, he could have been *lying*.

I forgot about it the next day and met up with Prusaious to tell her all about the ball. She told me I was crazy and I should obey Pete's wishes if I did not want to get hurt. I only laughed, being as stubborn as I was, and scoffed. He did not mean what he said. He would not have been that serious. She agreed about the chain though, only there to haunt me and make me as timid as a feral cat. I told her how tired I was and how weak I felt for reasons unknown. I told her how I wanted so desperately to break free from Pete's rule and I was sick and tired of being his puppet. She did not respond to what I had told her. She did not know what to say, so she brought my attention back to the ball and began to point out dresses that appeared in every window we passed. I had not considered what I would wear.

"What kind of ball is it?"

"I'm not sure. The note didn't say."

"Should you wear a mask then?"

"If it was that kind of ball, I'm sure there would have been an indication to bring one."

"Then what are you going to wear?"

I thought back to my closet, to things I had not worn in months, to brand new things I recently bought. I thought of the red dress in the back of the closet, the way it almost glittered in the right light and the way the colored ostrich feathers trimmed the very bottom of the skirt. However, it came with a matching mask and looked incomplete without it.

"I have no idea." I sighed and pulled at the chain around my neck that was growing so irritably cold and chafing my skin.

"Maybe you should wear *that*."

She pointed to a window where a marvelous gold dress trimmed with white fur at its sleeves and neck was displayed. It came with a matching shawl of white fox fur. Altogether, it was too pretty for someone to stage it on a plastic doll, but more of a person should have been wearing it, to compliment its beauty.

"Put that on and you'll outshine all of those snobby rich immortals."

"I don't know. It seems too flashy."

"No, that's perfect. Come on, let's see how it fits."

She pulled me inside to see the storekeeper.

"I want to see a dress, the gold dress with the fur in the window."

The shopkeeper glanced up to Prusaious with a raise of her eyebrows.

"For you," she inquired, her voice carrying a heavy accent.

"No, for my friend." She elbowed me.

"No one has even come in to look at it. You want it?"

"I don't know. I want to try it on though."

"It is a very expensive dress. Very pretty dress." She said.

"I do like it."

"You can go into the room over there." She made a gesture to the back of the store. "I will give you the dress to wear and you come out when you're finished."

I nodded, taking the dress into the other room. While I put it on, I listened to Prusaious and the shopkeeper talk.

"The dress is made of silk. The fur is real. I have been trying to sell it, but I have no luck. It is a beautiful dress. Would your friend buy it?"

"I don't know. She is going to a ball to meet someone."

"Then the dress is perfect!"

I came out of the small room, surprised the dress fit me so well.

"You like it?"

"I do, it is very beautiful."

"You will take it then?"

I could tell by the look in the woman's eyes that she was so willing to sell the dress. I knew how expensive it was and so did she. She was waiting for someone rich to stumble into the store and buy it. Why, it seemed as though she was poor and waited to get such a sum of money just to feed her family.

"You will take it?"

I looked at my reflection and turned around, examining it thoroughly. I still wasn't so convinced, even for the price she was selling it for, but I knew the chain was sticking out violently against the soft fur. I couldn't help but let my eyes gravitate to that one spot, like the dress itself meant nothing.

"Does the shawl come with it?"

"No, it is sold separately."

Yes, this woman needed the money that came out of this dress. I tucked the chain behind the fur and looked it over again. I knew somehow if I could get the chain off and it wouldn't be a bother anymore, then I could really appreciate the dress.

"You will take it?"

I hesitated, looked it over one last time.

"Yes I will."

I watched the woman's eyes light up in astonishment. "It suits you well."

"I suppose," I mumbled rushing off to the dressing room to take off the dress.

I paid it in full and watched as the woman's hands holding the gold coins shook with disbelief. Her eyes showed total gratitude, for she could not even utter another word. Prusaious couldn't help but smile. She helped me carry the heavy bag all the way back to the palace and waited for me to try it on again, just to see it again, but I sat up against the staircase, pulling furiously at the chain. I couldn't take it any longer. She turned into her wolf form to use her nails and sharp wolf teeth to aid me in taking it off. She pulled and choked me nearly half a dozen times without a slice. Only *he* could get it off.

"It won't come off."

"It will. Give it time." She hooked her claws into the links stepped back and I resisted the pull. It still wouldn't budge.

I shuddered, feeling its chill as though Pete himself was giving me an icy glare or laughing with pleasure at my failure.

I huddled before the roaring fire, with Prusaious now curled beside me. The heat caught onto the chain and it grew hot, so hot my skin suffered a burn. The chain was malleable now though and we could finally manipulate it. Prusaious pulled one last time; it broke and she turned to throw it into the flames.

"What will you wear around your neck now?"

I shrugged. "I'm sure there is something nice that will go with it. I might not even have to wear anything though."

"So why are you going to this ball?"

"There is this immortal that's going to be there. His name is Sebastian."

The wolf backed up cautiously. "I know who he is. He's trouble. You stay away from him. You stay away from the Prince of Light."

Chapter 42 - Prince of Light

"Sebastian, you stay away from him. He's nothing but trouble."

"Why? What's wrong with him?"

Prusaious began to pace and eyed me suspiciously. "You bit him, didn't you?"

I held my breath, felt a sweat form over my body.

"Well? Did you?"

"No…I…I almost did. Is that bad?"

"Is that *bad*? Have you noticed how weak you are? That's why! He might have had you drink his horrible…weakening blood."

"How is it weakening?"

"He is the Prince of Light. His blood is all but good and he would let any vampire bite him to feel his own power rise. He only wants you for your fangs, Chenille. Don't trust him. You saw what he could do."

"I don't understand."

"He only wants you so he can feel stronger."

"He's not all bad."

"You don't know him. I have heard wild, ludicrous stories about him, passed on from wolf to wolf. He's bad news and everyone in the North knows it. He is evil. He only lusts power. His brother is different…not evil…but he doesn't do what Sebastian does. He's not as bad."

"So what do you suggest I do?"

"You stay away from him. You don't dare come in contact with him. He wants you there just so he can feel powerful, but if you stay out of sight, he won't bother you. You should just forget the ball and not go, for your own safety."

"I'm going. I *need* to go. If I don't, I'll go crazy. Pete doesn't let me have any fun. The least I need is some pure fun and this is it. I am going, and not even you can stop me."

"You're right, I'm not. You can go, just be aware."

"Oh I am now. Some *Prince of Light* is going to pull my strength away? Trust me, I felt bad before I even met him."

"I doubt that."

"What kind of stories have you heard? What have the wolf to wolf stories told you about him?"

"He looks for vampresses and when he finds one, he'll pretend he's your best friend."

"And how do you know those stories aren't false?"

"I know. I have *seen* it."

I looked at her curiously. "What have you seen?"

"I've seen a vampress and I've seen him."

"Where?"

"At a hotel."

I tilted my head trying not to assume anything. "When?"

"Not long ago."

"So you're saying you saw a vampress at a hotel with Sebastian not long ago…in the North."

She did not speak, but lowered her head as if I was suspecting something.

"What did he call this vampress? Did she have a name?"

The wolf licked her lips nervously. "Annabel was her name."

I could hardly believe my ears. She had been watching me.

"You were spying on me!"

"No…no, I didn't know it was you!"

"You did! And you followed me! Admit it!"

"It was for your protection! Who knows what could have happened to you!"

"I didn't *need protection*…that's why I left in the first place. I was sick of it!"

"You didn't know what you were getting yourself into…what you are *still* getting yourself into."

"Did you take it upon yourself to follow me? Or did someone else tell you?"

"Someone else." Her voice dropped.

"It was Pete, wasn't it? You were spying for him. You are working for him!"

She backed away to the door, braced herself to make a run for it.

"And now you're still working for him! You're going to tell him, aren't you? You're going to tell him about my trip to the North and the ball, aren't you? You're going to rat me out?"

She was clawing at the door, trying to escape, but her claws couldn't grip the doorknob.

"Do you know what you are if you leave? You'd be a traitor! A traitor!"

"That's what *you* are!" She yelled back.

"You know what they do to traitors. *You* know!"

The doorknob turned with a satisfying click and she turned, her hairs raised.

"Yes. They are killed."

She turned back to the door and bolted. I knew she could not be stopped. She would not stop for anyone until she met up with Pete and told him everything. I had a choice. I still had a choice. I was still free and I could still go. I could worry about Pete later and I could just go and see to my worst.

Chapter 43 - Evaluation

I could only take precautions regarding who I saw as my friend and who was not. The people I knew as my friends were slowly declining and those who still were became harder to hold onto. I hadn't spoken to Amelia in weeks and Pearl and Taj' were still watching my son is if he was their own to protect him from Pete. They had not told me how he was doing. I felt they had deserted me in a way ever since the war. Nothing was quite the same, as if they were slowly fading, becoming less and less noticeable.

In the sunroom, feeling the warmth of the sun, I could not help but reflect upon what had happened with Prusaious the other night. The ball was tomorrow and I had not decided whether to go or not. I stayed awake, unable to sleep, just staring at the bag that held the golden dress, the all-expensive dress that gave a woman some money so she could eat. I could feel it intimidating me, beckoning me to try it on. I could hear it in my mind, trying to persuade me to wear it to Sebastian's ball. But what did I know? I was on the edge lately, thinking at any moment Pete was going to burst through those doors, or worse, Sebastian bursting through the doors.

There was no one to talk to. It was too quiet. There was only Pete's snowy owl Meleve, but she could not be trusted. She might fly out the window and hoot some sort of signal, calling for him to come home. There was Versailles, good Versailles. She could be trusted.

I made my way down to the barn and called for her. At first there was no reply and then she came, the pony at her heels.

"Hello. How are you?"

"Fine. You look distressed."

"Thanks."

"What happened?"

"Prusaious found out about Sebastian and she's telling."

"Are you going to go to the ball?"
"I don't know yet. Do you think I should?"
"Don't take advice from me. I'm just a horse with a horn. If you want advice, go see the big black snake."
"That won't help. He'd probably tell me that's what I get for not listening to him."
"What are you going to do?"
"Nothing, at least not right now."
"Isn't the ball tomorrow?"
"It is."
"You can go and take a risk if you want. I'd be happy to accompany you."
"Then I'll have the stable hands groom you and we will go tomorrow."

As soon as I ordered the groom to tend to Versailles, I walked around the palace grounds lazily for a while. Incoming clouds covered the sun, the cold drizzle expecting to turn into snow. It was common to have months like this, long periods of cold weather just after a brief period of warm, sunny days. Frost was beginning to settle by the time I had gone back into the palace. It was already freezing outside.

I got out the golden dress and tried it on again. It sparkled and glittered and I imagined it would catch all of the snowflakes as I arrived with Versailles to see the Prince of Light - to *impress* the Prince of Light. It was strange how I had more of a liking to him after Prusaious told me about him, but I suppose I could not resist.

My outfit was complete and Versailles would be too by tonight. Everything was set. All I needed to do was to wait for the morning to come and I would be free. Hopefully by then, Pete wouldn't be waiting at my bedside or follow me all the way to the North. I doubted that would happen. Prusaious could not run that fast and with the ice, snow and head-on wind, it would take her until morning to get to him. There was also the matter of finding him and telling him where I was and where I would be going and what my intentions were. By then I would be at William's castle, safely concealed between the people that would be there. There was absolutely nothing to worry me.

As I reassured myself, I felt myself relax, my thoughts dwindle, and soon I was happy, actually happy. I let the thoughts of the oncoming day race through my mind without further worry. The metal chain was off. Pete could not feel what I was feeling anymore, so I would not be questioned at this very moment. I was safe in my own mind, and knowing this, I took off the dress and dressed into warm clothes. There was a blizzard outside and I had no intention of going out. I could do whatever I wanted for this moment of freedom and would not be ridiculed, judged, penalized or in fear if I turned a corner too sharply and bumped into a familiar, dangerous face. I could break the rules, go against all of them. This was the moment, perhaps the only moment that I had to myself.

I wandered around the palace, ran through the endless corridors and welcomed myself into the forbidden room - the one Pete didn't let me in without his consent, the library. How could I be trusted? I had taken his book from his library and let a secret escape from its pages. I wouldn't blame him, but that didn't stop me now.

I stepped into the dome shaped room, the constellations of the stars painted on the ceiling, giving one the impression of looking up to the sky itself at night. The bookshelves were high against the walls from one side of the entrance to the other. From wood floor to painted ceiling, the books were stacked endlessly, one on top of the other. There was a small table in the middle of the room set beside a large chair identical to the one downstairs in front of the fireplace. I took a seat on the chair, and could almost feel Pete's presence. On the table was his book, slightly burnt and torn, but none other different from how I had remembered it before Pete confiscated it from me.

A servant came into the room, cast a weary glance to me and began to dust the books that hadn't been read in a while.

"You aren't to be in here, King's orders."

"He is away," I replied calmly, "what could he do while he is away?"

"You'd be surprised."

She guided her feather duster over the spines of the books and paused briefly to see if I was intimidated. She looked at me, searching my face for any hint of dismay.

I spent nearly the whole afternoon in that library, reading book after book, and placing them precisely as though I had not touched them. If one page crumpled or a book was in the wrong spot, he would notice. He would probably blame me for being in there because there was less dust in the air. I could only straighten it up to what I saw as perfection. Once I left, it was long past six o' clock and I knew the chef was still in the kitchen. I could ask for a five-course meal of anything to my liking and feast throughout the night if I wanted. The kitchen never closed. I went there myself, ordered up anything that came to mind.

Waiting for my fine meal, I sat at the large table able to sit fifty or more people comfortably. Figuring it would be too lonesome to eat by myself at such a large table, I considered otherwise. I had something small, just a sandwich for dinner. Tomorrow night I would have a large meal so it was best to eat light.

The palace was dark, the lights shut off and a chill seeped through the stone and crevices in the windows. The moon was high, still shining over the snowy landscape like a giant piece of ice in the sky. It was still windy, the whistling of the trees swaying from side to side and the branches scraping against the windowpane all echoed from outside.

It was warm in my room, warm and desolate. The only light came from a small wax candle on my bedside table. It was just enough to read an old magazine I had brought from Earth years ago from when I arrived on Catastrophe. Surprisingly it still held its shape, its pages torn, the binding still holding it together. I could not recall why I had it at all. There was nothing so special about it, no lines or phrases or advertisements I liked, nothing. Perhaps I had grabbed it out of panic to have something to read in case there wasn't anything to read here. I recalled how I was such a bookworm, how I loved every kind of document, parchment, old or new, copied and pasted, or simply handwritten. I loved it all. Something had detached from me. I didn't like to read anymore. I wasn't myself anymore. Reality was slipping and I found myself in a fog. I couldn't decipher what was true anymore. Nothing was making any sense ever since I had lost Lucian to the lock and key. Nothing was the same.

Pushing my imprudent thoughts from my mind, I put the magazine down and sat back, simply allowed my mind to clear and go into a fog. My body was twitching, but I couldn't see it doing so. It was strange; words couldn't describe it. There was a tapping at the window, a constant tapping, but not of a branch, more like a clicking noise, like a cricket. Now I was hearing things. I began to wonder if I was asleep and lethargic, or if the cook had put something on my sandwich. Maybe I was allergic to something. Maybe it wasn't that at all. The room began to spin around and I had to close my eyes. I couldn't take it, I wanted to scream, but I couldn't, no I couldn't, it was impossible. My body shook, wracking my bones and my blood felt icy under my skin. No, I wasn't dreaming. Something was happening to me. Something horrible was happening to me.

There was something in my mind, a psychological monster or a fever, that I could not escape. It toyed with my emotions and I could feel it. Whatever this was had a hold of me, was hurting me from the inside out, and I could feel its presence somewhere in the room, somewhere around me, if not right beside me. No, I knew. I knew exactly what was going on. Prusaious had just stopped running. Pete knew everything.

Chapter 44 - Haunted

My head filled with colors as what one would find on a painter's pallet. Pete had appeared before me, looking down with a smile. Black circles lined just under his eyes, showing how tired he was, but other than that, he seemed calm.

"Hello Chenille." He gave me another warm smile as my hands clutched the bedspread. When I didn't answer, the smile faded. I was too afraid to speak.

"Are you mad at me?" His eyebrows raised, his face becoming even softer.

"N…no," I stammered.

"What's wrong then?"

He gave me a half-smile, but there were no large obscure fangs showing themselves beside his other teeth. I drew in a breath, placing a hand to his chest before he could say another word. I could detect a slight fluttering at the side of his neck. His heart was beating. It did not make sense. He was an immortal…and so was I. Wasn't I?

"Chenille?" He talked without a traceable edge in his voice I was used to hearing when he was mad. In fact he wasn't mad…he wasn't even immortal.

"I'm ok." I reassured him, looking the other way.

He sat up and leapt onto the floor. His head turned up to the moon in an odd way and looked back to me.

"I know what's wrong." He looked back through the window again at Earth's moon. Funny, it looked so close, closer than it ever appeared from Catastrophe.

"You are afraid."

I could tell he could sense it. He knew all along that I was afraid of what he would do to me.

"You are afraid of being in the dark…alone."

"What?"

"Yeah, you know, all of those rumors of *monsters*. You don't really believe all that stuff do you?"

"I do. Do you?"

He gave me a glance of uncertainty and then shrugged his shoulders. "I never met one of them so there is no proof, but I can't be sure. No one can be trusted, you know?"

"Yeah. I know."

Something strange was going on. I had this conversation before with him. I had it a long time ago before I was a vampire and before I knew he was one. He seemed like a mortal to me now. I felt like a mortal. It was as if I had this conversation not so long ago though. At most, it seemed like only a couple of weeks or a couple of days.

That was ridiculous. Surely, this conversation had happened already. It wasn't happening *now.* It was becoming so clear now, just like a flashback.

He gave me a smile. "You can't let your fears get the best of you. You have to move on and face them. Whether you want to or not, someone is going to make you face them."

"What are you suggesting? I go out into the darkness?"

"I can help you face your fears. Come with me."

He put out a hand and though my mind was telling my hand to remain on the covers, it lifted and I watched it grasp his as though I didn't have a say.

"Come on." He was leading me through my house, without light to guide us.

Beneath the stars there was nothing for me to allege other than he was taking me to the backyard where that old willow tree was. It was far away so screams couldn't be heard.

"Sit here for me." I did as he told me. The trunk of the willow tree was rough against my back.

"How are you going to help me get over my fears?"

"Oh, right." His voice faded. "Stay there for now."

"Where are you going?"

"I'm giving you a little test. If you pass, you know you can stand up against your fears."

"And if I don't?"

"You never know what will happen." He said darkly.

"So you're just going to leave me?"

"Just for a little while. And when I come back we can go back inside."

"You promise you'll come back?"

"I *always* come back. Don't I?"

"You do."

"What do have to worry about then?"

"Where are you going to go? You're just going to leave me here until dawn?"

"No, just a little while."

"Why can't you stay with me? Or at least watch me from a distance where I can see you?"

"That defeats the purpose, *doesn't it*?"

"No. You can't make me stay here."

Slowly he began to back up.

"You wouldn't leave me here," I protested.

"Then come to me if you decide to change your mind, but don't be too quick to decide."

He said no more and walked away toward the house, the way he had come. In the back of my mind, I knew he was not trying to help me. This had happened already. He was not going to come back.

As much as I wanted to get up, to follow him, it was not possible. I was obedient, obedient in the sense that I would stay until he returned, risking my own fear of what could be lurking then what I already *knew* what was lurking. I could not dare to anger him.

I found a comfortable place against the tree and just looked up at the moon until I felt tired. I should have gotten up and gone inside. I would be warm underneath the covers, warm and protected in my own safe little room. If I had never left, if only I never met him, I would probably be safe in my room. I'd rather be safe and alone than accompanied with fear, accompanied by *him*.

The occasional hoot of an owl that nested in the old willow was all I heard. The sound of his voice did not triumph with return and alleviate my fears. I didn't hear anything at all. My eyes felt unbearably heavy until I couldn't take it. I couldn't stay awake even if I wanted to. Even though I was perfectly fine a minute ago, I felt so tired, like I hadn't slept in weeks.

I watched his shadow, a black spot on the ground, now a distance away, getting smaller and smaller. The farther he went, the more tired I became. It was only until I couldn't see his shadow anymore, when a dark cloud had drifted lazily over the moon to block its light, and I was out cold.

My head swelled again with all of these thoughts. It was all my imagination, just my imagination.

Chapter 45 - The Ball

It was the day - the day of Sebastian's ball. I was ready. Versailles was with me. Her mane and tail streamed behind her, decorated with pastel colored ribbons. I walked inside the palace and waited patiently for Sebastian. It was not even that I looked forward to seeing him, I just found this as a special escape, a perfect excuse, and this would prove that I would not, under any circumstance, be told what to do.

People were flocking by the hundreds into the palace and still I saw no familiar faces. Once the space around the wealthy and me narrowed, there was silence, a call for everyone's attention, and a man appeared at the top of the staircase. He began to talk and at once, I found myself growing bored. The old man chanted on and on about something I could care less about, when suddenly the palace doors opened.

"Here comes my son and his wife," the man boasted.

My heart skipped a beat but then I sighed at the sight of William and Catherine. "And my other son." His voice dropped in disappointment, only to a harsh grumble of words that spelled regret on his forehead.

Sebastian walked in alone, which I found unsurprising. He was glancing over the crowd of people as he walked before us all, following behind his brother. He stood beside his father, silent and disrespected by him, moved his eyes, slowly scanning below as his brother gave out a grand speech. I was listening, but his words didn't sink in or make any sense. I was still watching Sebastian who now stood with a slight smile on his face. I looked around, following his glance to who he could be looking at, who he was smiling at. And then I smiled back - it was me.

How pathetic was I? *Running* from a maniac, I could clearly not outrun. I must be out of my mind to have come here. Although, this was not the first time I ran away. What would he do *this* time? Would Sebastian be going too far? I did not love him, but I needed to get away, to feel loved even by some immortal rather than a hated king. I *needed* this.

The people now departed, for William's speech had ended. Sebastian had disappeared from his place at the top of the stairs and rushed to meet me, but surprisingly, Catherine got to me first.

"Annabel, I am so glad you came. I was so disappointed when you had left in such a hurry the last time we spoke." She said in an Irish brogue.

"Yes I know. I had an emergency and I needed to return home."

"It sure was lucky that *Sebastian* got that letter to you." She rolled her eyes. "The poor boy's been mad trying to find out if you'd come or not. Lucky you did. He's been waiting for you."

My eyebrows narrowed. "Waiting for what?"

She gathered my hand in hers and gave it a gentle pat.

"I will explain, but first let's go to the dining hall. William must be looking for me."

I glanced back to see Sebastian standing alone and confused, still waiting for me.

"Come now Catherine, must you keep our guests waiting?" William chimed as we entered.

"My apologies."

"We may all enjoy our meal now. Everyone sit."

"You sit next to *me* Annabel." Catherine said quickly and patted the open seat beside her.

She shook her head, stared at Sebastian who sat down beside his brother. They made a toast, but I could see he wasn't speaking after that. He paid no regards to his father who sat at the head of the table, only a few seats away from him.

Catherine rolled her eyes to me, tossed her red curls over her shoulder. "As I was saying earlier," she began, "the boy's been going crazy since you left."

"I hardly know him, what could he be so crazed about?"

"Oh, no don't even joke about it!" Her face became filled with concern. "I have been woken by him yelling in his sleep, all the way from down the hall."

"What does that have to do with anything?"

"He calls for *you*, Annabel."

"What do you mean?"

"He has yelled words of regret, and lies. He said he had dreams of you coming back to poison him. He has told me he is *drawn* to you." She laughed quietly and lowered her voice. "So I went to listen to him speak in his sleep. I needed to know he was not losing his mind. I listened with the door open just enough for me to hear. Do you know what he said? He said he loves you Annabel. He said he loves Annabel, the vampire." She looked at me, swallowed hard, fear building in her eyes as she waited for a response.

"He is mistaken and so are you."

"It isn't true then?"

"Why, are you suspecting it *is*?"

"I...I don't know...vampires hardly ever come to the North...because many werewolves live here."

My jaw tightened, but I managed a smile. "I am not. Why would a vampire come here, to the North?"

"Yes...my apologies Annabel." She glanced down at her plate and to me again. "Please, if you will excuse me."

She got up and began to walk away. She looked back uneasily as though I told her I *was* a vampire. A waiter served me food and I could only look at it. The aroma made my head swell, but my appetite was not present.

"Annabel." I looked up all too quickly. "You came back."

I did not respond, but simply pretended I had not heard.

"You're not hungry?"

I shook my head.

"Still no appetite?" Sebastian gave a slight chuckle. "That's no surprise."

I held my fist beneath the table, angry at my own thoughts that flooded into my head.

"I didn't think you'd come."

"I wasn't going to."

He was quiet for several seconds only to catch sight of Catherine returning. "I'll see you later?"

He slipped a piece of paper into my hand casually and walked off.

"Did I miss anything?"

"No, nothing at all."

I fumbled with the small piece of paper and tried to read it while I distracted Catherine with casual conversation.

Meet me outside near the pool. Follow my scent.

I looked up at him and scowled at his words. The second course came around and a servant replaced my plate. Sebastian got up just as dessert ended and sauntered away. After a long time, as not to seem suspicious, I left as well. I did follow his scent outside and looked around in the darkness. I couldn't find him. A cold drizzle was beginning to fall as I turned my attention to the illuminated pool. There was light coming through a sliding glass door that led to a distant room in the palace. Sebastian was in the room with his mother and father. By the looks of it, I could see they were arguing. I could hear their shouts, even from behind the thick door.

"She isn't even a princess," I heard his mother say.

"You can't marry her." His father concluded.

Sebastian angrily protested and turned, followed his parent's glare to see me standing in front of the glass door. He rushed forward and I ran as fast as I could, overwhelmed by everything. He wanted to *marry* me. No wonder he was talking in his sleep. This was too much. He *loved* me? I didn't understand. We barely knew each other.

The cold drizzle continued to fall. I ran quickly around the perimeter of the pool, but I could feel his presence behind me and stopped. He wrapped his arms around me from behind. My throat was tight as I cried with agony.

"It's going to be ok," he said.

He didn't get it. He thought I was just disappointed I could not marry him and that I loved him, but this was not the case. I would have to run away somewhere else now. I would have to run or be caught by the Eternal Mate I hated and suffer for what I had done.

"No, no it's not."

"I can fix this."

"You aren't good enough for her."

I didn't look up since I wasn't surprised. I knew it was *him*.

"Come here Chenille."

"Chenille? I thought your name was Annabel."

Pete laughed. "Yes, come along *Annabel*."

"She is staying here. I am going to marry her."

"No you are not. She is happy with me, isn't that right?" There was a long pause. "Isn't that right," he repeated.

"It seems she isn't so happy after all."

"What do you know? She is just confused as usual." He put out a hand to me. "Now come, you know you are making the wrong choice."

I could tell he was about to launch out in full attack if I didn't come and so did Sebastian. He loosened his grip easily, not wanting to fight. I felt him grab my wrist and gave it a tug to let my own judgment decide to go with simplicity or by force. I didn't move, feeling safe in the immortal's care.

"Who is it going to be?" It was a trick question.

I could feel Sebastian pulling me back now, wanting to fight. "Vampire," he breathed.

I knew what he was thinking and I held my breath. If they fought and he got hurt, his power would rise, just as Prusaious warned.

"Don't even waste your time with me." Pete growled.

I was sure Sebastian was smiling behind me. He wanted to mess with him so bad. He wanted Pete to bite him.

I slipped away from Sebastian and stood quietly where I felt the outstretched hand grab me and prevent me from escaping.

"I'm sorry Sebastian. He would destroy you…and I couldn't let that happen."

"He can't destroy me. He's not more powerful than me." He tried to egg him on, but Pete simply did not care. He had what he wanted. There was no longer a reason to fight, not that Pete would waste his time anyway.

I felt his arm wrap around me, locking my own decision into place. "You don't know what you have cost me…my own dragon for this nonsense? No, I won't have this anymore." He looked up as if he said the same to Sebastian.

"I have a surprise for you Chenille, a surprise I have promised. You remember it, don't you?" He said it close to my ear as though embedding the words into my head.

"Don't open your eyes until I say."

The noise around me began to fade, even Sebastian's plea, and one noise more horrible than the last began to fill my mind. I opened my eyes without warning. My family was there, every single member. "You can open your eyes."

They had all taken their wolf shape, the fur on their backs all raised like a bunch of rabid animals. My father stood on his hind legs.

"I like your Eternal Mate. We think alike."

"How is that?" My voice trembled with defeat as my eyes turned up to look at Pete's face.

"We see you as a traitor in our eyes. We see you as a disappointment to our species."

"You are all insane!"

"Oh is it us? Are *we* the insane ones?"

I looked up at Pete long and hard, my lips pressed together angrily. "How long have you been working with them?"

"Only for a little while."

"You liar! Traitor!"

"You regret meeting me now?"

"I've regretted it from the start."

"Surprise, surprise." He held something to my chest, though I didn't dare look down. I already knew what it was. He wasn't kidding, at least, I was sure he wasn't.

Creatures began to gather around. Taj', Pearl,

Prusaious, and Calvin were the only few I could spot out, but I knew there were more there I would probably recognize. They all stood behind the barrier of werewolves, awaiting the *fall of the Queen*.

"Goodbye Chenille."

"You wouldn't...you can't."

"Yes I can. I can do anything my heart desires."

"And you want *this*?"

"Yes. I want this."

"Then let it be."

I raised my voice so the creatures could hear and held onto Pete's hand before my chest. I could feel it shaking ever so slightly. I knew there was something in him, something that wanted me to live. His conscious, whatever was good of it, was telling him otherwise to what he was deciding. I had a chance, but knowing him, it was very slim, so I held my head high and kept my importune pleas in my mind.

"You do what you want that is good for you. You know what choice to make. So let it be." I looked up at my Eternal Mate and then back to the creatures. "Long live the King."

Chapter 46 - After the Ball

It was all over in only a minute's time. My eyes opened and I saw my body in his arms. I was just like a spirit ready to be reincarnated, but I was not so quick to reincarnate myself. I stood, waited and watched to see what would come of Pete and his disposition. Versailles came out of nowhere, the pastel ribbons flying behind her as she ran for him, too late. Beside her was Phantilla, who let out a scream so loud even I could hear it.

"You upset the balance of all things good!"

Versailles shot forward, pointed her horn at him and backed away, realizing she was too late. Phantilla, now outraged, flapped her heavy wings and began to attack him. Her golden beak struck his neck as the unicorn kept the wolves at bay.

"How do *you* like it? How do *you* like it?" The star screamed, her golden beak poking him even harder.

He did not fight back, but simply let the swan do her worst, and stayed defenseless. After the star attacked him, he carried my body away, left the bridge, and disappeared. Wherever he had gone did not look familiar to me. I would have gone to look around the place, but I could only go so far from my body.

"Oh Chenille what have I done to you?"

I sat down beside my body and listened to him.

"I know you can hear me," he said. "It was for your own good. I can't have you running off…I know I'm not good enough for you. I know you hate me…and I know Fitzray and Lucian…even that other immortal were better than I would ever be. But I can change…I will."

"No you won't." I whispered ghostly. I knew he could hear me.

"I will, I will. You have to trust me."

"I never did. I won't trust you now, after all you've done."

"You have to reconsider. You have to reincarnate

yourself."

"I have a choice?"

"Yes, it's up to you if you want to be reincarnated or not. If you don't, Catastrophe will suffer, like Phantilla said. The balance is broken. I can't rule without you."

"You should have thought of that before."

"I wasn't thinking. I wasn't even myself."

"What if I don't come back?"

"Chenille you have to...*you have to.*"

"You would be all alone, wouldn't you? You would rule alone and things would never be the same."

"Chenille please, what do you want me to do for you? What do you want me to do so you can come back?"

"You don't really know what you have until it's gone."

"What about your friends? What about your child?"

"I know he is safe with Taj' and Pearl."

"What about me? You don't think I could get him, and raise him as my own?"

"You could, but remember it is I who makes the decision to come back or not. If you leave this room, I will too."

"What about your horse and your dragon?"

"Set them all free."

"And what about your family?"

"They got what they wanted. If I came back, it would only make matters worse. Why should I come back? I don't need you. What have you ever done for me? You turned me into the creature I am today. You gave me no free will. You created me and caged me only for me to become Queen and serve as your slave. Perhaps today you have finally given me what I want - freedom. I couldn't have given that to myself even if I tried. It needed to be from you, and you finally set me free. This is an opportunity Pete, one I will either take advantage of or throw away for later regret."

"No, you won't regret. I will live up to my promises."

"I am still waiting from when you said that the first time."

"You have to give me a chance."

"I have given you one too many."

"So you are just going to leave? You are going to give up all the power I worked so hard to get?"

"How was being Queen any different for me? You can keep your power."

"You are making a mistake. You are making…a mistake."

He lowered his head now, in defeat, with nothing else left to say. He could persuade me no more and simply stayed quiet, breathing shakily over my body and holding it as if I was still there occupying it.

There was a noise. The door opened and a golden light flooded in. The door slammed shut without a trace of what could have entered, but there were screams coming from behind the door, like what nightmares and creatures of the imagination sounded like. There was a flash of gold and light slowly began to shroud the room, slowly from the door, spilling over to the corners and making its way inward to the center of the room. Pete lifted his head, disregarding the spilling gold light that now crept up the walls. There was a figure there I could see, holding a golden sword in his hands. I could not see his face. Pete rose at sight of the figure, backed away from my body, and slowly sank to his knees in surrender.

"Annabel." The voice said darkly.

I knew who it was now. The golden sword rose in the air and came down on Pete. He was useless without motivation or anger to fight anything. He stumbled back to one of the patches of darkness, a black stream of either blood or poison, I could not tell, formed at the corners of his mouth. He was defeated, unable to reincarnate, but simply remained deprived of power, now left weakened without a queen - without an Eternal Mate.

I drifted down to Pete, tried to get close to him and called his name, but I could only go so far from my body. The gold light too was keeping me in the center of the room, preventing escape. The figure came up to my body, one hand still holding the golden sword, the other shaking me. The figure did not understand that the body that rested on the bed would not wake, would not breathe. I drifted away from the golden sword, but the gold light was rushing in from the sword and the room was losing its darkness. I could see my body becoming very tense as though it reflected the way I was feeling. And I could feel an unbearable pain on my shoulders from the figure shaking me so hard, and the gold light became more intense, so much I lost my sight. I could only see darkness now.

"I will free you Chenille." There was a low groan from Pete and I could not hear his voice after that. I could not hear anything after that. I was screaming.

"I don't want to be the Queen of Catastrophe! I don't want to be the Queen of Catastrophe!"

I was the only one that could not hear the smack of an open door. Pete opened the door and screams filled the small room. The gold light vanished, the darkness took its shape over everything, and my mind went blank.

Chapter 47 -Arise Again

I opened my eyes, saw Pete there before me, and let out a yelp, backing away before he could get near.

"Catastrophe…I don't want to be the Queen of Catastrophe!"

I shook my head, trying to rid the long painful nightmare from my mind and my family who had come to spell my death.

"You were asleep. You must have had a bad dream, but you are all right now. I am here."

I backed up against the willow tree's trunk in disgust. "How could you say that?"

"Relax, what's gotten you so shaken?"

"Stay back…I…I know your secret! You're a vampire!"

"What does that have to do with anything?"

"That means I am your Eternal Mate." My head began to spin recalling all of the detail from the nightmare. "There was a phoenix and a unicorn…and I was queen of it all! And I became a vampire and had to go across the Bridge of Secrecy to my brother only to find out that my family was a bunch of werewolves. And it was all because of you…all because you bit me."

"Let me guess, were there dragons too?"

I sat against the tree confused.

Pete shook his head and neared my ear. "What a vivid imagination one must have to have such a dream as that. You know I love you and I would never hurt you." There was almost an edge of sarcasm to his tone.

"But that's what happened, I swear!"

"I wouldn't doubt it for a minute."

"How long have I been asleep?"

"About an hour…or two." He said.

"You left me here didn't you? And you came back."

I sighed somewhat disappointed the whole dream was not real, even though it felt so.

He put a hand gently to my shoulder, a wonderful scent wafted around him and he came so close as to be only a breath's distance away.

"Wait. How old am I?"

I heard a deep chuckle begin to form at the back of his throat. "Let me think. You are eighteen. Any more questions?"

"How old are you?"

"I am nineteen." I felt his fingers lightly press against my shoulder and I flinched from a pain in my neck.

He smiled, neared closer and kissed me. I waited to taste poison, waited for it to come, but there wasn't any at all. There was nothing strange like sickening black poison or thick black blood. It was ordinary as though it was a kiss from a mortal. Just then, as he broke away, there was a trace of something on my lips. I could taste it faintly and as I licked my lips, I almost doubted it. No, it wasn't poison, not poison at all. It was blood.

Afterword

"You did this. You are a vampire."
"No I'm not," he replied calmly. "What's wrong?"
"I just thought-," I began, quickly shaking my head. My lips were so badly chapped, they bled, and at once, my hand flew to my mouth.
"You thought wrong. I am no monster." He put a reassuring hand to my shoulder. "Vampires don't exist. At least not now," I heard him say beneath his breath.

I looked around, feeling the chill of the night come over me. The moon was full tonight and cast a beam of white light over the willow tree. Something was shining in the distance. I turned to Pete and pointed at the object. At once, he stood and gathered it in his hands to bring it back to me. It was a large piece of silver carved out to form two dragons.
"What is that?"
"A necklace."

Just then, Pete's cousin Louie came over. He noticed the necklace and took it in his hands to examine it.
"Will you look at this? What a piece of art this is." He rolled it repeatedly in his hands and smiled, handing it back to me. "Something like that is known to hold amazing powers. If you wear it, it might grant you wealth and good fortune."
"You seem to know a lot about it."

Louie shrugged his shoulders in response.
"Put it on Chenille."
"Let's go back inside. Dinner is about to begin."

I followed them back into my house to where everyone had gathered around the dining table. As I took my seat, everyone looked at the large silver dragon necklace. Louie sat next to me, lowering his voice.
"It once belonged to a princess." I looked at him surprised.

"Pete planned on giving it to you earlier but I suppose he dropped it when he saw you asleep against the old willow." He paused to glance at the necklace. "Some say it is a gift to symbolize the friendship of two people, hence the two silver dragons. The crescent moon made of diamond behind them represents the tranquility and peace between them." He paused to run his hands over the silver dragons. "When Pete saw you sound asleep near the willow he came and got me. You know how he can be sometimes, he always thinks of the worst. With that wild dog running around the neighborhood, he was frantic. You should have seen him."

I looked over to Pete who had heard what Louie said and smiled.

"He's glad you're ok. We all are." He looked to the family.

"It is a beautiful piece isn't it?" I chimed showing it to my family.

They all seemed to agree that it was remarkable and looked over at Pete who had clearly impressed them with his gift to me. I felt a ping of joy as I clutched the necklace.

"Don't flatter yourself *Queen of Catastrophe,*" Louie whispered, his lips brushing against my ear. "You have no idea what you just got yourself into."

Glossary

Important Creatures, People, Places, and Terms from Opulent

Characters

Alexander Silver- vampire. Married to Luna Silver. Fitzray and Pete's father. Turned Fitzray into a vampire. He was killed by Pete.

Amelia- vampire, Eternal Mate of Caspian. She is forever 18 years old. She is also Chenille's best friend. She lives on the outskirts of the City of Lights.

Annabel Richards- what Chenille calls herself while she is in the North.

Aura- female giant snake with purple eyes. She is the younger sister of Magnificent and Sylvarian and is the daughter of Taj' and Princess Pearl.

Calvin- vampire. He is Chenille's best friend. He is forever 17 years old. He lives far from the City of Lights.

Caspian- vampire, Amelia's Eternal Mate. He is a very good healer. He is forever 24 years old. He is Fitzray's best friend and was once in his clan. He is the doctor of the City.

Catherine- Irish immortal, Prince William's wife. She is forever in her 20's. Lives on Alfur, in the North.

Charlene- female white bat. She belongs to Fitzray.

Chenille East- vampire, reject of wolves. Child of Denver East and Serena East. She has bonded with Fitzray, and Lucian. Eternal Mate of Pete Silver. She is forever 18 years old. She is the Queen of Catastrophe. Lives on the border of the City of Lights on Inesious.

Citrus- small female orange dragon.

Denver East- werewolf bonded and married to Serena East. He has two children, Zaire and Chenille. He is forever 55 years old. He is the pack leader of all werewolves on Catastrophe and Earth.

Father of Time- phoenix, bonded with Mother Nature. His daughter is Princess Pearl.

Felia- an old woman that poses as Moran's grandmother while Pete and Chenille are at the old farm.

Fitzray Silver- vampire bonded with Chenille. Child of Alexander Silver and Luna Silver. He is the brother of Pete Silver. He is forever 18 years old. He is Prince of Catastrophe and was once a healer. Lives on the border of the City of Lights on Inesious.

Jasper- large white dragon bonded to Lucian. Refers to his owner as Master.

Jeff- mortal. He is Violet's brother and is an adopted son of Tetchra's. He is 18 years old. Lives on Earth. He purchases Chenille during a vampire auction on Earth.

Hickory- chestnut pony that belonged to Fitzray. Age is unknown. Lived on Earth.

Lazuli- female white unicorn. She had one foal - Versailles. She was a great friend of Princess Pearl. She died from being captured and having her horn cut off.

Lucian Noir- half-blood, bonded with Chenille. Son of Rainier Noir and Nell Noir. He is Pete and Fitzray's cousin.

Luna Silver- mortal. Married to Alexander Silver. Is Pete and Fitzray's mother.

Meleve- female snowy owl. She belongs to Pete.

Minx- large male, blue dragon bonded with Chenille. He refers to her as Mistress.

Moonscale- white male dragon. He was Fitzray's first dragon and gave him a Dragon's Soul. Pete sliced his wing once he had flown over the side of the Bridge of Secrecy to save Fitzray and was killed.

Moran- what Lucian calls himself when he is in disguise at the old farm with Chenille and Pete.

Mother Nature- mermaid bonded with Father of Time. Her daughter is Princess Pearl.

Ms. Brown- caretaker of Fitzray from infancy to eight years old.

Mullein- large male, black dragon, bonded to Pete. Gave Pete a Dragon's Soul.

Nell Noir- mortal, married to Rainier Noir. Lives on Earth.

Obsidian- giant phoenix. He was the last giant phoenix. He was killed from being poisoned by Tetchra and fell on the Bridge of Secrecy – destroying it.

Pete Silver- full-blood vampire that does not need a Ceremony to be reincarnated. Is Chenille's Eternal Mate. Child of Alexander Silver and Luna Silver. He is Fitzray's brother. He is forever 19 years old. He is the King of Catastrophe and lives on the outskirts of the woods bordering the City of Lights on Inesious. He has lived on Earth before.

Phantilla- a celestial star in the form of a glass swan with a beak made of gold. Her age is unknown. She travels back and forth from Earth to Catastrophe.

Prince Dafar Alan- immortal, married to Elisma Alan. He has two sons, William and Sebastian. Lives on Alfur.

Princess Elisma Alan- immortal, married to Dafar Alan. She has two sons, William and Sebastian. Lives on Alfur.

Prince of Light- Sebastian's other name. He is called so because of his strange powers that enables him to control light.

Princess Pearl- mermaid, bonded with Taj'. Child of Mother Nature and Father of Time. Lives in the Frozen Waterfalls. She can see the future by using the Frozen Pool at the base of the Frozen Waterfalls.

Prince William- an immortal married to Catherine. Son of Princess Elisma Alan and Prince Dafar Alan. He is Sebastian's older brother. He is forever in his 20's. He lives in the North, on Alfur, with Catherine.

Prusaious- werewolf. She is forever 18 years old.

Sebastian- immortal, son of Princess Elisma Alan and Prince Dafar Alan. He is forever in his 20's. He is also known as the Prince of Light.

Serena East- werewolf, bonded and married to Denver East. She has two children, Zaire and Chenille. She was forcibly turned into a werewolf and was killed by Denver.

Serpentine- a gold dragon that helps young Fitzray when he is growing up from reincarnation.

Taj'- the oldest of the remaining giant snakes. Bonded with Princess Pearl. He has two sons, Magnificent and Sylvarian, and three daughters, Aqua, Aura, and Serendipity. His parents are unknown. He is also called Lord of the Sea. He once lived in the City's reservoir and now lives in the Frozen Waterfalls.

Tetchra- shape shifter responsible for 'bonding' mortals and vampires. She kidnapped Fitzray as an infant. Age is unknown.

Timothy East- werewolf, not bonded. He is Chenille's cousin. He is forever 19 years old.

Valiant- blue jay by night, phoenix by day. He was found by Chenille when he was a baby. He was killed by the strange powers of the Star Pool.

Verna- vampire. Luna Silver's mother, young Fitzray's great-great grandmother. Over 80 years old. She lives on Catastrophe.

Versailles- female gray unicorn. She is Lazuli's daughter. She was born premature.

Violet- mortal, 14 years old. She is Jeff's younger sister and is an adopted daughter of Tetchra's. She lives on Earth.

Willow- a mermaid, friend of Princess Pearl.

Zaire- werewolf, not bonded. He is the son of Denver and Serena East and is Chenille's brother. He is forever 19 years old. He was killed by Taj' who threw him over the side of the Bridge of Secrecy.

Places

Alfur- large continent. Also known as the North.

Bridge of Secrecy- the bridge connecting Catastrophe to Earth.

Catastrophe- large planet, nearly twice Earth's size. Connected to Earth by a bridge suspended between the two planets.

The City of Lights- the largest city on Inesious. Also called the City.

Clesta- Catastrophe's orange moon that shattered from the destruction of the Bridge.

Frozen Waterfalls- located a few miles away from the City. Also where Taj' and Pearl live.

Inesious- the largest of Catastrophe's continents.

Nalani- small rundown village just outside of the Ticktay Mountains.

The Palace- commonly referred to Pete, Chenille, and Fitzray's palace.

The Star Pool- an invisible pool that reflects the stars. It has mystical powers that can show the future. Located north of Nalani.

The Ticktay Mountains- the largest mountain range on Catastrophe.

Verneil- a planet that Pete created and was destroyed.

Verneil- Catastrophe's blue moon that appeared after Clesta's shattering.

The Woods- the outskirts of the City.

Important Terms

Black Book- also known as Pete's old journal. Pete wrote it, recording important facts about vampires.

Blood Ceremony- when two vampires create a bond. This must happen for reincarnation to be possible. Two vampires, Eternal Mates or not, can perform a Blood Ceremony.

Bond- referred to two species (usually a vampire or werewolf) forming a pair. It usually involves drinking the blood of their chosen partner.

Ceremony- also known as a Blood Ceremony.

Dragon's Soul- a chain with a charm made from a dragon's scales and precious metal. It is presented to a dragon's Master or Mistress. This is the ultimate gift of loyalty a dragon can give.

Eternal Mate- a vampire responsible for turning a mortal or half-mortal into a vampress. As a couple, each vampire is considered to be an Eternal Mate to each other.

Half-Blood/Half Mortal- commonly referred to those that did not transform completely into a vampire. Can be killed even with a Ceremony. When killed, their heart is left behind and can be used to turn a vampire or vampress into a half-mortal.

Immortal- a person who grew up on Catastrophe and cannot be killed. It is unknown how people become immortals, though some can be born immortal by two immortal parents.

Moon Ceremony- when a wolf turns a mortal or half-mortal into a wolf. This can only be done on the night of a full moon.

Mortal- person born on Earth and can be killed.

Phases- emotions that a vampire goes through after the completion of a Ceremony.

Poison- a natural substance produced by a vampire. It can have various affects on a vampress. A vampire will produce poison to numb a vampress or mortal when feeding or during a Ceremony. Color of the poison varies from vampire to vampire but is commonly black or clear and depending on the power of the vampire, can sometimes glow. A vampress also produces a very small amount of poison, but will not affect a vampire. Male wolves also have poison, but only enough for one Ceremony per life.

Reincarnation- if a vampire or wolf completes a Ceremony and later dies, it will come back. It will be born an infant, grow, remember, and within a few years will return to their original age. They must reunite and complete a Ceremony with their Eternal Mate shortly after so reincarnation is possible again.

Sebastian's Ball- when Sebastian threw a large party and invited Annabel (Chenille) to Alfur.

Vampire- name for a male vampire, or the species as a whole.

Vampress- a female vampire.

Werewolf- part human that can change to a wolf form; is immortal and needs a Ceremony to become reincarnated.

About the Author

Isabelle Gallo's eternal love for fantasy inspired her to write *Opulent* when she was twelve years old, influenced by a multitude of dreams that portrayed a beautiful world - inhabited by characters that brought her dreams to life. Isabelle lives in New York with her family. Born premature, at only one pound, she has overcome countless challenges through love and support from her family and friends. She is currently at work on her final novel in *The Opalescent Collection.*

www.ingramcontent.com/pod-product-compliance
Lightning Source LLC
Chambersburg PA
CBHW020612310726
48979CB00008B/1450/J

* 9 7 8 0 6 1 5 6 0 0 6 9 7 *